# REVELATIONS

TERRY JAMES

**Revelations**
Paperback Edition
© Copyright 2018 Terry James

CKN Christian Publishing
An Imprint of Wolfpack Publishing
5130 S. Fort Apache Rd. 215-380
Las Vegas, NV 89148

cknchristianpublishing.com

eBook ISBN 978-1-64119-246-0
Paperback ISBN 978-1-64119-300-9

# REVELATIONS

# ACKNOWLEDGMENTS

My love and appreciation to all who mean so much to my life—as a husband, son, dad, honorary dad, and friend.

Margaret, Terry, Jr., Nathan, Kerry, Angie, Dana, Jeanie and many friends like Todd and Mike brighten my life in so many ways, I've lost count.

To my Mom, Kathleen James-Basse, my very special love and thanks for blessing my life beyond measure.

My profound gratitude to Geri Ungurean for masterfully helping in promotion, publicity and distribution of *REVELATIONS.*

Thanks to Lauren Bridges for her part in bringing the novel to publication.

To Jesus Christ be the Power, Glory and Honor Forever!

# PROLOGUE PART I

"**Y**ou've chosen the bottom of the barrel profession in the eyes of those who will read your stuff."

His journalism professor's words echoed in his thoughts while Tyce Greyson checked his camera.

*"News media types rate below politicians,"* the remembered words continued.

Melodious, Middle Eastern chants in the late afternoon brought an eerie sense of not belonging. Tyce Greyson felt far out of his element, even though he had, during the last 3 of his twenty-seven years on the planet, occasionally covered stories in Jerusalem as an independent journalist.

His next job was already a done deal. He would work as a staff reporter for a Little rock, Arkansas television station.

This would be the last such assignment as an independent writer he would undertake for the foreseeable future. He approached the Western Wall—the so-called *"Wailing Wall."* He wanted to get as many shots as possible while the sunlight remained. The piece would be written for a Jewish magazine based in Washington D.C. He was anxious to get the job done and eventually fly back to New York, then into *Hill Billy Airport* as those of his circle called the Little Rock airport named after Hillary and Bill Clinton.

*"Maybe we are out of touch with our audiences like they say. Maybe that's why the low rating,"* he considered.

He took several quick shots of people in mid-eastern garb and let the thought drop.

Greyson entered a crowded area of worshippers. He angled for the one spot he saw that afforded the least restricted camera view of the most holy worship site in Judaism.

When the worshippers began crowding around him the view of the wall became blocked. He cursed beneath his breath and held the camera above his head to keep it from being bumped. The worshippers advanced and he turned sideways to escape the milling swarm. Finally, he found himself free and was pleased to have a better view of the wall than before.

Greyson took several shots while moving around the newly found open area. He checked each photo before taking another series of shots.

He began studying the last of the photographs, his attention disrupted when touched by a hand on his left arm. He looked at the shorter man, whose eyes were wide and glistening in the late afternoon sunlight that slanted from the horizon.

The man lifted himself on tip-toes to get to a point nearer the taller, younger man's face. His aged, bearded face beneath the Kippah he wore projected extreme urgency. He spoke in heavily-accented English.

"Israel is the sign," he said in a near-whisper.

The eyes seemed to thrust the words into Tyce's

brain with laser-like intensity. "Israel is the sign," the man repeated in a whisper but with more passion.

After a moment of glaring, the religiously robed man shuffled to a few feet away. He turned to again look into Greyson's puzzled expression. This time his words thundered into the journalist's thoughts.

"Israel is the sign of the end."

# PROLOGUE PART II

I've been blind for decades due to a hereditary retinal disease called *retinitis pigmentosa*. My occupation is that of a writer. Public relations in corporate settings was my work until the blindness became total. Books dealing with dark, mysterious themes became my passion once the disease took my eyesight completely.

Foretelling of things to come has dominated my writing life, tugging my creative juices in directions I neither can control, nor want to control. That is all held in the hands of a higher power. There's nothing that can change the truth of that reality, and I wouldn't want it changed if there was a way.

Proof of the control of this higher power—to me at least—came on a *Good Friday*. My heart stopped, and I was suddenly confronted by another-worldly gallery of young, jubilant beings.

They were human in appearance but exuded unearthly...I guess you would say...ethereal, even heavenly radiance.

They were beckoning me. They wanted me to become a part of them-to tell me their astonishing, secret things. Their allure was mesmerizing. But, everything faded to black and I was again under the human hands of the physicians. They frantically worked to keep me among the living.

The doctors said it was the *widow maker.* They were amazed that I lived, since my heart had stopped three times and had to be restarted each time by defibrillation paddles.

Thoughts of that dynamic throng of young, glowing beings and what it all meant kept me up into the early morning hours for months. Answers began to trickle into my understanding one Friday morning nearly a year later.

The interview for my latest book had been hastily arranged by the publicist for my publisher. I stuck my hand out to shake the reporter's hand when he was ushered into my study.

"It's great to meet you, sir," he said, then introduced me to the camera operator who came with him.

Our interview was wrapped up in less than 20 minutes and the reporter, after thanking me for my time, said, "I've read not only this book."

Being blind and not being able to see his action, I presumed he held up the copy of the book about which we had just interviewed.

"I've read a number of others."

"I'm honored," I said.

"I've read yours and they inspired me to pick up some other books on prophecy."

"Oh? So, you've become interested?" I said

"More like obsessed. I've been reading the Book of *Revelations...*"

*"Revelation,"* I interrupted.

"Sir?"

"It's *Revelation...*singular, not plural," I instructed. One of my pet peeves.

"Oh, yes. *Revelation.*"

"Lots make the mistake," I comforted.

*"Revelation...* Not *Revelations.* I'll have to remember that," he said, chuckling.

"I'm reading the Bible in conjunction with your books and others on Bible prophecy. Also, other books by authors writing from perspectives not particularly Biblical."

"What do you plan to do with this...research? Any particular project you have in mind?"

My question unleashed thoughts that obviously he had kept bottled within.

"I was in Israel less than a year and a half ago," he said. "Do you have a few minutes?"

"Sure."

"Let me send my camera guy back to the station."

He did so, then turned his thoughts back to where he left off.

"I was taking some shots of the Temple Mount area in Jerusalem. This strange, Jewish guy...I guess he was a Jew, based on the get-up he wore... He, just out of nowhere, came up to me and said 'Israel is a sign of the end...'"

A moment of silence caused us both to reflect upon the words.

"Did he seem like a kook, do you think?"

"Could've been. His eyes were wild looking. But, I've been kind of haunted, I guess you could say, since he said, 'Israel is the sign of the end.'"

"So, that's what set you on this course of research?"

"Yeah. I guess that is what has poked at my curiosity

about all this prophecy business," he said after a moment of consideration of my question.

"Where do you think your...curiosity...is taking you?"

He laughed when I asked the question. "I came to interview you, and now you're interviewing me."

"Sorry, a writer's curiosity. You know what that's like..."

"Yes, sir. I'm glad you're curious. Maybe I can get some direction."

We each awaited the other's next words. He spoke finally.

"I've been with the Little Rock station since the encounter at the Temple Mount. CBS wanted me to get that experience before going to network."

"That's quite an opportunity..."

"Yeah. it's kind of intimidating, though."

"Oh? Sounds like you've made it."

"Well, not if you look at it from my vantage," he said. "You're always under the microscope. Or that's how I feel, anyway."

"You'll do fine," I said, not really knowing anything much about his business—except that I viewed all mainstream media with a high degree of skepticism.

"Wish I shared your confidence," he said.

I started to give my opinion on mainstream news media but held my tongue.

Again, there was a pause before he spoke.

"I'll begin working at network in about two weeks. But, first I'm going to pursue this...this prophecy itch I have...."

"How so?"

"I'm going to Patmos. I'm booked on a flight there for next Thursday."

"Patmos, huh? Well, that's a heck of a good place to

begin thinking on things prophetic," I said. "Ol' John did pretty well considering things to come from that island."

When the young reporter left my study with a handshake and my well-wishes, I sensed in my core being something profoundly spiritual pass between us. I envied him the future toward which he moved.

It was like the torch being passed. There was no way of knowing that torch would be coming back my way.

# CHAPTER 1

The flight to Athens then the travel by ship to the port of Patmos seemed as if it would never end. He was tired, but the prospect that lay before him assuaged the fatigue. He looked at the rocky landscape that rose in the distant to form a rugged, mountainous terrain.

"Mr. Tyce?"

The man approached with a smile, his right hand outstretched.

"Yes. I'm Tyce Greyson," Greyson said, automatically offering his own hand.

"I'm Stravos, your driver," the shorter man with the olive-complexion said with a bright smile in a Mediterranean accent.

Greyson loaded his duffle bag of clothes and cameras in their leather cases into the back of the old van, then himself into the passenger side.

"See," Stravos said," glancing into the rearview mirror. "The tourists will be loading, and you will be already up the mountain."

"I do see that," Greyson said, turning to look at the crowded scene of people and vehicles just beginning to get organized for the travel to the *Cave of the Apocalypse.*

"Skala is always like that when they debark the ships," the driver said, shaking his head. "It is good you called for Stravos."

Greyson smiled, saying nothing. But he was more than glad he took a colleague's suggestion and contacted this native to the region. Thus, we avoided the traffic congestion, just as he had been promised.

There was no traffic ahead on the narrow, asphalt road while the man herded the van toward the tourist site that was the traditional cave in which St. John was said to have penned the book of the Apocalypse.

"Mr. Tyce," Stravos said, glancing at his passenger while wrestling with the old van's steering wheel. "The Monastery of the Apocalypse is for the tourists. It is very nice and pretty. Very clean and interesting."

The journalist cast a puzzled glance at the serious expression on the face of his driver, who spoke in an equally serious tone.

"You would like to visit the *real* cave of the prophet John..."

Stravos' words were hushed and stated in questioning inflection—almost whispered. His dark eyes and thick brows narrowed in concentration when he made the inquiry.

"What do you mean? There's another than that one?" Greyson nodded toward the mountain top.

"There is another," the Greek said with a vigorous nod. "It is almost certainly the *actual* cave."

Greyson studied the driver's face. He was forewarned about getting hustled by the locals.

12

"And, you are the one person who knows the location of the...real...cave?"

The question came in a tone that said Greyson felt he was being hustled.

Stravos' countenance fell. He stared ahead at the road in the distance.

"I... I am sorry, Mr. Tyce." He said quietly. "I will not further bother you..."

Greyson felt the sudden rush of shame. He deserved to feel so disciplined.

"No... No, Stravos. It is I who am sorry. Please go on...Tell me about this...cave."

The little Greek straightened, instantly forgiving the American journalist. His words were now energetic, excited. "My cousin, Velly Ornoisis and me...We have known of the cave since childhood. It is on the other side of the mountain. There are very few who go to this place."

When Greyson made no response, Stravos continued.

"To the Monastery cave it is about 20 minutes when we come to the end of the road. To the cave...the *real* cave of the Apocalypse…we drive another fifteen minutes, then must walk for thirty minutes. It is somewhat difficult, but not too much so."

His friend in New York had told him Stravos could be trusted. Tyce Greyson sought the words that could ask the question without hurting the Greek's feelings.

"Did you take Bill Shaklin, my friend that recommended your services, to this cave?"

"No... No... My cousin Velly and me...we have taken no one to the real cave of Apocalypse. You are the first I have told."

"Why me?"

"Your friend, Bill, he call and tell me that you are

doing research. You want to find out about truth of the cave of Apocalypse. Velly wants to help you. Stravos wants to help you, also."

Upon reaching the small clearing where Stravos could park the van, Greyson surveyed the mountainside. There would be plenty of time later to go to the traditional site of St. John's vision. Tyce placed the camera carrier's strap over his shoulder, then the second.

He let his eyes follow the little stone-strewn pathway that narrowed in perspective and disappeared into the dark grey of the Patmos landscape. He searched the rocky ridges of the 300-foot-high surface that sloped toward the mountain's summit.

The cobalt-blue Aegean sprawled across the horizon in the distance while they climbed the mountainside pathway. His guide scrambled easily upward, sometimes stopping and waiting on the puffing American to catch up.

"Now the climb becomes more difficult."

Stravos pointed in a direction where they must leave the pathway.

"Another fifteen minutes," he said, continuing to point up the mountain.

Two minutes later Tyce stopped to assess the jagged terrain.

"If St. John climbed this, he couldn't have been an old man like they say."

Stravos seemed to ignore the comment.

* * *

"This is the most difficult part. There is another path ahead. It becomes easier," the Greek said, moving in the direction he had pointed.

They accomplished the rest of the climb in relative silence. The Greek pointed in the distance to one point of interest or the other that lay below.

Greyson's skepticism again surfaced. It was highly unlikely a ninety-something year-old man would be forced to climb to this point. The journalist, himself, felt his heart pounding, his breathing labored.

Even the Romans wouldn't force the aged John to climb this rugged terrain—unless they hoped to execute him through fatigue.

But, he remembered, the terrain was much different in those ancient times. The area had many palm trees and other vegetation, according to the history he had read. And, the Roman soldiers had to bear heavy loads on their shoulders. Moving a thin, old man in such a manner to this high point wouldn't necessarily be unthinkable.

"See! There...ahead!"

Stravos pointed to a dark spot in the stark mountainside.

"That is the true cave of the Apocalypse," he said, picking up the pace as he scrambled toward the recess among large, gray boulders.

Upon arrival they paused at the cave's mouth. Tyson removed the several bags from his shoulders and surveyed first the cave's opening, then the view of the area below. He noted that the vast Aegean would have dominated John's horizon. If this was the cave of his exile, the old prophet certainly would have had this great sea as the main backdrop for his thinking while dictating his visions.

Still, it was highly unlikely. Supplying even just two people—John and his assistant to whom he dictated—

15

would have been an on-going task with the grueling climb...

John, it was thought, was in the place of exile on Patmos for about 18 months. The soldiers would have had to supply the prisoners.

But, Rome required much more difficult and even deadly tasks of its forces. This might have been considered a plum assignment by a Roman soldier...

"See, here." The Greek's words interrupted Greyson's thoughts.

Stravos beckoned for him to come to just inside the cave's entrance.

"Look at the stones," The Greek shined his flashlight beam and pointed to a series of rocks that formed steps to a second level within the cave.

"They climbed here. Come," he said, asking the journalist to follow him up the stone steps.

They stood moments later, on an almost flat surface of stone. The Greek bid him to come to an opening in the rock wall.

Tyce had to bend forward to fit through the opening.

The Greek's eyes were wide with enthusiasm. "Look! This is where the prophet wrote. This is the window through which he saw his visions!"

The hole to which the Greek pointed looked to be several yards wide and more than a yard high. It was a natural formation just above a smooth, rock surface that indeed looked as if it could have served as a writing table.

Tyce sat on a stone just below the table's surface and checked the view.

"Yes. It is ideal for something like you describe," he said.

"And, see...here..." Stravos moved quickly to another wall where several niches had been carved by nature.

"This is where they kept things."

Greyson examined the recesses carefully but offered no agreement.

"What do you think?" Stravos looked to see Greyson's response.

"It is certainly an interesting cave."

"It is the *true* cave of St. John, Tyce."

The journalist said nothing in reply to the Greek's insistence, but continued to explore the cave-room.

Stravos followed him, watching to see Greyson's reaction to each area he touched and into which he peered.

"Someone used this cave for something," Greyson said, as to himself. "There are markings...here...and here. They were made to mark off days or for some other purpose."

He put the flashlight beam on the spot. He pointed to a few vertical lines that were etched into the hard surface on one smooth place on the wall.

"Yes! Yes! These are where the prophet marked his days," Stravos said excitedly. "See, here... Here are many more."

Greyson moved to where the Greek pointed.

"And here..." The little man moved to yet another surface to point to vertical etchings and to other markings obviously made by human beings.

Greyson knelt to fidget with the camera he brought with him to the room. He took several shots of the markings. He then took photos of the room from several angles. Next, he trained the camera's lens out the window-opening above the table-top, recording the vista the opening offered.

"This will be interesting to compare to the traditional site," Greyson said, checking the camera's recorded photographs.

"This is the *true* cave of the visions," the Greek said in an almost pleading tone.

"Could be, Stravos. I'll need to include it in the piece I'm writing for sure. I'll recommend that they come here if a documentary is produced from the project."

"They make a movie?"

"Maybe. We'll see. It's a fascinating cave, Stravos. Thanks for bringing me here."

The little Greek smiled brightly. "You tell the movie guys that Stravos is their guide?"

"Yep. Sure will," Tyce said, patting Stravos' arm and smiling. "Now, I need to get some more shots of the entire cave area and outside toward the Aegean."

Stravos scurried through the opening into the larger, elevated room.

The journalist prepared to bend sufficiently to get through the opening. He reached to a ledge above and to the right of the opening, clutching his camera in the other hand to keep it from bumping against the stone edge.

Sudden movement against his hand startled him. He jerked away from the opening. Something curled around the hand and his arm. His hand felt as if molten metal was being injected into its most fleshy parts.

He screamed in pain and with realization that he was being bitten. He flung his arm and hand downward and to the right. Still the snake clung to the hand.

He grabbed the thick, gray, viper near the back of its head and pried its fangs from where they were sunken into his flesh. He slammed the reptile to the hard surface and it slithered quickly out of site.

Stravos, seeing Greyson stepping quickly around the room holding his hand in a dance of panic and pain, raced to help.

"Snake bite!" Tyce screamed, holding the hand at the wrist and grimacing.

"Oh, holy mother," the Greek said, trying to hold the stricken journalist's elbow and arm.

"You must be as still as possible," Stravos said, trying to remain calm. "The less movement, the better..."

He led the journalist to the stone by the flat, rock table beneath the cave window opening.

"There is no tower," the Greek said in a frustrated tone while his eyes darted in search of a solution.

"What?" Greyson said, grimacing, the pain over-whelming. The hand had ballooned and was turning blood-red.

"No cell phone tower," Stravos said.

His eyes brightened. "You have satellite connection?" The Greek searched for the words. "Connection to internet?"

"Yes," Tyce said. "My device is in the backpack."

Stravos was back in less than two minutes, the device in hand.

"I email my cousin Velly Onenisis. Tell him to get help right away!"

Tyce Greyson's senses darkened. The intensive burning in his bitten hand faded. The throbbing pain with each heartbeat began to subside.

His fear and panic dissolved to total darkness but in the next instant leaped to surreal consciousness. From the blackness came swirling, convoluting, colors of every description and brilliant shards of illumination that provided understanding beyond human thought processes.

A chilling wind blew in waves against his body. He stood on the shore of a heaving, churning sea. He turned to look back up the mountain. There, high above, was the cave—the cave from which he had viewed this shore and sea.

Roaring noises from the tumultuous body of water caused him to turn again, and look at the huge, dark waves that arose and fell in thunderous, crashing collapses.

Something grotesque lifted from the boiling waters. A gargantuan sea monster, it's great head bobbing and swinging from side to side—its enormous teeth dagger-like while they gnashed, sea foam and lava-like drool pouring from the sides of the blood-red mouth.

It raised higher, until it's entire, hideous, dragon-body was exposed.

It began tramping slowly toward the shore...its fiery, serpent's eyes affixed upon his own, terror-stricken eyes.

## CHAPTER 2

"He's coming around."

The woman lifted the patient's right eyelid with her thumb, then lifted the other eyelid.

Tyce Greyson's thoughts moved from the dark fog when the hospital room's light made clear the doctor's face.

"There you are," the doctor said, a brief smile passing her lips while she spoke in an uplifted tone.

"Don't try to talk for now," she said. "let's just let things come back slowly."

"What things?"

The journalist's words were slurred while he tried to make sense of the situation.

"You've been...out...for quite some time," the woman said.

"Where am I?"

"You're in a Boston hospital."

"Boston?"

"Yes. You've been comatose for more than a week...

You don't need to talk anymore for now. We'll have time for explanations once we get you back to your old self."

* * *

"It's great to have you back, Tyce!"

George Brantt offered his right hand. Seeing his reporter's still swollen right hand, he grabbed Greyson's left and shook it.

"Yeah. It's great to be among the living," Tyce said, accepting first Brantt's welcome, then the greetings of several others of the network's staff.

"That was quite a trip we sent you on," the news executive said. "You know we don't pay hazardous duty pay for snake bites while spelunking, don't you?" Brantt teased.

"'Well, I would have definitely asked for hazardous duty pay had I known...'"

Brantt talked, holding on to his reporter's arm while walking him into his office.

"That must've been some bad snake. What kind was it?"

"They don't know for sure. It was a pit viper. With hemi toxin that works through circulatory system. If it had been one with venom that attacked the nervous system—had neurotoxin like the cobra—I guess I wouldn't be talking with you."

A moment of silence between them brought reflection on how serious the reporter's ordeal had been.

"So, you don't remember anything after you...blacked out?"

"About two minutes or so after the bite, I felt everything darken, then I had a vision, or hallucination. No, it was very real, not like I was out of my head."

Tyce paused to remember. "I was on the sea shore...below the mountain side where the cave is...the creature... it was a massive sea monster...like a dragon. It was coming for me...then I awoke in Boston."

"Well," Brantt said, patting him again on his shoulder. "You're okay now, and that's what matters."

"Yeah. I don't seem any the worse for wear."

"We plan to do something on the Patmos caves...both St. John's Cave and St. Tyce's Cave," Brantt said.

The news executive cocked his head slightly after sitting across from his reporter. His tone and expression became more serious.

"Tyce, some would say you're still too wet behind the ears for an anchor spot in a market as big as the *Apple...*"

After waiting a few seconds to let Greyson absorb his words, Brantt said, "But, I'm not one of 'em. I want you to co-anchor our local affiliate. The big one..."

* * *

EVEN WITH THE nod by and backing of George Brantt, network protocols would have to be followed. He would have to do the demos to be reviewed by the committee.

These weren't his favorite things to do, but he had done many of them. And, since the boss wanted him in the 7 p.m. and 11 p.m. co-anchor chair for the network's largest local affiliate, there would be no problem. Unless he blew it...

The thoughts ran through his brain. He had lied to the doctors—to George Brantt. He still felt the aftereffects of the snake bite and recovery. But, they weren't anywhere near debilitating. He could handle a fifteen-minute demo session.

The only problem with recovery was the visions

blurring for a second or two. That, and headaches that sometimes wouldn't go away no matter how much medication he took. Still, such headaches were few and far between. And, they were getting even fewer and further apart.

"Tyce!"

The man's enthusiastic greeting snapped him out of his thoughts.

"Lou!" Tyce returned the greeting with equal energy.

"Man! It's good to know you're okay," Louis Buckley said, giving Greyson a hug.

"Thanks. Good to be back."

"So, it's the big time now," Buckley said poking Tyce's shoulder gently with a fist.

"Well, not exactly. But, it's a great place to launch."

"You bet it is... And we are here to see to it that it's a spectacular lift-off!"

Minutes later Greyson sat behind the red and white anchor desk that appeared on the screens of millions of viewers each night. He read the news script both from the triple-spaced copy on the papers he held and, alternately, from the prompter nearby.

"Great! Great!"

Buckley came to Greyson when the taping was finished, helping him remove several wires.

"Thanks. Hope that's good enough to get past the committee," Tyce said.

"Good enough?! It was great, Tyce!"

"Thanks, Lou. I need the affirmation."

"No, you don't. But, I'm here to affirm...It was a great demo piece. They'll love it."

"Have you met Mariel?" Buckley's question was put in a somber tone.

"Mariel? No, I don't think so."

"You're in for a treat. Mariel Gunn. She's *hot.* She's been brought up from St. Louis. She's been here for about two months. Don't you ever watch our show?"

"You know I haven't been in New York for more than one or two days at a time for a couple of years...She's *hot,* huh?"

"Well, she's a *hot* looker, that's for sure. But, we call her the Ice Princess," the broadcast engineer said with a quick laugh.

"How so?"

"She's a cold one... Unapproachable..."

"A girl has to be careful," Tyce said with a grin. "Especially with guys like you around."

"She's a know-it-all, on top of her frigidity..."

"Sounds like somebody got rejected," Tyson teased.

"Yeah, well... let's not judge lest we be judged... let's see how you and the Ice Princess gee and haw, as my ol' farmer granddaddy used to say."

* * *

TYCE MOVED from the microwave oven with the plate of steaming spaghetti and meatballs and mashed potatoes that had several minutes previous been a frozen dinner.

He made his way to the small living room of his apartment, sat the plate on the coffee table beside the laptop and returned to the kitchen to retrieve a bottle of peach-flavored, diet tea.

He would have to be back at NYOK no later than 9 to prepare for the 11 p.m. newscast. He had the same feeling as always in his gut. Queasy. And this was by far the biggest market of his career.

* * *

MEANWHILE, as always, he would spend every spare minute working on the book. He watched the screen display the title and text beneath, while sipping from the tea bottle. He forked a bite of meatball into his mouth, and quickly had to drink from the tea again to cool the overly-hot meat that burned the center of his tongue.

"The Israel Prophecy." He read the title of the book manuscript silently, thinking, like every other time he opened the document, about how the title might be improved.

His idea for the story came soon after the encounter in Jerusalem. The bearded man, obviously an orthodox Jewish Rabbi, according to his attire, quietly had moved to beside him while he stood taking photographs at the Wailing Wall.

The man crowded close to him so that Tyce felt as if the Rabbi was urging him to move away from the position he had chosen to observe.

There was no one within 15 feet of either of them, so it wasn't like there was a crowd, thus space at a premium.

The man kept looking at him while Tyce took shots with his camera of the Temple Mount area, the Rabbi finally standing slightly on his toes to put his bearded face near Tyce's left ear. The Rabbi had spoken in a volume just above a whisper, so he could be heard over the chanting sounds from those in prayer.

"Israel is the sign," he had said.

The man's intense, piercing eyes burned even now in his memory. "Israel signals the end," the Rabbi said a second time.

The man had said nothing more for almost a minute, then walked away a few feet. He had turned and spoken for the last time before quickly moving into a crowd of similarly clad Jewish religious men.

"Israel is the sign that it is the end," he had said in accented-English.

He reflected silently on what the brief encounter on that bright, Jerusalem day had meant. His thoughts had run from it meant nothing—just an eccentric, religious Jew bending his ear—to somebody, somewhere above was trying to tell him something. The whole Patmos experience, the snake, the coma, just added to the strange sensations whenever he dwelt on the matter.

While he had always been more than just a *"news reader,"* as many of the local TV news anchors were accused of being, his interest in news surrounding Israel had fueled his ravenous curiosity since the day the Rabbi whispered in his ear *"Israel is the sign..."*.

Tyce brought up a second document on the laptop. "Israel prophecy/notes".

He scanned down the document until he found his note: *"The prophecy—built around one prophecy."*

His research since the encounter at the Temple Mount led to an astonishing conclusion. Israel was the only nation to be found among the nations of world history that had been completely erased from the map and then come back into existence. And it did so almost two thousand years later.

Not only that, it had lost its language and had that language—Hebrew—reestablished upon its rebirth.

Even beyond that fact...Israel was reborn in precisely the manner many scholars—particularly theological scholars—believed the Old Testament foretold.

He looked at his notes for the scriptural reference then flipped through the pages of the Bible he picked up from the table. He found the book of Isaiah and whispered the scripture while he read.

*66:6A voice of noise from the city, a voice from the temple, a*

*voice of the LORD that rendereth recompence to his enemies.
66:7Before she travailed, she brought forth; before her pain
came, she was delivered of a man child. 66:8Who hath heard
such a thing? who hath seen such things? Shall the earth be
made to bring forth in one day? or shall a nation be born at
once? for as soon as Zion travailed, she brought forth her children. 66:9Shall I bring to the birth, and not cause to bring
forth? saith the LORD: shall I cause to bring forth, and shut
the womb? saith thy God. 66:10Rejoice ye with Jerusalem, and
be glad with her, all ye that love her: rejoice for joy with her,
all ye that mourn for her:*

The words were like a laser burning into his realization.

*6A voice of noise from the city, a voice from the temple, a
voice of the LORD..."*

The scripture was speaking directly to him. It
couldn't be missed. The strange little, Jewish religious
man... He spoke the words that day at the Temple Mount
in Jerusalem...

"Israel is the sign..." And, again the rabbi said before
disappearing into the crowd at the Wailing Wall, "Israel
is the sign of the end."

The Jewish state had, in fact, been reborn in a single
day exactly like several millennia ago. The prophet Isaiah
said it would happen.

* * *

TYCE GREYSON PUSHED the up button on the elevator. He
smiled at the pretty, young woman who smiled back as
he stood aside to allow her exit.

The scent she left behind was pleasing, and the
fragrance of her perfume, for the moment, lingered,
taking away the hard edge of his anxiety.

The elevator stopped on the third floor, and several people entered, the pleasant odor emitted by the coffee in the Styrofoam cups the new passengers held replacing that of the perfume.

"You are the new guy," one of the new, fellow, passengers said. He shifted the cup from his right hand to his left, reaching to shake Tyce Greyson's hand.

The journalist quickly jerked the hand away.

"Sorry. The hand is injured," he said. He shook the man's right hand clumsily with his own left.

"Yes... I'm Tyce Greyson," he said, smiling. "I was bitten by a snake, believe it or not." He held up the bruised and swollen hand.

"Bernie Maddox," the shorter, balding man in his fifties said. "Yes, I remember now that George Brantt said you got bitten...While in the Aegean, I believe, on assignment."

"Yes. On Patmos."

"I'm general program director," Maddox, looking ruffled, with his sleeves rolled up, but wearing a tie, said. "That means that they assign me things that nobody else wants to do."

"Don't you believe him," the considerably younger man standing beside Maddox said. "He's a slave-driver around here. I'm Phillip Edison, the so-called sports director," he said.

"I've seen your takes," Maddox said. "Very good!"

"Nice of you to say... I'm looking forward to being a part of NYOK," Tyce said.

"Your last anchor job was in Little Rock, huh?"

"Yes. I was at KTHV for about eight months."

"You'll find New York an interesting market, I think. It's almost like network... Kind of like Little rock, I suspect," Maddox said with a chuckle as the elevator doors slid apart and he held the doors for Tyce to precede him into the brightly lit hallway.

"Well, I spent just under a year at Jackson before Little Rock," Tyce picked up on the program director's facetious banter. You haven't seen laid back until you've spent time in Jackson."

"Jackson, Tennessee?" Edison asked.

"Mississippi," Tyce said, pseudo-somberly.

"Well, it's great to have you with us," Maddox said, patting the new man on the back. "First time is always a little nerve-wracking, as you know. But, you'll soon be a star!"

"Yeah...Well, I'll just settle for being accepted," Tyce said, leaving the three men who walked in the opposite direction he had to take to get to Studio A.

He walked through the doorway after pushing open the thick, sound-proof door. Technicians and others moved about the large studio, some making last minute adjustments to items surrounding the anchor desk where he would, within the next thirty minutes, be seated.

"Welcome to NYOK, Mr. Greyson," a man wearing jeans and a flannel shirt said. He removed the headset-microphone combination from his ears and walked quickly to shake the new arrival's hand. "Marcel Rollins," he said, smiling.

Tyce jerked the hand out of danger. "Injured hand," he said, showing it to Rollins. "Please just call me Tyce," he said, seeing several others approach to take their turns in welcoming him.

Rollins forewarned the others against trying to shake hands with the new arrival.

"We've about got everything ready to go," Rollins said, turning to look at the area the others continued working on after introductions to the station's new co-anchor.

"It's an all new set," Rollins said. "We're kind of proud of it."

"It's beautiful," Tyce said, walking with Rollins to the outer edge of the big, colorfully appointed desk, behind which two new, burgundy leather chairs were positioned several feet apart.

"You will sit in this one," the man in his early 30s said, moving to behind the chair he indicated. The same chair from which Greyson had earlier recorded the demo.

"Don't ask me why they want you in this one rather than the other," Rollins said with a grin. "These guys all think they have the answers to everything," he said with a laugh, waving the clipboard he held toward the general direction of the glass surrounding the anchor desk's left side.

"Well, it makes no difference to me," Tyce said with mock sincerity. "Just so I get more face-time than the co-anchor."

The remark brought a rumble of laughter from Rollins and the other people working on the set. There was self-deprecation in the new guy's remark, despite its overtly, ego-centric declaration. Tyce Grayson was a "*good one,*" as the undercurrent vernacular went amongst the "*worker plebes*" of NYOK Five-TV.

"Uh-oh...The princess has made an entrance," Rollins said, low enough in volume so that only Tyce could hear his words.

Tyce turned to look in the direction of the big door he had himself entered several minutes earlier. A slender young woman strode quickly toward the glassed-in area of the studio. She paid no attention to Tyce, Marcel Rollins, or to anyone else in the room, instead going directly to the door to the studio's control center. She opened the door, then walked through the opening and let the door close behind her.

"I'll see if I can get us an audience," Rollins said, bringing muted laughter from workers going about their last-minute business in the studio.

"You haven't met Marial yet, have you?" He said, looking back over his shoulder at Tyce while they walked toward the door she had just entered.

"No. I've only heard her name. She didn't show at either of the two meetings we had," Tyce said, following Rollins.

"That's typical. Don't feel badly. She's like that."

Rollins opened the heavy door and led the way into the long room with the glass that looked out on the news set.

Grayson's co-anchor stood in front of one of the control room's technicians. She gesticulated vigorously, with her perfectly manicured fingernails of bright crimson flashing through the air while she talked. She stopped her rant to the man when she noticed the two men begin walking toward her and her partner in the one-sided conversation.

"Marial..." Rollins urged Tyce toward his partner-to-be by pushing gently on his arm.

"You need to meet the other member of the team, seeing as how the show starts in about twenty-two minutes," he said matter-of -factly. Tyce understood Rollins was enjoying forcing the young woman to meet her new co-anchor whether she wanted to or not.

The smile was brief and tight. The face was indeed beautiful, make-up right in every respect, surrounded by perfectly coifed blondeness.

Greyson extended his left hand, while holding up his

right for Marial Gunn to see. "Hurt hand," he said without further explanation.

Her feminine grip of his own offered left hand was cold and quickly retracted when the greeting was made.

"Here's your copy," she said, handing Tyce several pages of large, bold, triple-spaced type. "Of course, it's all on the prompter," She looked at him with her eyes affixed on his and paused a few seconds before again speaking.

"They think it's best if I do the lead for the first few programs," she said, her tone all business.

"Yes...Yes, that will be fine with me."

"Good. You will do just fine... Dice, is it?" she said with another tight smile.

"Actually, it's Tyce..."

"Well, Tyce... You will do just fine. I understand this is your first time as a full-time anchor," she said, looking at Marcel Rollins with an expression that silently, but unmistakably dismissed him.

"As full-time anchor, yes. I've filled in on a regular basis whenever needed while in Little Rock," he said, glancing at Rollins, who winked as he turned to leave. Tyce got the message that he shouldn't let the woman get the best of him.

"Little Rock..." Marial Gunn looked as if she was trying to remember. "Oh, that's where Bill Clinton came from, isn't it?"

"Yes...Hillary, too," he said in a light tone.

"Oh, no. Mrs. Clinton is originally from Illinois, then spent years in the northeast...not...Arkansas."

The word *Arkansas* lingered on her tongue like a mouthful of coffee whose excessive heat needed to be dissipated.

"Well, she belongs to the nation and world, really......"

His lightly given retort seemed to have missed being noticed by Marial Gunn. She spent the next few minutes instructing him on how, exactly, he was to address each of the several cameras they would have focused upon them in 12 minutes hence.

"NYOKTV is not Little Rock," she said, starting for the door into the studio." This is a market of more upscale viewers... The greater Metro area has some four to five million viewers. Nothing at all like your last broadcast area."

"Oh? You know the Little Rock market?" Tyce asked, trying to sound genuinely surprised that she apparently knew the market, based upon her earlier supposed not knowing about Little Rock.

"Well...No... not specifically. But I know about markets like that small, more rural demographic."

He followed behind her, admiring the perfect, feminine form, wrapped tightly in smart, business attire. She moved without a misstep in the 3-inch black, patent leather heels, gracefully avoiding the thick cables scattered about the tiled floor.

Less than five minutes later, sitting to her right and facing the camera directly in front of him, he heard in the earpiece: "*And, five, four, three, two, one...*"

Marial Gunn's face dominated the monitor screens of NYOK Studio A.

"We at NYOK Five TV are pleased tonight to introduce our new, Prime Five co-anchor."

She looked at Tyce Greyson, the cameras switching in synchronization between the two of them.

"Welcome Tyce Greyson, who joins us as co-anchor for the seven o'clock and Eleven o'clock week day news... Welcome, Tyce..."

Greyson's face alone filled the monitor screens as he responded.

"It's going to be a wonderful experience. For me personally and professionally, to serve our viewing audience, Marial. Thanks so much for the introduction..."

After 30 seconds of friendly banter, Marial Gunn gave the lead story of the hour.

Greyson read the next story and the cameras' red lights went dark when the broadcast went to commercial.

"How'd I do," Tyce, said, turning to look into his co-anchor's green eyes.

She said nothing, but returned an incredulous glance, before shuffling the script in front of her and preparing for the red lights to illuminate.

Tyce Greyson waited for his co-anchor to finish the brief story that opened the segment after the commercial break, his concentration on the camera's huge lens trained directly on his face.

When the red light flashed, the black lens grew while he peered into its depths. It became an enormous orb that siphoned his consciousness into a suctioning vortex.

His surroundings grew dark, until he, alone, stood on a strange surface he, through reeling senses, determined was wet, cold sand. When his eyes began to recover a degree of vision, he looked into a violent, billowing tempest. A raging sea that threatened a deadly tidal surge that would be upon him at any moment.

Light grew within the dark, tumbling sea. A surreal scene burst into his dumbfounded cognitive processor—his mind struggling to understand.

CHAPTER 3

T yce felt something cold and wet move across his forehead. His consciousness began its ascent until he realized his position on the sofa.

"Tyce...Tyce..."

The voice was familiar.

"He's coming around," George Brantt said to the others in the room.

"Tyce...You okay?"

Brantt gently patted Greyson's cheek with his fingertips.

"You okay?"

The journalist's eyelids fluttered and finally opened fully.

"What's going on?" Greyson's words were weak but grew stronger. "What...What happened?"

"You passed out," George Brantt said, a concerned look on his face while looking into Greyson's eyes.

The journalist's head pounded, the pain centering

somewhere in his forehead. He shut his eyes, still struggling to completely recover his senses.

"You okay?" Brantt repeated, again patting Tyce's
cheek.

"Yeah. I think so."

He tried to sit up, using his elbows to rise.

"Woah! Let's just relax for a bit," Brantt said using his
hand to nudge Tyce to stay on his back.

"Passed out? I was about to begin reading the news
copy. It's the last thing I remembered... before that
strange... a vision. It was of that scene at Patmos... The
shore... the sea... a storm. Then..."

When Greyson winced with pain in his forehead,
Brantt again tried to keep him on his back.

"Take it easy, Tyce. There will be plenty of time to
talk about it."

* * *

HE NOTICED THE QUICK GLANCES, the abrupt turning of
heads. The smiles of greeting were issued somberly by
those who were usually the friendliest of the New
Yorkers in the building.

After a thorough exam by a doctor he had been given
a sedative then driven to his apartment. He had slept
more than 10 hours. Awakened by a phone call that asked
him to come to the NYOK studios, he moved down the
hallway less than an hour later toward the meeting.

"How are you, Tyce."

George Brantt gripped Greyson's arms and squeezed.
He looked deeply into Tyce's eyes.

"Never felt better," Greyson said.

"Good...Good."

Brantt guided Tyce toward the meeting room.

"We want to go over that broadcast, Tyce. Now...don't be shocked at what you see and hear."

Greyson's facial expression told the program director further explanation was needed.

"While you began giving a flawless stream of information, it was... not what was written in the news script."

"What? You mean I actually broadcast? I thought I'd passed out," Greyson said, stunned at Rollin's words.

"Let's review the tape."

Rollins motioned to a technician to prepare to show the previous night's broadcast.

The monitor screens on the edit room walls lit up. The words on the screens displayed the day and date of the tape in large, black letters against a light-yellow background.

"Roll it."

When Rollins issued the order, the screens changed to the image of Marial Gunn, glancing to her left. The video cut to the head and shoulders of Tyce Greyson looking directly into the camera.

"Today marked the twenty-first anniversary of the city's *Clean Streets* program... And, the mayor says it has been a success."

The screen changed to New York's mayor being interviewed for 20 seconds and then cut back to Tyce Greyson's image.

"Watch," Brantt said. "This is where it starts..."

The journalist watched his image projecting from the monitor take on a radiant glow. An aura of indefinable effulgence, making his face appear almost like a caricature of his true countenance. His blue eyes now looked to be entirely black, so large did the pupils become. He spoke in a deeper, less hesitating cadence than his usual delivery.

"A nuclear weapon was used against the Syrian city of Damascus. It is the first such weapon to be used other than in testing since Nagasaki, Japan was bombed in nineteen forty-five."

Greyson sat forward, his mouth open in astonishment at his own pronouncement.

He watched himself on the monitor screen while his image collapsed forward then against the chairs right armrest. Marial Gunn reached to try to help her co-anchor. The screen snapped to black.

Neither man said anything for several seconds. George Brantt spoke, finally.

"The report from the hospital says everything checks out. They can find nothing amiss."

Tyce stared at the still dark monitor, unable to verbalize his thoughts.

"They said the snake venom and so forth has long since cleared your system, Tyce. Unless it was a toxin that has effects, they know nothing about," Brantt said.

"My God... And that went out to all of New York?" Greyson spoke to himself more than to George Brantt.

"I'm afraid so..."

Brantt's tone became one of encouragement. "Look, Tyce. Stranger...much worse... things have happened in broadcast. Remember when Rather stomped out of a live broadcast? One guy once began a strip show right on camera... Yours was because of lingering after effects of a serious illness. That's all. Marial explained to our viewers about your being bitten by that snake and your recovery. We've been getting lots of sympathy emails and calls..."

Greyson glanced at his friend and smiled briefly.

"Thanks, George. You're a friend."

"Well, I want you to take the rest of this week off. We will begin afresh next Monday at the seven o'clock evening news."

\* \* \*

HE SIPPED from the bottle of peach tea, while reflecting on the conversation that introduced him to the prediction—the *prophecy*—that began bringing enlightenment. That began bringing the Jewish Rabbi's whispered words into focus.

Visits to several book stores resulted in his collecting several volumes on the nation of Israel, both ancient and modern. Subsequent searches on the Internet—using terms the books provided—made the matter clearer. Israel was unique among the nations of the world. The facts were undeniable, intriguing. It was again a nation after being destroyed and its people scattered around the world. Its language was all but eradicated. Then, suddenly, in a single day, Israel was again a nation, its language again the national language. Even by secular, historical assessment, the nation's rebirth was nothing short of miraculous.

One of the book's author had pointed out to him over coffee one day in Dallas that the prophecy was fulfilled precisely. The prophet Isaiah had made the prediction hundreds of years before the birth of Christ.

Tyce's thoughts were cut off by the I-Phone chime alerting him to a caller.

"Tyce Greyson..."

"Marial Gunn, Tyce." Her words were quick, her tone business-like.

"What may I..."

"Just a few suggestions for the show." She cut him off, launching into the suggestions.

"You move your arms a bit too much when shifting to the paper," she said. "This tends to distract the viewer's attention from the presentation of the story."

He was silent for a few seconds, before starting to respond.

"Oh? I guess I..."

"You also tend to move your head from the prompter to the paper too rapidly. It gives the impression of jerkiness. Everything should flow smoothly, not in a herky-jerky movement, if you understand what I mean."

Greyson felt his cheeks redden but caught himself to keep from retorting with anger.

"I studied the tape of your audition and thought you would want to know. We want our audience to know they can expect the same professionalism they are used too."

"Oh, yes... I agree..."

His response was mild in tone, control of his elevated temper returning.

"Good...good."

There was silence on her end, he felt compelled to say something...anything.

"Thanks for the constructive criticism. I'll work on those things."

Still, there was silence on the other end.

Tyce said, "Is there something else?"

She spoke after another several seconds of silence.

"Are you okay?" Her tone was softer, almost one of concern, he thought.

"Yes. I'm okay."

More silence before she again spoke. "Well...that's good. That's very good."

"I'm told you will return to air next Monday."

"A week from this coming Monday, yes. George insists I take the week off."

Silence dominated the line, before Marial spoke somewhat hesitatingly. "I was wondering...If maybe we could meet...maybe for lunch, sometime before our next broadcast together."

The *Ice Princess*, asking *him* for a lunch date? The thought crossed his mind like receiving an electric shock when one placed one's finger into an empty light socket. He thought to ask her the meeting's purpose. But, he thought better of asking the question.

"Sure. That would be great. When...?" her tone returned to being more business-like.

"I'll let you know," she said, cutting him off. "I mean...I'm just not sure about my schedule. I'll call soon."

\* \* \*

SHE WAS A BEAUTIFUL WOMAN. Marial Gunn's pretty face lingered in his mind while he tried to stop thinking about her surprise invitation to lunch. He needed to get back to the book. To thoughts of Israel...To the words of the little Jewish man...

Coverage of news always got back to Israel—to Jerusalem. The cameras, the microphones might turn away for a period. To report on other pressings issues and events at the top of the news cycle. Always, though... always they returned to capturing news involving Israel, of Jerusalem at its center. Every presidential administration had tried to establish peace in this region surrounding the Temple Mount. Always they failed.

The Rabbi's words echoed in his memory, "Israel is the sign of the end..."

Greyson pushed back from the laptop, continuing to look at the words on its monitor screen.

"The Israel Prophecy."

Should he change the title of the project to, "Israel the Sign"?

He walked to the small kitchen. Retrieving a bottle of *Advil*, He squeezed the cap, twisted it and poured the capsules into his palm.

When he had washed them down with the tea, he massaged his temples to try to quell the headache that had again begun throbbing.

The I-Phone chimed, and he searched beneath some papers until he found it.

The voice was almost frantic on the other end when he answered.

"Tyce! Are you watching the news?!"

"No, George...What..."

"My God, man! Damascus!"

"What about Damascus?"

George Brantt's voice became shaky with emotion as he said in a near whisper, "They've nuked Damascus!"

# CHAPTER 4

"The Russians are threatening all-out war. The administration says any attack against Israel will be considered an attack against the United States."

Tyce Greyson listened to the back and forth in the news room in the CBS building. The city and nation were electric with talk of the Damascus destruction.

"Tyce Greyson?"

The woman's words snatched his concentration from the conversation between two of the network's most recognizable reporters.

"Yes. I'm Greyson."

"Mr. Bressnick is ready for you."

The journalist followed the woman through a series of doorways and into a large office.

"Tyce! Come in. Sit down."

The short, balding network executive beckoned him to be seated on one of the two, large sofas in front of the enormous desk.

"Get you something to drink?" William Bressnick asked with a brief smile.

"No. Thank you."

"I think I'll have one, if you don't mind."

He punched the intercom button and gave his secretary his order.

"You are quite the talk, Tyce. Your broadcast from the other night has gone viral."

Bressnick awaited the journalist's response, which was slow in coming.

"I didn't know... What's it all about?"

"That...prediction... That's what! You said Damascus would be nuked. And, so it was. It's the most profound military action since Truman nuked Hiroshima and Nagasaki."

Tyce's thoughts moved quickly over the purpose of his being called in to network. What did they want?... obviously, they wanted something.

"You are being called a prophet. I have a half-dozen requests to line you up for interviews. Some of the top journalists in our business."

"A prophet!" Tyce's words were spoken with a laugh.

"Your...*prophecy*...is almost as big a story as Damascus's being nuked."

Greyson said nothing, stunned into silence by Bressnick's words.

"We want to do a feature on this.What would you call it? This phenomenon," the executive said, watching his secretary approach with the gin and tonic. He nodded his approval to her.

"What do you think?"

Tyce shifted his glance toward the carpet in concentration.

"I don't know what to make of it. I don't remember making the statement about Damascus being nuked."

"Makes no difference. Your face and words are in every venue you can think of. We need to use it in the right ways."

Ratings. The word entered his mind instantly. The network salivated at the thought of the ratings the whole story might bring. Still, it was understandable. It was the business they were in—who could get the highest ratings. And, the broadcast networks were suffering greatly from the fractionalization of the news business. Cable and cyberspace had forever changed their near-monopoly.

"I know that George gave you a week off. But, we would really like for you to do the news on NYOK Five beginning again tonight. Are you up for it?"

"It's fine with me...If you don't mind risking my going off on a tangent again."

Bressnick laughed. "You seem perfectly fine now, Tyce. Let's get back to the affiliate broadcast for now. There's no telling where this will lead for you."

* * *

A LITTLE MORE THAN an hour later, he stood in a room just off Studio A of NYOK Five. He looked over several pages he had been handed. They were briefs from across the world telling of his broadcast predicting Damascus being hit with a nuclear explosion.

his "prophecy" as it was put in some of the briefs, was as much the story as was the fact that Syria's capital city was now in radioactive rubble.

Almost in third place was the fact that Russia and the

United States were threatening each other over Israel's being blamed for the attack.

But, it was unproven exactly what nation or terrorist group did the deed. The first fingers of pointing went automatically in the direction of Israel.

"You are back a week early, I see."

He looked from studying the pages to see the pretty face of Marial Gunn.

"Not my choice," he said.

"Well, well. You now have instant celebrity." Her words were harsh, and disapproving.

Tyce made no response but challenged her accusation non-verbally with eye contact and unemotional facial expression.

"It is really weird, though," she continued. "This happening... your *prophecy*...only a day earlier."

The word *prophecy* was spoken with a tone dripping with sarcasm.

He was spared having to respond when the familiar voice caused both himself and Marial to turn and face Bernie Maddox.

"Terrific! I'm glad to see you here early, Tyce."

The general program director carried a sheath of papers. He plopped them on a nearby table then moved closer to talk to his co-anchors.

"This thing has gotten out of hand. This broadcast will be seen by more people than the Super Bowl," Maddox said, only half-joking.

"Why? What's so special about...?"

Maddox interrupted Greyson's question.

"You are the *big deal*," Maddox said poking a finger into Greyson's shirt. "They're calling you *the prophet of punditry,*" Maddox said laughingly.

47

"Punditry? He wasn't in the role of a *pundit*," Marial Gunn said. "He was doing a news broadcast."

Bernie Maddox looked at Marial, said nothing then looked again to Greyson.

"Anyway, Tyce, every affiliate in the nation will be tuned to our broadcast at eleven tonight."

"What about the seven o'clock?" Marial asked.

"We want to make sure things are in place, technically, technologically," Maddox said. "There's not enough time to set it up for the seven o'clock newscast."

"What do they expect us to do at eleven?"

Greyson's question brought an animated response from the general program director.

"They just want to see you, Tyce...The man who can see the future!"

"Ha!"

Marial's pseudo-laugh made Maddox break into genuine laughter. "No. We want you to give a brief...maybe ninety-second...explanation of what happened. But, we would like the explanation couched in kind of mystery, if you know what I mean."

"No, I don't think I do know," Tyce said.

"Nor do I," Marial Gunn put in.

"We would like you to just give a brief description of the visit to Patmos—the place where St. John had the vision. Tell them a little about that experience, the snake bite, then the vision you, yourself, saw that day. Also, the one along the same line you had that night you gave the...*prophecy*".

"I've got to go."

Marial Gunn turned quickly on the stiletto heels when she made the announcement in a disgusted tone.

Tyce smiled inwardly, watching with interest the

lovely feminine form walk quickly away, the stilettos clicking on the hard, studio tile.

* * *

AT FIVE MINUTES BEFORE SEVEN, both co-anchors were seated in the burgundy leather chairs. Each poured over the sheets of news copy they held and checked the teleprompters.

"Remember, camera two will frame your head and shoulders when camera one cuts from my completing the opener." Marial Gunn, without looking in his direction, issued the reminder.

"Yes, thanks." Greyson knew she was still worried about what she considered his spastic movements that she said distracted viewers.

The co-anchors heard in their ear pieces "*And five, four, three, two...*"

The red light on camera one came on and Marial read from the prompter.

Tyce Greyson looked into the black camera lenses, concentrating on the opening line he would read. The red light illuminated, and he negotiated the first several lines of the story about the pending Metro Transit strike that loomed. Then, he felt it coming on. He tried but couldn't stop it. His senses faded to dark while the big lenses of camera Two grew, became immense—completely encapsulating.

Gale force wind blew against his body, chilling him to the bone. Foam from the sea doused him with each heaving wave. The storm swirled in every direction while he stood amid the maelstrom upon the churning waters in some unfathomable way.

The very fabric of the billowing, foaming scene

before him appeared to rip apart. Light glowed iridescently within the opening. A terrible, nature-rending cataclysm projected from the widening tear in the dark sea and storm-blackened sky. It was a scene of destruction, at the same time ancient, and modern in its violence.

His nostrils burned, and his lungs felt as if they were expanding to the point of bursting. He shook his head and tried to swat away the thing that was inflicting the discomfort.

"He's back," the voice said, sounding as if it spoke from an empty, 50-gallon metal drum.

"It's just smelling salts," the EMT said in a soothing tone. "We 're just trying to bring you around."

Tyce Greyson sat up, resting on his elbows. His mind struggled with what was happening to him.

"Easy now."

The medic looked into his patient's wildly rolling eyes.

"You're okay, Mr. Greyson. just take it easy.

\* \* \*

"THE COLISEUM WAS TOTALLY DESTROYED in the massive earthquake that struck Rome."

Tyce Greyson watched himself on the TV screen. His face had the familiar, eerie glow like in the previous broadcast utterance. The words were spoken in a manner unlike his own.

"It's the same everywhere. It's being shown constantly across the country... Across the world. The Italians have especially taken notice."

George Brantt listened along with Tyce Greyson to the network executive's words.

"Every news outlet on the planet is running this 30 second...*statement.* They are calling it a *prophecy.*"

Bressnick and Brantt looked at the journalist, awaiting a response. There was none.

Greyson's thought was only that he didn't want to be at the center of the...whatever it was.

THE DOOR to the small lounge opened and Bernie Maddox made the announcement between moments of trying to catch his breath.

"A major quake just struck Italy. The epicenter is Rome!"

TYCE WALKED into the apartment's cramped living room. he placed the bowl of raisin bran to the side of the laptop.

The TV screen several feet behind the laptop's raised cover/screen displayed his own image.

He pushed the button to unmute the television audio.

"Are you finding it difficult to go anywhere these days without being recognized?"

The ABC morning show co-host posed the question and the screen next displayed Greyson's face.

The Journalist shook his head negatively. "No. The public doesn't recognize me any more than before this...this hoopla."

"Well, it's certainly more than *hoopla.*" The host's voice raised in apparent amazement that his guest didn't seem to understand the significance of things going on in his life.

"You predict the first nuclear destruction of a city

51

since 1945. You predict that the coliseum in Rome would fall because of an earthquake. These things happen within hours of your predictions. That's more than *hoopla,* Mr. Greyson...Don't you think?"

Tyce pointed the TV remote at the screen and pushed the mute button before his image responded to the TV host's question.

His life was about to change, and it played constantly on his mind. He didn't want celebrity. Not because of his own modesty and humility. Celebrity, especially of the sort these episodes were producing, meant he would have less time, and less privacy for writing. He cherished his private time. No phones, no visitors, no interruptions. A writer had to have time alone. It was a lonely business, as one famous writer had put it. Maybe Hemingway.

He needed privacy now. The face of the little Jewish man played over and over in his thoughts.

*"Israel is the sign of the end..."*

The final words of the man in the Rabbinic garb ran through his mind again, while his eyes were focused on his own image on the TV screen.

He pushed the off button. He would not be disrupted by his own face, a face that was becoming more well-known by the minute because of such interviews.

His I-Phone chimed, and he looked disgustedly in its direction. He would have to mute it next to stop the interruptions.

"I'm finally free," Marial Gunn said in a resolute tone. "What does your schedule look like, for...say...lunch around noon tomorrow?"

He was both startled and lightly amused at her abruptness. The thought quickly ran through his mind that he would tell anyone else "no". He wanted to be right here, in front of the laptop, writing on the book at noon tomorrow.

"Sure. Noon tomorrow will be okay. When, and where?"

* * *

HE SIPPED LIGHTLY on the Vodka Collins then stirred the drink with the little straw-stirrer. The restaurant milled with the Manhattan lunch crowd. It was a bit noisy for his liking, but such scenes were always interesting.

Each table was peopled by a different story. His reporter-curiosity made him wish he could read lips.

He saw her when she first entered the restaurant's main room. Dressed exquisitely as always, her very presence seemed to magnetically pull the attention of the many eyes in the place. Or maybe it was just *his* eyes that enjoyed the profound allurement.

He stood at the table and began waving at her, seeing she was looking for him.

"There you are," Marial said with a quick smile, seating herself across from him.

"And, there *you* are," he said trying to pay her a compliment with his intonation, without being too overt.

She cast a fleeting look with the green eyes that reflected suspicion of his being chauvinistic in his unspoken compliment. Her expression then softened, apparently letting her suspicion fade.

He could see that her concentration was on something she wanted to ask. Finally, after a few seconds, she did so.

"How did you know those things were going to happen?"

The question, rather than surprising him, made him smile. She thought the predictions were magician's trick.

"Our union won't let us divulge our sleight-of-hand methodology," he said.

He thought better of it the moment he said it. Now she would be angered and that would be the end of their lunch date. To his surprise, she laughed in a barely controlled giggle.

"No! No... You couldn't fake that. I didn't mean to imply that I thought it was a trick. I guess I am asking how do these predictions begin? One second you are reading the news. Next thing we know you're in some sort of trance. Do you feel these...these episodes coming on gradually, or..."

"No. I just suddenly wake up, lying flat on my back. Reading the news is the last thing I remember before coming to consciousness."

She studied his expression, her reporter's curiosity wanting to probe into his thoughts.

Their attention was interrupted by the waiter taking their order. She spoke again when the waiter left.

"Tyce, I understand that network is sending you back to Patmos for the documentary series."

"Yes. They want to begin filming in about two weeks. At least that's the current schedule."

She hesitated in asking the question, almost as if it pained her to ask.

"Do you think you might convince them if I could go along as part of the project?"

\* \* \*

WILLIAM BRESSNICK HELD his right hand on his co-anchors left shoulder while he walked Greyson into his office.

"Tyce, Facebook, Twitter, all of social media is going nuts with this thing. It's insane. You're the biggest topic since Trump to dominate all that media. It's growing by the minute!"

The journalist said nothing, doing as the executive instructed when they reached the sofas. "Be seated. Get you a drink?"

"No, thanks. Had my limit at lunch."

"Liz, hold my calls," Bressnick said into the intercom, then returned his attention to Greyson.

"This thing has taken on a life of its own," Bressnick said excitedly. "I know that's a cliché, but in this case it's an understatement. It's phenomenal!"

"I'm beginning to think so. I'm not enjoying it..."

"Not enjoying all of this attention?! My boy, it's an opportunity few, maybe nobody, has ever had to...to establish a new paradigm in the production of docu-mentaries."

"Well, I am excited about the project. And, I would like to get even with that snake..."

Bressnick laughed. "Yeah. There's that!"

Greyson's tone became more somber. "You know, Mr. Bressnick, this weird... the eerie matter of these broad-casts...these predictions... I have no idea of what it's all about. I constantly ask myself if it has some religious meaning...some spiritual importance that I need to deal carefully with. A responsibility I've been given."

"We don't intend to deal carelessly with it, Tyce. You can be assured. You will have your say. Your requests and even your demands...if they are reasonable... will be taken into consideration."

Greyson said after several seconds, "Well, my first request, is that we take Marial Gunn along with us to Patmos."

* * *

THE SOCIAL MEDIA had not settled down, even though the last six broadcasts of NYOK 5 TV News were done without a new prediction by Tyce Greyson. He had turned down all but two interview requests, both on major broadcast networks. Bressnick and the other executives didn't want their new star-prophet giving the cable competition fodder for winning higher ratings. He would just have to be reclusive, Bressnick had told him.

It was more than okay with him. He found solace behind the keyboard of his laptop. This was exactly where he wanted to be. Working on the book...

He ruminated about the past few days. How she had reacted when she next saw him after Bressnick had added her to the list of people assigned to go to Patmos for the documentary work.

Marial had touched his arm, squeezed it, then continued caressing it with her fingertips while she talked. "Mr. Bressnick told me that you specifically wanted me on the project. It was a really nice thing to do, Tyce. Thank you."

Her beautiful features played now within his memory —the meeting with her just before the broadcast that night. The newscast had gone off without a hitch. His thoughts of late about her had driven from his mind anxieties over the possibility of having another vision, and over the incomprehensible matters that had ruled his life since leaving the Aegean island.

He read silently from the book he picked up at a

prophecy conference. That was what they called the meetings. The people who studied eschatology—the study of end times.

Before attending his first series of meetings in Dallas he had considered such things to be a bit kooky. After talking and interacting with the speakers and attendees —and listening to the presentations-—he decided these were not kooks. Although he wasn't a convert to their way of thinking, there were good reasons for the things they believed. Too many things had transpired...continued to transpire, that validated the possibility that there was something to this Bible prophecy business.

In every case, the speakers, the regular attendees at the meetings, all came up with one conclusion so far as he could tell.

Israel was the number one signal that the world was very near the time of Christ's second coming.

He saw again in his mind's eye, that day at the Wailing Wall near the Temple Mount in Jerusalem. The little Rabbi, he had whispered in his ear, with passion that still burned into his memory.

"Israel is the sign of the end."

Greyson turned his attention again to the book he had purchased at one of the book tables. He read again the author's words he had gone over with a yellow highlighter.

*"Jesus had just given the many signals of His return in answer to His disciples' question: What will be the sign of thy coming and of the end of the[age]?*

*Christ had gone over those signs in detail. He then said, 'And when you see all these things begin to come to pass, then look up and lift up your head, for your redemption draweth nigh.'"*

He opened another of the books from one or the

other of the prophecy conferences he had attended recently. He thumbed through its pages until he found the passage of his search.

"The primary reason we can know that the nation Israel is at the center of Bible prophecy fulfillment is very clear. The Israel of Jesus' day and up to about 135 A.D. existed until the time of the Roman Emperor Hadrian. Israel at that time was cut off from being a nation and the Jews were dispersed into the whole world.

Daniel the prophet had predicted Israel's downfall and reestablishment as recorded in chapter 9 of the Old Testament. Jesus, who is God, and had given Daniel the Old Testament prophet the prophecy in the first place, foretold the nation's downfall when He talked with His closest followers that day on the Mount of Olives: And Jesus went out, and departed from the temple: and his disciples came to *him* for to shew him the buildings of the temple. And Jesus said unto them, See ye not all these things? verily I say unto you, There shall not be left here one stone upon another, that shall not be thrown down.' (Matthew 24: 1-2)

Jerusalem suffered destruction in 70 A.D. by the Romans, when Roman soldiers, under General Titus, son of Vespasian the emperor, tore down the Temple. The Jews were severely persecuted and hunted down until they made their last stand at Masada. Hadrian, then the emperor, crushed all Jewish survivors that rebelled, and the rest fled into other nations.

There was no Israel—no Jewish state—until Midnight May 14-15, 1948, when Israel was reborn as a nation.

We know there had to be a nation called Israel at the

time of Christ's Second Advent. There also had to be a temple.

Daniel foretold: *... And the people of the prince that shall come shall destroy the city and the sanctuary..."* (Daniel 9: 26)

The city is *Jerusalem* and the sanctuary is the *Temple.*

We also know that there must be an Israel and a Temple because Jesus said there will be a Temple in which Antichrist will enter and claim himself to be God.

"When ye therefore shall see the abomination of desolation, spoken of by Daniel the prophet, stand in the holy place, (whoso readeth, let him understand:) Then let them which be in Judaea flee into the mountains.' (Matthew 24: 15-16)"

The Apostle Paul expands on this *son of perdition* as recorded in 2 Thessalonians 2: 3-4.

Greyson retrieved the Bible and rifled through the pages until he found the words of Paul.

"Let no man deceive you by any means: for *that day shall not come,* except there come a falling away first, and that man of sin be revealed, the son of perdition; Who opposeth and exalteth himself above all that is called God, or that is worshipped; so that he as God sitteth in the temple of God, shewing himself that he is God."

GREYSON STOOD AND STRETCHED, then kneaded his temples with his thumb and fingertips. The headache was back, and he was out of Advil.

When he reached the lobby of his apartment building he saw several reporters he recognized. They were arguing with management. They wanted to go to his apartment. He slipped from the elevator to the exit leading to the back of the alley in the building without being noticed.

He walked quickly down Seventh Avenue in the direction of Times Square, his thoughts tuning out the busy New York City sounds.

His last attended Bible prophecy conference moved through his mind. One speaker—he couldn't remember the name—had spoken on Second Thessalonians. On chapter 2 of the Book.

The word *"Day"* in the prophecy..."*That day*"... The speaker had said that the term *"Day"* referred to the *Day of the Lord.* This would be a terrible time, the speaker said. It would be the time Jesus, himself, referred to as recorded in the prophecy in what the speaker called *"the Olivet Discourse".*

Jesus foretold that it would be the worst time that had ever been or would ever be again.

The terms *"man of sin" and "son of perdition"* referred to the *Antichrist*—the man who would be the word's las and most terrible dictator.

The *man of sin* would, the speaker said, go into the Jewish Temple. He would stop the sacrifices and make the Jews stop worshipping God and would kill the priests. He would then declare himself to be god and demand that all the world worship only himself. It would be a time more horrible than Hitler's Nazi regime.

The journalist crossed the street when the light changed and, after walking another block, descend the stairs and entered the pharmacy.

When he was seated in the small restaurant near the drug store, he popped several of the capsules after the waiter brought water.

"Tune on whole wheat and coffee," Greyson said in answer to the waiter asking for his order.

There was now no temple on the Temple Mount. He remembered a lecture by the speaker that managed to traverse his brain, despite the raging headache. There would be a temple built. There would have to be one built atop Mount Moriah because Bible prophecy said so.

There was no doubt about it—the speaker was telling the facts. The Temple Mount was—had long been—the one spot on the planet that presented the greatest danger of igniting world-wide conflict and nuclear war.

A sudden rush of people though the restaurant's doors started him from his thoughts.

"There he is!" A female reporter's shout directed the attention of everyone in the room to Tyce Greyson's table.

* * *

"It's getting intolerable, George."

Tyce spoke to George Brantt between glancing at the news copies he held, then at the program director.

"I'll have to give up the apartment. They won't leave me alone for a second."

Brantt, standing beside the sitting Greyson put a hand on his shoulder.

"Bressnick knows about the pressure from the gaggle following you and hanging out around the apartment. He's arranging a secure suite just a building or so away from CBS."

"A suite! I can't afford a hotel suite," Greyson said. "I can barely afford the shoebox I'm in now."

"Those are the perks, my boy," Brantt said authoritatively. "That's what celebrity is all about. CBS is footing the bill."

Twelve minutes later Marial Gunn burst through the door to studio A. She was uncharacteristically late. Her normally perfectly made-up face appeared reddened, her blonde hair, normally affixed in perfection, a bit disheveled, a few strands loosened and in thinly curling ringlets against her lovely jaw line.

Tyce liked the look. But, it would soon be changed.

She entered the little space off the Green Room, where she would get make-up and the hairdo made right again.

"It's been some kind of day," she said, hurriedly sitting in the burgundy chair beside her co-anchor.

"You okay?" His question expressed genuine concern and Marial nodded affirmatively and smiled appreciation of his asking.

The recorded voice of the booth announcer alerted the television audience that the NYOK 5 seven o'clock news was about to begin, and the co-anchors heard the familiar countdown.

"Five, four, three, two..."

He heard Marial Gunn's voice begin the first story. it would go for 40 seconds, then it would be his turn.

He glanced at the sheet he held between his hands, checking the monitor screens then the prompter.

Her words faded, as did his visual effort—the attempt to see the large, black, copy on the white pages.

Rather than continuing to see the text on the page, a hole began burning in the center of the blackness that replaced the white page.

People sat within a cylindrical-shaped conveyance. The passenger tube moved ahead at a rapid speed, the people within their seats reading newspapers or in conversation.

Radiance from a light source that could not be determined illuminated the cabin in an eerie iridescence.

The passenger tube suddenly seemed to erupt with violence. The scene became one of panic. The passengers lurched wildly within their seats, screaming while trying to hang onto anything that would provide stability.

Water cascaded from a rupture in the cabin's forward-most parts, filling the chamber and drowning those in its path.

"Tyce...Tyce!"

Marial Gunn's voice was the next he heard. It was distant, calling to him as if in an echo chamber.

"Tyce!"

Marial held him, her arm stretched across his chest, trying to straighten him in the studio set's anchor chair.

She looked around, desperately asking for help.

Momentarily, several technicians took over the job of keeping Greyson upright. Marcel Rollins patted Greyson's face with fingertips. He looked around to get the attention of one or the other of the men trying to help.

"Get us a doctor or somebody!"

"WE'VE REVIEWED THE TAPE," William Bressnick said. "We've tried to warn the people in London."

Tyce Greyson sat in the chair facing the monitor screens as requested by the network executive.

"We've tried to tell them about your... your statement," Bressnick continued.

"What did I say this time?"

Greyson held a cold compress the medics had given

him against his forehead, trying to get the pain to subside.

"Here it is," Bressnick said, pressing a button on the control board to begin the recorded words.

*"The Chunnel train, Eurostar, was destroyed, all fifty-seven passengers drowned by the waters of the English Channel."*

Tyce Greyson sat, stunned, his own revelation causing the staccato pounding in his head to increase.

"My God... Have you heard anything?"

"The broadcast went out only an hour and a half ago. We've been trying to reach somebody over there. To tell them to beware. But, everybody we've talked to says there is no report of any accident involving the Chunnel train."

Bressnick picked up the buzzing phone from the control console beneath the wall of monitors.

He stood, his eyes wide, his mouth agape, after answering the call. He slowly replaced the receiver on its cradle. He spoke almost in a whisper.

"Just thirty-five minutes ago...the Eurostar was destroyed in some sort of Chunnel explosion while on the way To France. Apparently, all fifty-seven aboard were killed."

# CHAPTER 5

"There are some on Twitter and other social media blaming Tyce."

William Bressnick sat at the head of the long, mahogany, conference table while speaking.

"There are always the crazies, but they are, by far, in the minority. Mostly, people want to know more about all of this." The gathering of network executives was sent, through teleconference, to executives farther up the chain of command.

Tyce sat half way down the table on Bressnick's right. His thoughts ran the gamut, from the worry that the unwanted celebrity would ruin his life—had already probably done so—to the beautiful features of Marial Gunn. He remembered her caring touch to his cheek before leaving him with the medics. The cool, slender fingertips against his face.

"You take care of him," she had said, before leaving the room.

Bressnick spoke again. "So, I believe this documentary series will be well received. Even those who think

Tyce is somehow responsible will be fascinated by the programs."

"Tyce, what do you think about all this?"

It was the voice of the network's president high above in the building. "I understand you're feeling a lot of pressure from the press."

Greyson straightened in the conference chair, trying to clear his mind of his thoughts about Marial Gunn.

"At least there is some distance, a buffer between my every waking moment and them."

The CBS president was amused.

"'*Them.* I remember an old black and white movie called *Them.* They were giant ants. Voracious ants," he said in a tone of amusement.

"Yeah, well... Maybe they're not quite that bad. But, now that I'm in the new digs, they can't get to me as easily. Thanks for that."

"Good... Good," the executive said.

"So, are you ready to take on this assignment? To go back to Patmos?"

"Yes, sir. Looking forward to it."

"He says he wants to find that snake and get even with it," George Brantt put in from across the table, bringing laughter from all in the room and from the network's head executive.

\* \* \*

ISRAEL'S *IDF* was on its highest alert. Damascus lay in ruins and Syria's chief allies; Russia and Iran threatened the Jewish state with retaliation.

Rome and many of the ancient ruins had suffered great damage from the earthquake, the coliseum all but destroyed.

Yet the talk of everyone in New York, in the nation—even internationally, was the local co-anchor of a CBS news affiliate. Tyce Greyson *was* the news.

William Bressnick was excited.

"Do you realize that this documentary series will make all others seem insignificant? Your newscasts are seen by an audience larger than that of the broadcast networks and the cable news outlets combined. We have no choice but to put security around you for the foreseeable future."

Tyce didn't like the idea but said nothing.

"It's only reasonable, Tyce. There are lunatics out there in today's world."

"I've never been threatened...except by the news hounds," Greyson said, feeling the headache coming on again.

"We've hired a security firm. They will assign a few of their people. They will be discrete."

Greyson said nothing but fumbled through the attaché case to his right to find the bottle of Advil. Bressnick stood and walked to the desk to punch the intercom button.

"Liz, bring us a glass of water, please."

Moments later the journalist downed the water and the capsules.

"We want you to do one more broadcast from NYOK before we head for Patmos," the network executive said. "We will do some heavy promotion of the Patmos series in this broadcast."

* * *

THE SCHEDULE WAS SET. They would fly out of JFK at 12:45 p.m. the next day. But first he would do the news broadcast, preceded by and followed by promotion of the upcoming documentary series: *Patmos Apocalypse.*

He watched the laptop's screen as the computer pulled up the document.

*Israel, the Sign*

The tentative title given the manuscript ran through his mind, whispered by the voice of the Jewish man in the religious garb. It was as if the little man in the religious get-up had dictated the title. Greyson could think of none better.

Bressnick had promised him time and funding for pursuing research on the book. He would do the research in Jerusalem and other places in Israel. He could do so between times of filming the documentary, which he would narrate for the most part. Telling his story and going over the dramatic *prophecies* he had uttered since the bite by the viper.

The remembered words of the short, rotund, television preacher he had become fond of watching on Sundays thundered in his head now, while the text scrolled on the laptop's screen.

*"Have you noticed how Israel is condemned by practically every nation in the U.N? Have you noticed that even though Israel does nothing through aggressive actions toward the Palestinians...and the PLO and other Islamic-Arab actors in the area to murder Israeli Jews,.it is the Jews, it is Israel who is called the aggressors...the occupiers...the murderers?"*

The questions burned into his reporter's curiosity. It was always the Arab states, the Islamists, that declared they would completely eradicate the Jewish state. They vowed to push every Jew into the Mediterranean.

The Arab coalition had indeed attempted to do just that on the historically notable occasions in1948 at Israel's rebirth into modernity. The Arab forces, under

Nasser then Sadat had tried to destroy Israel in 1956, 1967 and 1973. They continued their blood-vow to erase Israel from being a nation.

Despite these rants, the rest of the world—with few exceptions—continued to declare Israel the problem. Israel must give in to the Palestinian demands that declared they wanted Israeli territory in exchange for peace. Yet the Arab enemies would never even recognize Israel as a legitimate state.

The Texas preacher's words echoed again in his mind's ear.

*"The world hates Israel because that is the people out of whom the savior of the world...Jesus Christ...came into the world to seek and to save lost humanity. The Old Testament prophet, Zechariah, said it all in giving the end times declaration..."*

The preacher had held up the big Bible, then placed it on the pulpit.

"Zechariah the prophet foretold the following," the preacher had said before reading from the scripture.

"The burden of the word of the LORD for Israel, saith the LORD, which stretcheth forth the heavens, and layeth the foundation of the earth, and formeth the spirit of man within him. Behold, I will make Jerusalem a cup of trembling unto all the people round about, when they shall be in the siege both against Judah *and* against Jerusalem.

And in that day will I make Jerusalem a burdensome stone for all people: all that burden themselves with it shall be cut in pieces, though all the people of the earth be gathered together against it."

Tyce remembered the hours spent at the United Nations building. The constant diatribe against Israel. The delegations that got up from their seats when

Benjamin Netanyahu or other Israeli spoke before the assembly. How the vote against Israel was overwhelming in most every case when the Jewish state was at the center of controversy.

The Zechariah prophecy could already be considered to have come true, he pondered, looking again to the laptop's screen.

His own life was now being drawn irresistibly into the end of days drama, or whatsoever one might call it. Why and how had it happened? he had always considered such as in the same category as UFOs, ghost stories, and other matters. Things better suited to the fiction writers' pursuits than to journalists in pursuit of truth.

The Bible, he respected the Bible, having been raised a Catholic. But, as a journalist—a realist—the Bible was to be looked at as a great literary work, not as the very Word of God, as the Texas television preacher would have it.

Yet it was happening to him. Why him? The Patmos visions, or whatsoever they were... The sudden celebrity from the...prophecies?

They had come true, those predictions, predictions he didn't even remember making during those news casts.

And the next newscast was now less than an hour and a half away. The final newscast before heading to Patmos and to Israel and Jerusalem in pursuit of... trying to find out what might be his own part in all of this strangeness.

His thoughts were interrupted by noises in the suite's foyer.

When he moved from the computer in the direction of the sounds, he was startled by the voice.

"Just stay put, Mr. Greyson. We just want to talk with you."

The larger of the two men, both dressed in dark suits, spoke in a calming, voice, tinged with an intonation of condescension.

"How did you get in here?"

Tyce's words were ignored by the intruders.

"Just relax. We are from national Security. We need to ask some questions. May we be seated?"

The men walked into the small room.

"We won't be but a minute," the same man said, while he and the other man seated themselves.

Tyce, contemplating how they got past his CBS-appointed security people, stood, saying nothing, then slowly seated himself in a chair across from them.

"Where are you from? What agency? The NSA?"

"It really is of no concern to you, Mr. Greyson...*Tyce*... May we call you Tyce?"

Greyson said nothing, looking to the man who spoke then to the silent man, who stared at him, a deadpan expression on his face.

"We are here, Tyce, because these...these *visions?*... These things you are predicting...They are presenting problems..."

The agent fell silent, apparently awaiting Greyson's response.

"What problems am I presenting to national security?" Tyce's question was laced with irritation.

"We are somewhat concerned that these...*predictions*...could exacerbate...could add to the civil unrest, which, as you know, is growing because of racial and ideological differences going on at present."

"How so?" Tyce's words displayed his growing irritation over their intrusion.

"We want to...*preempt*...anything of a volatile nature that might result from these... visions of yours. We need to prevent panic that these...predictions you make might cause."

Greyson said nothing, deciding to make the man explain how they planned to "preempt" his future statements.

"We would like to .... *observe* you for a period of time. We would like it to be...*voluntary*... We request that you not broadcast for the next several weeks. That you let some of our *experts* in psychoanalysis work with you in getting an *understanding* of what this... *gift* of yours might entail. From the standpoint of being a threat to, or an enhancement to America's national security."

Tyce Greyson's inner-mechanism of self-preservation kicked in. He would tell them anything they wanted to hear for the moment.

After several seconds of pause, the journalist said, "Sure. For America and our national security. Anything I can do."

\* \* \*

WILLIAM BRESSNICK WAS LIVID. He paced, red-faced and cursing.

"The audacity of this administration to interfere with the free press! It won't stand!"

The network executive listened then while the network's chief executive officer's voice spoke over the intercom speakers.

"Tyce, so you told these agents that you would do as they demanded?"

"Yes, sir. But it was only so they wouldn't force me to go with them."

"Good thinking," the voice said. "We have made written objections and taken legal steps to continue with the broadcasts, un-encumbered by government inter-ference."

"Any push-back from the administration, or anybody?" Bressnick's question was given after sitting and sipping from the coffee cup held between his fingers and thumb.

"Not only has there been no push-back, but they denied any knowledge that the encounter in Tyce's suite had taken place," the voice said from the intercom speakers.

"Well, it wasn't one of my patent visions, believe me. It really took place."

Both executives laughed at Greyson's words.

"Yes, and speaking of which, we will do the final broadcast tonight before you head for the Aegean. We have some significant promotion for the documentary project. We will begin, announcing your return to the cave where all this began. I've seen the promotion. It's quite amazing. We've come up with the final title for the series. We've changed it from *The Patmos Apocalypse,* to *Revelations.* Great title, huh?"

The network's president paused, awaiting response. hearing none, he spoke. "Tyce, we are really getting serious now about security. I'm sorry, but you can never tell what these clandestine services people will try to pull. There will be people around you at all times, but it will be as discreet as possible and as unobtrusive as we can make it."

* * *

TERRY JAMES

MONITOR SCREENS STRUNG along the wall were alive with video and narration. Lightning, thunder and rolling, boiling clouds generated by technological wizardry gave the scenes the appearance of apocalyptic rage.

"That should hook 'em," Marcel Rollins said, watching the angry clouds swirl above the scene of a tumultuous sea, while the narrator pronounced, "The man who sees the future is now among us."

The scenes switched to Tyce making the predictions in the broadcast segments, then back to the heaving sea and stormy skies.

"The making of *REVELATIONS* gets underway as Tyce Greyson revisits the ancient Greek Aegean island of Patmos, where St. John received the visions of Apocalypse two thousand years ago."

"Wow," Rollins said quietly, glancing at Greyson sitting next to him. "That's some promo!"

Rollins looked past Tyce and stood from his chair.

"Uh-oh. There's the princess. Better get things moving," he said, walking to meet Marial Gunn who had just entered Studio A.

He talked briefly with her before walking on toward the glass that surrounded the studio news set.

Marial approached, her look one of concentration.

"What's this I hear about government agents...?"

Her question brought a quick, dismissive smile to Greyson's face.

"It wasn't much of anything. They are afraid I'll cause national panic. They want to study me for a couple of weeks."

"Study? You mean like in psychoanalysis?"

"Yep, I guess that's their idea."

"Do you think they will go further?"

"I really don't know their real idea behind the session

we had. Regardless, we are going forward with the trip and with this broadcast."

Marial 's expression softened. Her tone became quieter.

"They tell me they've put security around you. That's pretty serious."

"Yeah, well, not as serious as all this weird vision stuff. Whatever is going on, I've got to take it to the limit, as they say."

She gave a look of complete agreement.

"Good, Tyce Greyson. Good for you."

*"And five, four, three, two..."*

Marial Gunn looked into camera 1 and read from the prompter. The story ran for a minute and 45 seconds before she turned to her co-anchor for a bit of light-hearted transition to the story of a new effort at helping the homeless within New York City get food and housing.

After 3 minutes of the story, the camera's red light went dark and the promotion of Tyce Greyson's upcoming trip to Patmos filled the monitor screens of Studio A.

Tyce watched his co-anchor take in the promotions, admiring her loveliness. She was, he considered, undoubtedly the most beautiful woman in the city.

She seemed mesmerized by the scenes playing before her. Where normally she would be shuffling papers and marking the pages of news copy with a highlighter, she now sat, her intense gaze affixed upon the promotion. The scene that ended with the words emblazoned across the screen over churning clouds and sea.

"REVELATIONS "

*"Standby...And... five, four, three, two..."*

The red camera light came on and it was Greyson's turn.

"There were fireworks today in the U.N. General Assembly when the Israeli ambassador to the United Nations accused that body of having a, quote, Anti-Semitic mind-set. This prompted the entire delegation representing the Arab Emirates to walk out."

The words on the prompter began to disintegrate before his eyes. His vision darkened, and his thoughts faded to black.

His next conscious indicator was of emerging from a dark abyss. He ascended until voices joined in his awareness.

"Tyce! Tyce!"

The EMT urged him to full consciousness while the strong odor of ammonia singed his nostrils.

"Tyce! I think he's coming too," the man holding the packet beneath Greyson's nose, said to the several people gathered around.

* * *

"I've asked Marial to sit in with us, Tyce. She's been quite concerned about you."

George Brantt seated himself in the console board chair and started pushing buttons. The largest of the monitor screens on the wall above them lit up.

Brantt's words helped soothe the headache that had been with him since the newscast and losing consciousness. She was concerned about him. The thought pleased him very much.

"What did I say this time?"

His question was issued with disgust in his tone.

"I wanted to let you watch it, rather than just tell you.

First impression might jog something in your thinking as opposed to just telling you and letting you mull it over before actually hearing the newscast."

"So, you've already seen it?"

"Yes, I've gone over it several times, " Brantt said.

"What about Marial?"

"First time for her to review the newscast. Bressnick will sit in, too."

Both men turned to watch William Bressnick and Marial Gunn while they walked into the control room.

The network executive came to Tyce and patted his shoulder.

"How're you feeling?"

He asked the question while seating himself to Greyson's left.

"Don't know yet," Tyce said. "I'll be okay when the headache is done, I think."

The co-anchors' glances met. Each smiled greetings but said nothing.

"So, let's have a look," George Brantt said, manipulating several buttons.

The screen showed the date and station name of the newscast. After a few seconds Tyce's image filled the screen and he read the news item.

"There were fireworks today in the U.N. General Assembly when the Israeli ambassador to the United Nations accused that body of having a, quote, Anti-Semitic mind-set. This prompted the entire delegation representing the Arab Emirates to walk out."

They watched his face take on a yellowish pallor, and his pupils dilated, making his eyes look like black, glistening, orbs.

"Look at his face," Marial said from Tyce's right while watching the replay. "What's happening?"

The men said nothing, watching intently while Greyson's mouth moved, and the words issued in a guttural, staccato announcement.

"A nuclear device from a long-ago crashed B-52 bomber accident detonated in waters off North Carolina's coast..."

They watched Tyce Greyson collapse after uttering the words, Marial Gunn trying to catch him as he fell from the chair toward her position on his right.

"Have the people been warned?"

Greyson's question was urgent.

"Yes. The governors of the coastal states have been told. Everybody from the president to the military to FEMA are in process of being told."

Bressnick said, after Brantt had spoken, "They are looking at precisely where they believe nukes were lost."

"There were more than one?"

"We're not sure," George Brantt said answering Tyce's inquiry.

There were several seconds of uncomfortable silence. Tyce finally spoke.

"The other times...after the broadcasts...the things happened within hours..."

"The newscast took place a little over two hours ago. There's no word on anything," William Bressnick said.

"Are you okay, Tyce?"

Marial gently squeezed his forearm.

"You don't look well."

# CHAPTER 6

"There's no word of any problems off the North Carolina coast."

Marcel Rollins walked from the front of the plane to where Tyce Greyson sat.

"It's been about," Rollins looked at his watch. "About twenty-two hours since the newscast. Still no explosion."

Tyce said nothing, letting the possibilities run through his mind.

Maybe the...*gift* ... was gone. Maybe the snake's venom was out of his system. He smiled inwardly at his foolish thought. Whatever it was, it had nothing to do with the snake bite... maybe.

He closed the laptop and stood to place it in the overhead bin above his seat.

Maybe it was just that the...the predictions would now take longer to unfold... to come true. Maybe...Maybe there would be no detonation. He hoped with all that was within him that that was the case.

"Tyce, I found out that your girl will arrive at Athens International tomorrow evening, Athens time."

"She's not my *girl,* Marcel," Greyson said with mock irritation.

"Well, you're the only one who has been able to break through the Ice Princess' glacier-facade."

"Wish you would stop calling her Ice Princess."

The broadcast engineer stifled a laugh.

"Yeah, okay, sure... So, she's not your girl... So, how should I refer to her?"

"How about just Marial?"

Rollins moved so Tyce could return to the seat near the window.

"Okay. Okay. I'll say no more. By the way, we are headed into a bit of weather, they're telling me."

He looked out the window to his right, seeing the darkening skies ahead. The *Gulfstream CBS* had chartered had provided a smooth flight since the noon liftoff from JFK. It was highly unusual, William Bressnick had informed, for the network to charter jets for anything. But, this project was of such importance that they wanted schedules to be met precisely. Commercial travel wouldn't do.

Also, Bressnick had said, the logistics required special travel arrangements. There had to be the constant security, which meant extra people on the trip. The top people at network saw it as the most important documentary project ever planned.

He wished Marial was on the flight. Her face was in his thoughts constantly over the past days. She would join him...join the project tomorrow night in Athens. The thought pleased him very much.

He had gotten little sleep over the past 18 hours. Drowsiness tugged at him now while he watched the clouds ahead grow nearer and felt the ride become bumpier with each passing minute.

80

The wing moved up and down quickly while the air through which it sliced became ever more turbulent.

Flying had never been a thing to fear. He had been through many a stormy ride. Although, he considered, his confrontations with storms while flying had always been in the big, heavy jet aircraft, not the luxurious, but much smaller *Gulfstream.*

He watched while the wing just outside the porthole became ever more difficult to discern. The plane had entered the dark, swirling clouds. The air pockets through which the G-6 plowed shook the plane, the seat beneath him unable to buffer the jolting ride.

Opaqueness produced by the storm engulfed his vista. He felt his inner senses fading—as if they were melding with the darkness outside the porthole. He suddenly knew that, yet another episode was intruding upon his reality.

He could do nothing to stop the strange, cerebral convolutions. he realized in his last, fleeting moments of conscious thought that reality was about to be overtaken.

The dark, swirling curtain ignited, a pinpoint of light brighter than the Sun bursting at its center. The ring of fire surrounding the hole in the fabric burned wider until a scene of people on their knees filled his astonished realization.

Hundreds of people knelt, their heads bowed before the massive, pure-white light that shined so brightly the form it shrouded could only be faintly discerned. The figure of a man stood within the effulgence before which the throng bowed.

Tyce Greyson's brain pulsed with the sights and sounds it struggled to comprehend. A cavernous voice echoed deeply from somewhere within the vision.

*"My people...called by my name...have brought forth Kingdom Intervention..."*

His next inner-cerebral sight burned with super-white iridescence from the center of the dark vision-fabric that had closed upon the conclusion of the echoing words.

The word emblazoned in flaming yellow and orange letters upon the blackness: *Spared.*

Reality instantly returned, Greyson now seeing clearly the aircraft's right wing just outside the porthole.

The thought came without having to search for meaning. He had just been told through the vision that prayers had spared the people the nuclear explosion would have destroyed.

* * *

"WE DON'T THINK the bomb not going off will affect ratings for the REVELATIONS documentary."

William Bressnick's voice spoke over speaker phone that Marcel Rollins held while he and Tyce listened.

"And, maybe it will yet go off, God forbid," the network executive said.

"It won't."

Greyson's declaration was emphatic, causing a pause before Bressnick again spoke.

"Oh? How can you know?"

"Another...vision... or whatever it was."

"Really?! When?"

"Somewhere over Europe. I was looking out the window at the storm and I had another of the episodes."

"What did you see, or experience?"

"This figure of light. It was a human figure shrouded by the most brilliant light imaginable. It spoke—at least a voice that I heard said that people called by my name have brought forth kingdom intervention."

Again, there was pause on the other end.

"What do you think it means?" Bressnick said.

"The people I saw...hundreds of them... They were on their knees. They were bowing before this figure of light. They were praying, I think...I know they were praying to this...this figure of light."

"I can't buy into the religious stuff. How do you know that has anything to do with the bomb not going off like you predicted?"

"I just know it. That's all I can tell you."

THE TRIP to Athens had been tiring, even for a man of only thirty. The experience in the storm above the European continent had added to the fatigue. It had, like the visions before, been emotionally draining. Probably, he thought, had taken a physical toll as well.

Tyce looked in the bathroom mirror and examined his face. He was aging, the puffy places beneath his eyes taking on an ever more lined look of an older man. But, the age pouches always went away, he considered, to assuage his unpleasant thoughts of growing old before his time. He would look and feel much better when he had gotten a night's sleep.

The documentary project would begin the filming process in two days. The crew would spend tomorrow going over the shooting schedule and all the details. He would study the parts he was to narrate.

Marial would join them tomorrow evening...

He let his thoughts of her move within his growing

drowsiness. The reunion would be something he could look forward to...

His I-Phone chimed, and he answered.

"Tyce, Bressnick and Brantt have been on the phone with some BBC guys. They want you to interview with one of their premiere programs."

"When? We have a tight enough schedule now," Greyson said, shutting off the hotel room's light while exiting the bathroom.

"Tomorrow at eight, London time."

How would it interfere with the dinner he planned with Marial? The troubled thought quickly traversed his thinking.

"How long will the interview last?"

"Don't know. I think they are like the old Sixty Minute format. Several segments of ever how many minutes."

"Guess there's no choice. Okay. I'll do it."

* * *

MARIAL GUNN APPROACHED after leaving the secured section of the Athens's airport terminal. Tyce stepped forward from between George Brantt and Marcel Rollins to meet her.

Her radiant smile was all he saw, the only thing in the terminal. She was his total object of attention.

When he reached his hand to take hers, she pushed it aside with her fingertips, instead wrapping her arms around his neck and hugging him tightly.

Tyce felt his face redden with the heat of emotion. It wasn't embarrassment at the public display of affection. He felt the rush of something he hadn't sensed in his 30 years of life. She was everything he wanted...needed, to make him complete.

The hug lingered, and when she pulled away, he saw her eyes glisten with tears.

"You okay, Marial?"

He held her at arms length, looking into the green eyes, beautiful, even filled with tears.

"I'm okay...Just am glad to see you," she said, her voice breaking slightly.

He said nothing but pulled her to him again.

"I'm glad you're here," he said, then, still holding her with one arm, turned to let the other men greet her.

"I'll be writing some of the scripts," Marial said while sitting between Tyce and George Brantt in the back seat of the taxicab. "It's something I haven't done for a while, but it's something I've really been wanting to do. Even thought about taking a script-writing job in Hollywood once."

"Oh? Why didn't you?"

"New York, and a chance to enhance the old career as a broadcast journalist," she said with a facetious lilt in her voice.

"Well, I'm sure glad you turned down Hollywood," Tyce said, reaching to take her hand and squeeze it. He continued to hold the hand while they talked.

"Well, it would have just been for that one film, with no real promises of future work beyond that. Plus, I was warned over and over about the...*casting couch*..."

There was a moment of silence before Tyce said, "Well. You made the right choice in my humble estimation."

The cab pulled into the drive beneath one of the hotel's porticos. Tyce, Marial, George Brantt and Marcel Rollins got out and walked into the big lobby.

"Those men," Marial Gunn said, turning to indicate three men dressed in suits. "They were at the airport looking at us. "Now they are here, still looking at us."

"It's security. I'm afraid they are with us indefinitely. Network is concerned the bogyman might be out to get me."

She said nothing, but he could see worry briefly change her expression.

"They can take care of any problems, I'm told," he said, continuing to move across the expansive lobby floor with Marial at his side. He decided to change the subject.

"We've got about thirty minutes before the BBC people expect me. We will do the interview in this building. They have a make-shift studio that will allow for a live broadcast. They will film an interview for their weekly program, then get to the live broadcast. I think they said they will interview me live for their nightly newscast. That will only be for ten minutes or so."

The elevator doors slid open and several people exited. One of the passengers touched Tyce on the arm, stopping him from moving forward into the elevator.

"You're Tyce Greyson, aren't you?"

Before Tyce could answer, the man was roughly pulled aside by intruding arms. The man grunted, a startled look on his face.

The security man held the man, examining him with their eyes.

"It's okay," Greyson said. "Let him go."

The man straightened his clothing, his expression changing to a look of anger.

"What's going on here?"

He cast glances at the men who had grabbed him and then at Greyson.

"Sorry. These men are security. To answer your question... I'm Tyce Greyson."

The man again looked at his attackers while straightening his tie and coat, before speaking.

"Yes. Well, I'm with BBC. Name's Nigel Brisbin..."

"Sorry about the security," Tyce said. "Nice to meet you."

"I've come to escort you to the studio," Brisbin said in a British accent. "May I take you there now?"

With filming of the interview completed in just over an hour, Greyson's make-up was retouched while he awaited going before the cameras for the live BBC audience.

Marial stepped into the small room.

"Bressnick says to mention the episode you experienced on the plane if you get the chance."

"If there's time. I'm only on for a few minutes."

"Well, that's his message," she said reaching with fingertips to brush his hair into place.

"We'll see how it goes..."

They wanted him to give an excuse for the bomb not going off. They couldn't afford to lose the momentum they had going for the documentary. They didn't want Tyce Greyson to lose the mystique of being able to soothsay. The thought amused him. It was what it was, and nothing could change what would or would not be.

THE MAKE-SHIFT STUDIO in the Athens hotel suite was remarkably like other broadcast studios. Monitors lined one wall and the bells and whistles of control seemed all in order while he seated himself in the black, leather chair.

Momentarily a lanky, older man with silver-white hair and mustache offered his hand.

"Reginald Formby," he said.

The familiar voice of one of the BBC's top news personalities explained the details of how the live interview would go.

The Brit, when he had finished explaining the program format, sat across from Tyce, crossed one lanky leg over the knee of the other and studied several pages he held between his fingers.

An engineer began the countdown to the live segment and Formby then spoke, looking into the camera.

"We have on BBC *World Scope*, tonight a guest who most will recognize, I think."

While Reginald Formby spoke in upper-crust British, the monitor screens changed from projecting his face to that of Tyce Greyson.

"His has become a most recognizable face of late. He is called the man who sees the future by some. I welcome Tyce Greyson to our segment tonight."

With greetings made and reciprocated, Formby ask his first question.

"Mr. Greyson, how do these...visions...begin? They have happened, as I understand, when you have been doing live broadcasts—like ours, here, tonight."

"Yes...All on live broadcasts. Except for the ...vision... on the flight to Athens."

"Oh? Please do tell us about it."

Marial looked to the main monitor screen that displayed Tyce's face. he shifted slightly in his seat across from Reginald Formby. his expression became one of deep reflection before he spoke.

"I was looking out the window to my right. We had

flown into...at least a portion of the storm. The outer edge of a storm. my mind began reeling, like always with these...these visions. Everything before me became dark...totally dark."

Tyce paused to think more deeply on the recollection.

"A hole of light appeared at the center of the darkness. it was like a ring of fire. it burned the fabric of that.... that blackness. it burned apart and in place of the darkness were people...hundreds of them. They were praying...on their knees. they were praying to this...this brilliant light that shrouded a human-like form."

The camera cut to Formby when he spoke.

"Really?! What was this all about, do you think?"

The main screen again filled with Greyson's face.

"I've come to believe they were kneeling before...before Jesus Christ."

The screen again was on Formby's face. his silver-white eyebrows raised in surprise.

"Christ? Why so? What makes you think it was this particular figure?"

"My upbringing as a Catholic, maybe. people bow before a religious figure. it's usually Mary...or Jesus. maybe another saint..."

"And what did this mean, do you think?"

"I heard a voice coming from somewhere within this...this whole scene... It said: *'People called by my name have brought about kingdom intervention...'*"

"And, how do you interpret this?" The program host's words asked the question with a raised level of curiosity.

"This...voice... was saying that the prediction about the lost hydrogen bomb exploding somewhere off the North Carolina coast would not happen because God's people had prayed. God had intervened."

"What makes you so certain of that?"

"I just know. And... there was the final thing that happened to end the vision. The word appeared upon the blackness that returned. It said, in red and yellow flame-like letters...the word SPARED."

The host hesitated, as if searching for a follow up question. After clearing his throat and fumbling a bit to ask his question he said, "Do you think this, perhaps, might be the end of the...these visions?"

Tyce considered the question for several seconds, his expression becoming one of being perplexed—unable to think of an answer.

Finally, he said, "I guess we will have to wait and see, won't we?"

* * *

"ALL IS SET FOR TOMORROW."

Marcel Rollins words interrupted Tyce's work on the laptop.

"The chopper will be waiting at the airport. The trip to Patmos will take about an hour and a half, they are telling me."

Tyce stood from the sofa and moved from behind the low table on which the laptop sat. He poured coffee from a carafe, then offered to pour Rollins a cup.

"No, thanks. Too much already," the producer said.

"Can everyone fit into the copter?"

Rollins grinned, thinking he knew Greyson's thought.

"There's room for the Ice Prince... I mean for Marial, if that's your question."

"That's a given...Else there would be no trip to Patmos for me," Tyce said, sipping then from the cup.

Rollins let the banter drop with a further grin.

"We will be taking two choppers. One is one of those big ones like Marine One that ferries the president around. The other is a smaller one. There's quite a bit of equipment we'll be taking."

There was a knock at the suite's entrance door and William Bressnick stuck his head in, talking while coming in the rest of the way.

"Just got word from BBC. They want you again tonight, Tyce. For a full thirty minutes live. Seems your ten-minute live interview whetted Europe's appetite."

"Thirty minutes? What can we talk about for thirty minutes?"

The journalist's question was put with a touch of irritation.

"Reginald Formby will have some interesting points to question you on, I assure."

"I had reservations for dinner..."

"This is important, my boy. This will help build toward generating interest in *Revelations*."

"I'll try to move the reservation," Tyce said with resignation.

She will understand. She knows the value of this kind of opportunity for publicity," Marcel Rollins said.

SHE EMERGED from the interior of her hotel suite, stunningly alluring while affixing a small piece of jewelry to her left ear. It was all he could do to keep from blurting his true thoughts. He fought to maintain his male equilibrium—to keep from saying something foolish.

"Marial...You are..." He paused, speaking then in a quiet voice, the words as if to himself rather than to her. "...absolutely beautiful."

She laughed, her eyes sparkling, her facial expression twisted in a pretty way with amused appreciation. His words were, for him, uncharacteristic. His manner of saying them was like a teen-age boy on a first date. She was, it was more than obvious, delighted beyond measure.

"You are sweet to say so, Tyce Greyson," she said, standing on her tiptoes in the heels she wore to kiss him on the cheek.

He looked deeply into her eyes, those sparkling, emerald eyes—an urgent desire building that he could no longer constrain. Their lips met as they melted into their first passionate embrace.

He was inwardly glad 20 minutes later while the cab raced toward the make-shift, BBC studio. If the program wasn't awaiting his arrival at 8 p.m. Athens time they would have...who knows? They had forced themselves to part for the moment, the last thing at that moment either wanted to do.

Tyce's thoughts were in overdrive now, while the buildings of Athens whisked by. He considered that to have fulfilled the temptation of their impassioned desire would have been to rush that which was much more than mere, hormonal drive. His feelings for Marial were never before a part of his experience. Something infinitely deeper than sensual urge.

"You and Marial getting pretty serious?"

Marcel Rollins' question snapped him out of his thinking about their tearing themselves from each other's arms.

"What?... Marial is...very special," was all he could manage as the taxi moved to under the hotel portico.

"Thought so," Rollins said with a grin, getting out of the cab and waiting for Tyce to join him on the sidewalk.

They arrived with less than 10 minutes to spare. The make-up girl started working on Greyson the moment he sat in the chair. Five minutes later he was seated across from Reginald Formby.

Formby gave a brief glance in his guest's direction, then studied the pages he held.

"Well, Tyce," he said, looking up from the pages. "Our viewers await. Shall we?"

"Anytime you're ready," Greyson countered.

Formby welcomed his guest in his well-known British voice. Tyce saw the camera's red light come on just behind and to the host's left.

"You depart Athens for Patmos tomorrow. Is that right?" Formby began, after the introductory remarks were completed.

"Yes. We hope to land on the island sometime early afternoon."

"And, you will be revisiting the cave you explored when you were there previously?"

"Yes. We will take the CBS film crew and begin work on the documentary series."

"And, what is the series to be called?"

"*REVELATIONS* is the title, and each of the episodes of the series will have subtitles. I've not been told any of the subtitles yet."

The British host shifted slightly in his chair, smoothing the material of the gray suit pants he wore. He cleared his throat before continuing, again shifting in the chair across from his guest.

"This series is *Revelations.* That is, with an *s.* The Biblical book is *Revelation*—singular." Formby's thought was meant to invoke a response.

Greyson paused to think on the statement before responding.

"Yes. It's a play on the name of the Biblical book. But, it is supposed to reflect on things that have happened..."

The host spoke in a way intended to further enlighten the TV audience about Greyson's description.

"You are too modest. This title refers to these phenomenal things you've predicted that have come true. *REVELATIONS* refer to these...prophecies...as some are calling them."

"Well, yes. That is the reason for the series title. But, it will cover much more than things involving me."

Again, Formby spoke in a forceful way.

"Well, there could be nothing that could top these...*prophetic utterances*... I should think."

Tyce started to respond to Formby's declaration. The large camera behind and to Formby's left, it's red light appearing to balloon in size and intensity, burned into his cognitive process. The now familiar veil of blackness fell, causing him to lose all awareness of his surroundings.

The dark fabric that had become his field of realization exploded in light at its center. It burned rapidly, scrolling apart, until was exposed a stunning scene that projected brilliantly into his astonished cerebral senses.

People on their knees... They looked into a sky of billowing, white clouds. Thousands upon thousands of people on their knees, their faces and hands lifted toward the sky...

The sky above them exploded into light brighter than the Sun and when the burst of effulgence dimmed so that he could see the scene, the people had vanished. only the landscape of rolling hills upon which they had knelt remained.

his vision again darkened to black. Another pinpoint

of light appeared at the center of the veil and it burned to yet another scene.

Many orbs of light hovered above a night scene in Manhattan. All lights of the city were out. The skyscrapers were illuminated so that he could see them only because they were made visible by the many orbs—the shining discs that moved slowly above in the night sky.

The orbs grew in brightness so that now they illuminated the Manhattan streets. People milled about. Not in normal fashion, but in a staggering, chaotic way, looking at the sky above... at the floating, brightly pulsing orbs.

He felt his body moving, as if being vigorously shaken. Words seemed to sharply pierce his reeling senses, as he struggled to come to grips with his circumstance.

"Mr. Greyson! Tyce! It's okay! You will be okay..."

his eyes met those of Reginald Formby, the British host of *Worldscope* trying to bring him around by shaking him.

Momentarily, others took over the job of bringing him to consciousness. He was again aware of his position in the chair.

"You just had another vision, Tyce," Marcel Rollins said. "What a vision!"

Greyson, still trying to get his bearings, tried to question Rollins statement.

"What...? Did I say something?"

"You sure did. But, for now, let's just make sure you're going to be okay."

# CHAPTER 7

Tyce sat stiffly in total concentration. His face projecting from the large monitor screen was nearly unrecognizable, so changed was his countenance. His words sounded deeply guttural—as if they were from someone other than himself.

"Millions of people disappeared while others watched. The phenomenon affected the entire planet. Panic and chaos ensued in the wake of the vanishings."

When his TV image finished the statement, it collapsed in the chair before Reginald Formby's hands and arms entered the picture. Marcel Rollins reached to flip the switch that caused the screen to go to black.

"You don't remember making the...prophecy?" George Brantt's question snapped Tyce from his gaze into the dark screen.

"Last thing I remember before blacking out is starting to answer Formby's question. Then I was witness to this scene when the darkness just... just came apart because of a fiery pinpoint of light."

There were thousands of people kneeling, their

hands lifted to the sky. The sky had pure white, billowy clouds. Everything became so bright that all else was obscured from view. Then, when I could see the scene again, all the people were gone. only the rolling hills where they had been kneeling were in view."

There was silence for a few seconds in the room before Brantt again spoke.

"Well, you've certainly gotten our attention with this one."

"There was more. Immediately the scene shifted to downtown Manhattan. All the city was in complete darkness. It seemed to be nighttime. Then, the buildings, the streets, the people became visible. The city was somewhat illuminated by these...these gigantic orbs of bright lights in the night sky above the skyscrapers.

The people on the streets were in a panic... frightened...while these...discs of light floated above them.

Then I guess I was coming out of it...I heard Formby's voice."

He felt the cool, slender fingers on his cheeks. Marial bent from behind him to put her face against his.

"I watched it," she said, continuing to stand over him with her hands on his shoulders. He reached to take her hand.

"It was the weirdest yet," he said, standing from the chair and turning to look at her.

"Mr. Bressnick wants to talk," one of the documentary crew members said, offering Tyce the phone he held.

He moved to one corner of the temporary control room while greeting the network executive.

Bressnick's question was to the point. "Was this...vision...like the others?"

"Even more vivid than the others. It was like watching a movie with outstanding special effects."

"No religious...interference this time, you think?"

Bressnick's words were said without levity in his tone when posing the inquiry.

"Well, there were people on their knees, as if they were praying. They had their faces and hands lifted toward the sky."

Bressnick was silent on the other end.

"Look, I don't know what it means. I don't even know what I say during these..."

"I know. I know... it's just that it would help with the project if..."

"If the thing would come to pass?" Greyson's lightly offered words cut into Bressnick's attempt to express himself in the matter.

Again silence, before the network executive laughed.

"Well...quite frankly, yes!"

"I'm not sure the rest of us would agree with you," Tyce said, glancing toward Marial, who conversed with the others.

"What do you think, Tyce? Do you sense this...vanishing...will actually happen?"

Greyson paused to reflect on the network executive's query.

"All I can say is that this one had a completely different feel...That is, it was more...eerie, I guess. It was more surreal than the others. More ethereal."

"It has already gone wild on social media. Everyone in media and the government are after me to let them at you."

"Well, don't let them...*at me*."

"No. Don't worry. let's just get on with filming the documentary. The suspense and intrigue will build. This was the best thing that could happen for the promotion of the series," Bressnick said.

Greyson spoke in a somber tone after a few moments of silence. "If what I saw during this...if it actually happens...I'm not sure the documentary series, or anything else will matter too much."

\* \* \*

Marial looked out the helicopter's window, seeing the Aegean sprawl 14,000 feet below. Spinney ridges of the small Cyclades chain protruded from the cobalt blueness like the humps of a gigantic sea serpent.

"Patmos is that larger one, there," Tyce said loud enough to be heard over the thumping of the helicopter. He leaned near her to point to a large mass of gray jutting from the Aegean.

Marial looked out the window then at him." Are you nervous, going back to where this all started?"

"Only thing I'm nervous about is that episode last night. I don't know what it means..."

"The last one of the...episodes...didn't happen. The bomb exploding off North Carolina's coast. Maybe this one won't come to pass."

"But, the vision seemed to clarify why the bomb didn't go off. The word *Spared, that appeared* after the scene of the people in prayer...The voice saying that their prayers were the reason..."

"Well, the people were praying in the vision last night, weren't they" she asked, leaning against his arm and laying her face against his shoulder.

Her warmth somehow calmed his uncertainty about the prediction—about the trip to the strange cavern where it all began.

\* \* \*

Stravos' broadly beaming smile greeted them when the huge blades stopped turning and they walked down the steps from the helicopter's doorway.

"Mister Tyce!"

The small Greek waved to get Greyson's attention.

Stravos grabbed the journalist's hand and shook it vigorously with both hands.

"You have a good flight, yes?"

"Any flight that you get back down safely is a good one," Tyce said, returning the Greek's smile.

Stravos smile widened even more, his attention turning to the woman at Greyson's side when he was introduced to her.

"This is Marial Gunn," he said while Marial put out her hand to take that of Stravos. "She will be working on the documentary with us."

"She your woman?" Stravos said, continuing to smile and hold her hand.

"No," Marial sighed in feigned disappointment. "Just his associate."

"Ah! Yes...Welcome to Patmos," Stravos said, seemingly oblivious to her words.

"The truck is here, as you see," Stravos said, waving his hand at the big vehicle behind him. "This will carry all of your equipment. And, I have men who will move it up the mountain. They will work very cheap."

Greyson put his arm around Stravos' shoulders. "I worked it out, so you and your men will be well paid for helping in everything we do while on Patmos. I'll tell you all about it a little later."

The Greek said nothing but smiled while looking

down while they walked and nodding his head, obviously pleased at what he heard.

"Have you been up to the cave yet?" Tyce said while they rode in Stravos' van that moved along the rough road ahead of the truck.

"Yes. We have made certain the serpents are not there," the Greek said, matter-of-factly.

Tyce laughed. "That's good...That's *very* good!"

"Yes, that *is* good," Marial said with enthusiastic agreement.

Their amusement seemed lost on Stravos, who took it as compliment while concentrating on the road ahead.

\* \* \*

TYCE SAT on the stone of the flat stone below the larger slab of natural formation. He looked out the cave opening, down the mountainside to the long, gray-brown beach. The Aegean lay beyond for as far as could be visually determined.

He alternately, between times of looking at the Mediterranean vista, read the script held in his hands.

He would have to memorize only a small portion— for moments during the filming when the cameras were on him. The rest he would read as narrative to be the voice over for the many intriguing shots the film crews hoped to capture.

But, he reminded himself, he must always read the voice-over portions with the same, conversational cadence and tone as when on camera.

"We're about ready to do a test or two," one of the crew said from near the small entrance to the upper cave room.

"I'm about ready, too," Greyson responded, looking in

the direction of the man. His eyes went automatically to the ledge above the cave opening. The ledge where the snake had latched onto his hand.

He shivered inwardly. It was a ledge that had been in his nightmares since...

"Tyce!"

Marial's face appeared in the opening. There was anxiety in her voice.

"It's happened!"

"What? What's happened?" he said, hurrying to duck, then follow her through the opening when she retreated.

"It's Bressnick," she said, handing him the satellite phone.

"Tyce Greyson," he answered.

"Tyce. It's actually happened! People...People everywhere...all over the world, apparently..."

"What? What happened?"

"They've disappeared...Vanished!"

He stood in stunned silence, trying to grasp Bressnick's words.

"Your...prophecy...or whatever it involves...It's happened!"

Still, Tyce remained mute. He felt as if the blood had drained from his face—as if he would faint at any second.

"You there?"

"Yes...Yes. I'm here."

"We've got to get you back here. I've never seen anything like the clamor...We will have to postpone the filming for now. This supersedes anything and everything!"

"What can I do, Bill? What do they want?"

He didn't know what else to say, sensing the hypotensive darkness grow within his reeling brain.

"I don't know exactly... I just know that you are central to all of this in the minds of...of everybody! The top network brass—not just of CBS, but of all of them— want you back here, in New York. That's not even to mention the government...the administration. They are demanding that we produce you for." The network executive let the thought die.

He handed the phone to Marial when Bressnick said goodbye, a faraway look in his eyes.

"What's it all about, Tyce," she said, grasping his arm and seeing his dazed expression.

"I... I haven't a clue," he said, turning to walk to the opening between the cavern's rooms.

He sat again at the stone table, his thoughts and eyes drawn to the scene far below and, then, to the sea beyond.

He reached to manipulate, to massage his temples between fingertips and thumb. A cerebral storm raged within his cranium. His head felt as if it would explode. When he next opened his eyes, they were drawn to the dark, boiling clouds. They rolled and tumbled above a sea now frothing with waves. Waves that even at his elevation above the tempest could be seen crashing and heard roaring.

Torrential rain blew just outside the cave's window. Below, the surf pounded in heaving, thunderous smashes into the beach and beyond.

His senses darkened while wicked, jagged lightning shards split the blackening skies atop the storm.

He saw it, then. a dark mass that raised from the tumultuous sea. It continued to rise until it was completely exposed.

The flashes of lightning illuminated the monster with an iridescent, chloros glow. The sea beast's massive head waved from side to side, it's roaring heard even above the storm's ear-shattering cacophony.

Massive jaws which he had seen in his previous vision held his attention in mesmerized paralysis, its curved, dagger-like fangs protruding from the blood-red mouth. The jaws and teeth gnashed, sea foam and greenish drool over spilling onto its glistening, reptilian scales.

The beast began walking on its tree-trunk thick legs, it's ponderous body dragging behind a spinney tail that swished powerfully, while it continued to move toward shore.

When fully emerged to stand upon the shore, the obscuring veil of rainfall parted in curtain-like fashion. His eyes were thus permitted full view of the Monster.

The hideous thing had transmorphed while moving from sea to land. The reptile-like features had changed into a head like that of a leopard. The snarling mouth was like that of a voracious lion. Between its ears were horn-like projections, with the central most horn considerably longer—higher than the others.

It's legs and feet resembled those of a gargantuan predator animal, with thick, enormous claws that, like its teeth, appeared made of metal.

Clouds that swirled angrily above the transforming beast appeared to form a tornado. From the dropping funnel ejected a dazzling stream of laser-like light. It struck the beast at the tip of the highest, middle horn between the ears. The entire scene upon the shore became one of blinding brightness.

When Greyson could next see the scene before his awe-struck eyes, the mighty beast was gone. There stood in its place upon the sand a solitary, human figure. It was that of a man. His eyes zoomed in like a camera lens zeroing in on its subject. He saw the face in detail. The countenance seared indelibly into his memory.

* * *

NEW YORK CITY 2 DAYS LATER

"When you were in the trans-state, you just kept saying 'The beast is on shore'..."

Marial Gunn stood beside the hospital bed. She smoothed Tyce's hair, a concerned look on her face.

"It' been two days since they brought me here?"

His words came in a near whisper. He felt as if all strength had left him. The touch of her cool hand on his cheek helped to bring his thought processes into focus.

"Yes. We've been here a little over 48 hours," she said. "Are you feeling a little stronger?"

"Not really. But, I'll be okay, I think."

"The doctors say you've had some sort of brain electrical short-circuit problem. It caused you to shut down physically as well as go into a light coma, they called it."

"Yeah, well... I feel like I've been shut down, that's for sure."

"I've explained to them the vision I had...as well as I could," he said, still trying to focus his thoughts on his situation.

"Yes. I was here when they asked their questions. The doctors finally ran them out of the room. You need rest...to regain strength."

"I guess I'll be grilled when I can be interrogated..."

"They are wanting to talk to you, that's for sure," she said, smoothing his hair again and touching his forehead to determine whether there was fever.

"Brantt said everything is falling apart. The economy has crashed..."

"That's not for you to think about right now," Marial said in a stern tone. "We just want to concentrate on your getting better."

He ignored her concern. "They said people are going crazy. That there is rioting..."

"It's the economy. Markets and many economic indicators were at all-time highs," she said. "Then this...disappearance of so many...has just brought everything crashing down and into chaos. Food distribution in the country...around the world....is disrupted."

George said people seem to have lost their collective mind."

"I heard a psychologist say it was a mass panic attack...a societal panic attack, I think he called it," Marial said.

"Well, to hear Bressnick talk about it, the powers that be want to talk with me because I'm considered in the middle of it all...Like I'm the cause of things going on..."

She patted his shoulder to calm him when she realized he was becoming distressed. "Shush. We will deal with it once you are better."

* * *

HE WATCHED the man pick up the large suitcase and begin walking toward the hospital room's door." You're taking me to CBS," he questioned, causing the man to turn to answer.

"Yes, sir. They want you to stop by before you go to your apartment."

The black SUV moved slowly toward the CBS Building, traffic even more congested than usual, Tyce thought.

"It doesn't look like much has changed in the traffic situation in New York," he said. Maybe is even more crowded than ever.

"They are saying that New York wasn't nearly as affected as others," the security agent sitting next to him said.

Tyce, looking at the pedestrian traffic, said, "Have you heard how many are missing?"

"From the city, or from the country?"

"Either...Both..."

"According to the news, they still haven't gotten anywhere close to getting a count. But I heard one guy...a government guy...say he estimated about eighty million in the United States."

"Eighty million!"

"Yeah, but, like I said, they have no idea at this point."

The SUV turned off Broadway several minutes later and moved more quickly down a side street. Soon the driver turned into a ramp and down into a parking garage.

"This isn't the CBS Building," Tyce said, calculating that the building was still blocks away.

"It's okay, Mr. Greyson," the security guard said. "We have to make a slight alteration in plans."

"What alterations?" His question was made with a tone of suspicion.

"Everything is okay. Just relax. We will have you where you need to be in a couple of minutes."

"I'll take care of your phone, if you don't mind," the other agent said after parking the SUV and coming around to join Tyce and the agent who had sat beside him during the ride.

"My phone? Why?"

"Never mind. It's for security," the man said, taking the instrument from Tyce's hand.

They arrived at a large door after ascending a flight of stairs, an elevator ride of 20 floors, and a long walk down a carpeted hallway.

Upon entering the dimly lit foyer, the men urged Tyce toward the interior, through an open door.

He looked around the large room, thoughts of what might be the reason for the detour moving through his mind. These were the same men who had accompanied him since CBS hired the security firm. The same men, along with two others, who shared the shifts it took to cover him during waking hours.

The network executives didn't operate this way, he considered, looking at first at one of his companions then at the other. He didn't ask questions. he knew...just knew...they wouldn't answer if he did so.

*"Bring Mr. Greyson,"* a voice from a speaker some-where near the room's ceiling said.

One of the security men opened one of the large double doors in one of the walls.

Tyce entered when the agent stood aside to allow him to pass through.

Several men in the room stood from chairs near each other. The shortest man among them, dressed in a dark gray suit and tie held out his hand.

"Thanks for joining us, Mr. Greyson," the man said in accented English, shaking Tyce's hand. "I am Nathan Sterne."

He introduced the three men who stood near him.

*I really wasn't given a choice,* ran through his mind. But, he said nothing. He nodded acknowledgement of the man's greeting.

"These gentlemen and I were hoping to ask you some questions," the man said, nodding toward the other three men.

"I was going to CBS headquarters to answer questions," Tyce said with some degree of irritation.

"Yes... Well, I apologize for ...the necessity to preempt that meeting. I... That is, we...believe our asking that you be brought here is of utmost importance. I assure that if it were not so important we would have not taken this action."

Tyce looked at the man then glanced at the others.

"Are you from the government?"

Sterne glanced briefly at the men who stood by him.

"Not the government you probably think."

Greyson remained silent, awaiting an explanation.

"We represent the Israeli government," Sterne said, watching Greyson's face for reaction. When he saw no change, he continued.

"We are aware of your...gift...Mr. Greyson...Tyce."

No surprise; his unwanted celebrity was widespread.

"I know that doesn't surprise you. Your... prophecies are known world-wide."

Again, Tyce remained silent, waiting for the man to get to his point.

"What you don't know is that we have known of you before...all of your fame. Since before you made your first prediction."

Tyce stood mute, not knowing how to respond.

"Mr. Greyson, Tyce..." The Israeli spoke with a tone of uncertainty in his accented voice.

"Do you believe in a higher power? Are you a religious person?"

Tyce's reply came after a moment to consider the reason for the question. "Not really, I guess."

"How do you account for these visions you have had that come true?"

"I believe in God. I'm just not sure he is hands-on..."

"Existentialism? Is that your belief system? There is a God, but he put the world in motion then just left it to its own devices?"

"Maybe he inserts himself when he wants to," Tyce said lightly.

"We Israelis...those of us who have fought in battle, have a term for that...as you put it...insertion of God into things. The term is *Michmash*."

Sterne smiled slightly, looking at Greyson's unchanged expression.

"It is taken from King Saul's son, Jonathan... From his victory against the Philistines. It was a miracle, like in so many of our wars- then and now."

Tyce glanced quickly at each of the men, then again at Nathan Stern.

"What am I doing here, Mr. Sterne?"

"We do owe you an explanation, and so you shall have it."

He waved a hand in the direction of his colleagues.

"We have been sent to tell you that you...you are in great danger of being forced into servitude by a diabolist group. They are...I am reluctant to use such an overused term, but perhaps it is one most easily recognizable- that is most easily understood. The term is *the new world order.*"

Sterne watched for Greyson's reaction. The journalist's expression was one of incredulity.

"I see you are skeptical," the Israeli said.

"The conspiracy theorists have been shouting it from the housetops for as long as I remember," Greyson said.

"And long before you were born, I assure you," Sterne retorted.

Tyce said nothing in return; his curiosity was piqued, however.

"We have something that, perhaps, will help convince you. That is, convince you that what we say about this new world order cabal is more than mere fiction."

"I'm listening," Tyce said.

The Israeli motioned to a chair. "Please, let us be seated while I further enlighten you."

When all were seated, Sterne continued.

"This...cabal...has one thing in mind, Tyce. They intend to drive a wedge between your country and ours...between the United States and Israel. Secondly, they intend to destroy America's sovereignty... to siphon, or usurp her tremendous wealth and resources."

Tyce studied the Israeli's face. The man really believed what he was saying. This had been the rant from many on the political right, especially over the last fifteen years, according to his study. He would listen further before tuning out and demanding he be driven to CBS headquarters.

"Has it ever crossed your mind why there is such a rage against this president? Why every element on the political left rave in unison against this administration?"

"They claim the election was stolen, for one thing."

"Ah, yes. That is the central, driving force of their antagonism. But, there hasn't been one scintilla of evidence that the charge is true...despite investigations, one piled upon another by supposed investigative experts of every sort."

"And, your point?" Greyson said.

"My point is, Tyce, that the true, underlying reason for the hatred for this president is something far more sinister than that an election was stolen."

"And what's that?"

"This nucleus group...this cabal of globalist fanatics...want to destroy your country. Until this is done, their globalist intentions...to build their new world order...their 'One World Order' is now completely stymied. It is on hold. This, they cannot, they *will not* abide."

"And, what have I to do with all this?"

The Israeli studied Greyson's face and saw genuine puzzlement take the place of skepticism.

"Mr. Greyson...Tyce... You have become famous, a celebrity, because you have seen the future. The people of America are fascinated with you at every level of social media and so forth."

"And what does that mean in terms of why these people want to involve me?"

"Because the people will, they believe, pay attention to what you say. Theirs has become an almost religious fervor for your...prophecies. And, with this world-wide vanishing...whatever it involves... people are asking, where are you? They will want to follow your words. They are frightened, and this cabal of globalists want to use your voice to convince the people that America must acquiesce to the United Nations call for America to join into the new order of things."

"I don't know what the...disappearance is all about, Mr. Sterne."

"Makes no difference. You will be forced to say what the globalist elite want you to say...Don't you see, they want to use you as a spiritual, a psychological battering ram to break through the American independent will."

Tyce considered the Israeli's words before speaking.

"I can't believe I'm that important in this, this disappearance, these globalist intrigues..."

"But, you are, Tyce," Sterne broke in. "You are key to their plans."

The Israeli shifted forward from the sofa where he sat with elbows on knees as he spoke with increased concern in his voice.

"This is a crisis of monumental magnitude, Tyce. The world is mad with grief and worry. Every young child, every baby, every fetus in the wombs of women all over the world were lost in this vanishing. This disappearance that you...Tyce Greyson...predicted only a couple of days before it happened. *You* are inextricably linked to this; thus to the globalist plans to use this crisis to construct their changed world order."

Tyce sensed a chill of realization. He was, indeed, at the center of everything involved.

"But, how do you know these things? What am I to do?"

"We ask...we plead with you to come with us, before the cabal can chain you to their cause."

"How do I know I can trust you? Why am I to believe that you might not have something even more diabolical in mind? Maybe you are Russian agents!"

The Israeli smiled appreciation for Greyson's caution and for his reluctance.

"I will simply ask you again. Do you believe in a higher power?"

"And, I'll repeat... not really, I guess."

"There is one at work, Tyce."

"I'll have to have more than your word for it, Mr. Sterne."

"Very well...Fair enough. Do you remember a trip to

the Wailing Wall at the Temple Mount in Jerusalem? Do you remember that as you were photographing the area you had a visitor? Do you remember?"

Tyce felt the cold flush of realization. The little Jewish religious man! His words resounding now in his memory. *"Israel is the sign of the end..."*

Tyce was silent, unable to respond.

"I can see on your face that you do remember. As a matter of fact, we know that you are in process of writing a book involving that visit to the wall. The words the rabbi gave to you that day was from that higher power, Mr. Greyson."

# CHAPTER 8

Israel must be a nation before Christ's return. The Temple Mount is all important. It will be at the center of world controversy as Christ's return draws near. Jerusalem will be the city that every nation on earth will be against. Israel is the sign of the end.

While he typed into the laptop, the thoughts ran through his mind in undulating recollection., in an uninterrupted chain of analysis.

His own involvement in all that was happening...it had to be connected one link to another. The visions...the vanishing of millions all over the planet. The Israeli's—Nathan Sterne's—words about a globalist cabal wanting to bring him into servitude to implement their plans. Their design to destroy America's sovereignty. To absorb and siphon its great wealth to establish their desired changed world order. All moved through his convoluting brain, convicting him of the course he must follow.

The Jewish Rabbi at the Wailing Wall, his wide eyes

ablaze with fiery emotion. The words that drove home to him what he must do.

*"Israel is the sign of the end..."*

Sterne warned him that the noose was tightening around his neck. They would never let him out of their grasp once they had him. He would have to make a choice. Was Nathan Sterne telling him the truth or did William Bressnick's words tell the real story?

Bressnick had, just minutes before, told him that CBS, and all of the mainstream broadcast outlets wanted to work in concert with government.

Tyce considered now, while looking at the laptop's screen, how the declaration was an oxymoron—if that was the right word to describe the incongruence. The networks had been...were still...at war with this president and his administration's agenda.

Why would they suddenly want to cooperate with this White House?

The *Deep State*, as it had become known. That was entirely another matter! The globalists within the many branches of government, particularly within the state department... Many were devoted to establishment politics. Wittingly or unwittingly, these often followed the Washington, D.C., internationalist line rather than the nationalistic line of thought. They were, in effect, globalists. America's sovereignty took second, even third and fourth place in their geopolitical thinking.

CBS...The other mainstream types in news and even entertainment... These would be on board with the *Deep State* types.

The realization hit. The way things were altered in that millisecond when the millions vanished; the president, vice president and many within the administration...they were also gone—disappeared!

The vanishing of millions in every country in the world... Everything was changed now. All bets were off on how anything would play out from this strange moment forward.

Bressnick's words over the phone replayed in his mind. The network executive was angry.

"Why didn't you come straight here? I told you we have people who want to talk with you...With us....so we can move forward."

"I thought it would be best to go to the apartment to recover some strength," he had lied. "Won't the meeting wait...?"

"These are people who don't like to wait, Tyce," Bressnick interrupted. "I'll expect you here, in my office at eight."

Pressure must be great upon the network executive, he thought. Bressnick was one not given to incivility. His tone had been uncharacteristically demanding, furious before hanging up.

The I-Phone sounded. He hesitated to look who was calling.

"Marial! Where are you?" he said.

"Question is, where are *you?*" Her words were laced with anxiety.

"I'm in a hotel room. What's wrong?"

"There are guys looking for you, Tyce. Big, government-type guys... in dark suits!"

"Where are these guys?"

"They are all over your apartment. I stopped by and they grilled me about where you are. They weren't nice at all."

Government-types... Agents from one national security office or the other. The thoughts ran swiftly. Sterne's warning that they wouldn't let him out of their grasp once they had him.

"Marial, are you still there? At the apartment?"

"No. I left as soon as they let me go. I was beginning to wonder if they *were* going to let me go."

"Things have changed. I can't let them find me. I will have to figure how to ...to get us together without allowing them to find me."

The phone chimed again within seconds of Marial saying goodbye.

Tyce studied the device to determine who was on the line. He decided to take a chance when the I-Phone didn't identify the caller.

"Tyce Greyson," he said, apprehensively.

"Tyce, it's Nathan Sterne. Are you convinced yet that you must join us?"

The Israeli continued when Tyce hesitated to answer.

"We know about the people who desperately want to force you into cooperating with them. That's why I wanted you to take the hotel room while you considered the things that we discussed."

"Yes. I'm convinced. But, what about Marial?"

"They are following her, to find you. It's good that you didn't divulge your location, although, they are even now working to locate your cell."

You must leave the phone and meet us in the lobby. We will pick Marial up and deliver her to you at the right time."

They had it all laid out—the way to evade the government men, or whomever. Marial was in their plans- that was good.

"What about my I-Phone? I have my contacts, my vital information on it."

"Tyce, we have it all. We can restore it," the Israeli said patiently.

"How? How can you have my years of information, of contacts?"

"Let's just say we have the data...All of it. It is secure. You must leave the phone. The best thing to do is to just put it in the lavatory...the commode. Flush it so it is totally inundated with water."

* * *

"THE WORST OF it involves the children." The Israeli spoke while sitting beside Tyce. They rode in the back seat of a big, black sedan toward a location they wouldn't discuss.

He remembered Nathan Sterne's words of 20 minutes earlier upon leaving the hotel. "We don't talk about our plans aloud."

"The children have completely vanished. Apparently, all of them," the agent beside him said. "People, especially women who were pregnant, have gone berserk. Even children yet born...fetuses are no longer there. They disappeared, too."

"And this is world-wide?" Greyson said.

"So far as can be determined. Yes."

Sterne spoke from the front seat.

"Did you see the news reports while in the hotel?"

"I caught only bits and pieces," Tyce said.

"The news is just breaking. You couldn't have heard that a growing number of people in news media and government are putting your name at the center of this phenomenon," Sterne said, half-turning to be heard above the road noise.

"Me? How can I be held responsible?"

Greyson's words spilled in a muffled laugh. He realized then that Sterne was serious.

"They believe your prediction somehow makes you responsible," the Israeli said. "That's how insane people, especially those in media and government have become. This phenomenon seems to have made all rationality disappear as well as people."

"What are they saying?"

"That you must be found and interrogated so that it can be determined what you know about this...crisis, as they are calling it."

The traffic became less congested while the car moved farther from the city. His sense of direction told him that they were no longer headed toward either JFK or LaGuardia. They were somewhere in the unpopulated area of New Jersey. That much he knew.

Darkness now dominated the landscape. a few, scattered, pinpoints of light dotted the deepening veil of nighttime. Finally, the car rolled to a stop.

When they had exited, sounds and smells informed his senses. The ocean was near, somewhere in the blackness.

"Over there," one of the Israelis said, pointing to a flashing red light in the distance.

"Let's hurry, Tyce," Sterne urged. "There's only a short window of time to do this transfer."

His first thought was to demand an explanation of their plans for him. An indefinable inner-nudge convinced him otherwise.

He didn't see the men at first. The black attire they wore made them indistinguishable in the darkness.

"Over here," one of the men said, taking Tyce's arm and urging him toward the sound of the ocean tide.

"We will leave you now, Tyce, Nathan Sterne said, shaking his hand. "Here are your new phone and laptop.

Everything is restored. It is all protected by technology of the most advanced sort. They will not be able to locate you through these." He handed him the computer and phone.

"Your personal belongings...all we could find...are on their way to Tel Aviv. This bag contains a few things we thought you might need, meantime."

He handed Greyson a duffle bag. One of the men in black took the new phone, the laptop case and the bag from Tyce.

"What about Marial?" he asked.

"We are working on that. Trust us," the Israeli said, again pumping Tyce's right hand vigorously.

* * *

HE WAS TAKEN TOTALLY off guard. He had expected to be flown out of New York. When he heard the ocean tide and smelled the fish smells he then had expected to go wherever they were taking him by boat.

It was indeed a boat. But not the kind he expected.

Tyce examined the interior of the submarine. He considered that staying confined in such tight quarters for weeks at a time, as did submariners, would be intolerable.

He didn't have claustrophobia, but the tiny berth, in which he couldn't fully stand, made him a bit anxious. Apparently, the captain of the vessel knew anxiety when he saw it.

"Mister Greyson," the well-conditioned man wearing a khaki-colored jumpsuit uniform said in an Israeli accent, holding out his right hand. "I am Yorbi Kosner. I am captain of the Rahav. Welcome aboard."

"Thanks. This took me by surprise," Tyce said, re-seating himself from his slightly bent standing position within the close quarters.

The Israeli naval officer sat across from him on a bunk attached to the sub walls by chains.

"Yes. It is very rare that we have such an assignment. It took me by surprise, also," Kosner said.

"How did you get a sub into our waters to pick me up?"

"Ah! They told me you are a reporter, and would have questions," Kosner said with a laugh. "We have our ways, Mr. Greyson."

"Exactly what is your mission, Captain Kosner?"

"Our assignment is to take you to somewhere near Nova Scotia. From there you will be flown to Israel."

There was silence between them for a few moments. Tyce could see the Israeli officer had unspoken things on his mind.

"Now, let me ask a question or two," Kosner said. "We...my crew and I... we've been underwater for most of the last month. We know only that you are someone who is now well known...famous...because you predicted the strange thing that has happened. The disappearance of so many..."

Tyce listened for what the man desired to know.

"What is it like out there now? We have heard bits and pieces. That there are tremendous upheavals across the world. We are, of course, quite concerned. We are not allowed to check on our families, our friends, until our assignment...our tour, is ended."

"It's chaos, Captain. Every baby, young child and even fetuses in the wombs of their mothers are apparently missing in this...whatever it is that happened. That alone is enough to make it a changed world. One much different than the one you left when you began your tour of duty a month ago."

He saw the sub captain's eyes fill with tears that began streaming down his face. He instantly regretted he had blurted the answer.

"I'm so sorry, Captain. I didn't mean to..."

Yorbi Kosner shook his head in negative fashion, waving a hand at him. "No! No. I had heard just briefly about this. I have nieces and nephews who are.... *were*...very young. My own daughter and her husband were expecting."

"I'm so sorry, Yorbi," Tyce said.

"The others of my crew must not know of this. It is difficult for them as it is, being away from family for so long- sequestered in this vessel."

"They won't hear it from me," Tyce assured.

Kosner straightened and flicked away the tears from his face with a finger. He cleared his throat and spoke again in a strong, unemotional voice.

"Now, Tyce... Can I answer any of your questions further?"

He mulled over the Israeli's words. "Do you know what your people are doing for my...colleague...Marial Gunn?" he said.

Kosner shook his head negatively. "Sorry. No. I've not heard that name."

"*Trust us.*" Nathan Sterne's words echoed within his thoughts. They didn't comfort at this moment. But, he had no choice but to trust...

* * *

"Mr. Greyson."

Tyce heard the female voice, its accented-English sounding in his ear as he felt himself being jostled awake.

"Mr. Greyson...We must be on our way," the woman continued.

"I will step in the next room while you dress," she said, closing the door behind her.

He sat on the edge of the bed. The trip to the little island just off Nova Scotia—to the landing strip, then the flight by military cargo plane to somewhere in Israel, left him fatigued. He ached from having slept so intensely but for so few hours. He checked his wrist for the watch that wasn't there. He looked around and remembered it was on the hotel room's nightstand.

It was 8:22 a.m., he surmised through eyes still trying to focus after coming to full consciousness.

In less than fifteen minutes the Israeli military officer knocked on the door. "You ready, Sir?" she asked before peeking in.

"Yeah... as ready as I'll ever be," he said.

He, the woman, and two men rode in the dark blue government sedan in downtown Tel Aviv. They moved into a subterranean parking area after entering the down ramp.

The man reached out to take Tyce's hand less than five minutes later. Greyson recognized the face but couldn't remember where he had seen it.

"Welcome to Israel, Mr. Greyson...Tyce...May I call you Tyce?" the man said in the now familiar accented English.

The realization hit him. It was one of the prime minister's closest advisors.

He had covered several press conferences when the Israeli delegation was in New York and D.C. This was an important member of the Jewish state's ruling party.

"Yendle Gesh," the man said, shaking his hand firmly and smiling.

"Sorry to have brought you here in this rough manner. But, it's a unique situation in which we find ourselves, as you are well-aware."

"Thanks for the ride, none-the-less. It was...unique," Tyce said with a fleeting smile.

The big Israeli roared with laughter. "Come! Come! Sit down and let us discuss the uniqueness of all this intrigue," Gesh said, nudging his guest toward a large, overstuffed, high-backed chair.

There was but one question on Tyce's mind. The Israeli answered it before it could be asked.

"Your colleague...Miss Gunn...Marial...I think is her name. It will be just a matter of a couple of days and we will have her here to join you."

"Is she okay?"

"Our people tell us she is just fine. There's nothing to worry about," Gesh said, his demeanor growing serious. "We hope to get her to Tel Aviv in a more conventional way than you arrived."

Tyce said nothing, awaiting what came next from Yendle Gesh.

With the others gone from the large, elegantly-appointed office, Gesh spoke with gravity in his tone, in the familiar baritone voice Tyce remembered from the press conferences.

"We have some of the best minds in medicine and psychology in the entire world. They are looking forward to looking into...this gift you have demonstrated."

"You mean like looking at a guinea pig?"

Tyce's words, to even his own surprise, came in a tone of irritation.

The Israeli's expression didn't change. He spoke calmly.

"There are those, I can tell you, Tyce, who want to dissect you, if necessary, to learn your secrets."

"Well, sir, I have no *secrets*. I have no idea where these gifts, as you call them, come from. Or, where they're going."

"You must admit that things for you in the states were becoming intolerable. There was nowhere anyone with your degree of fame could hide."

The Israeli studied Greyson's face, and he saw no change of expression.

"We offer you safe haven, you and your friend, Marial, from what would have almost certainly been a zoo-like existence in the United States."

Gesh's words were true. There was no place to hide. He had to *"trust"*, for now, at least.

\* \* \*

THREE DAYS HAD PASSED. There was no word about her. His meetings with the Israeli government top defense officials were getting on his last nerve. He was now in a demanding mood. It was time for them to do something for him.

"Unless you produce Marial Gunn, our business is finished."

The doctors glanced at each other warily, the female among the four of them speaking.

"He is right. We have been asking far too many questions. He has Marial on his mind. He can't help us if he's constantly concerned for her safety. We must insist they fulfill their promise to bring her here."

The others grumbled muffled agreement.

"The problem is, Tyce. We haven't a lot of authority...that is...influence with those who can get this done," she said.

"Well, we're through here unless she is produced, and soon," he said, resolved he had answered his last question.

Momentarily, the laboratory door swung open and several men entered. Unlike the scientists they wore business suits rather than white lab coats.

It was obvious they had been monitoring his inquisition. Their intrusion raised his irritation level while he watched them approach.

"Mr. Greyson, my name is Ariel Jacoby. My colleagues and I have a request of you on behalf of our nation."

A subdued smile crossed Jacoby's lips. He nodded to the doctors who had been studying the journalist. The group left the room when he dismissed them.

"The consensus of our scientists is that your ability to speak ...that is, to look into these future matters is triggered by one, specific, thing. Every case of these visions has involved a broadcast. Do you find that to be true?"

"Where is she now?"

The American's words were sternly put—uncompromising.

The Israeli continued without acknowledging his question. "So, we have set up an interview...a *live* broadcast. Perhaps this element-the broadcast element-will induce an episode of the phenomenon. Will you do this?"

Tyce stood and walked to confront the man that was his own height. He looked the Israeli in his eyes when he spoke. He said it slowly and calmly.

"Look...Mr. ..."

"Ariel Jacoby," the Israeli repeated his name, appearing unaffected by the confrontation.

"Mr. Jacoby... No Marial Gunn, no Tyce Grayson. Period. got it?"

Jacoby smiled. "Very well, Tyce." He nodded to one of his companions, who walked to the laboratory door. He motioned with his hand to someone in the room.

Marial appeared in the doorway, hesitated for a moment, then, tears streaming down her pretty face, ran to Tyce's welcoming arms.

CHAPTER 9

"Why do they want you to do a live broadcast? It will reveal your where-abouts to…"

"They want to know if doing the live broadcasts is what causes these episodes," he interrupted Marial while they walked hand in hand.

"Do you think that's what sets the episodes off?"

"Well, it's during the live broadcasts that I've made the predictions."

"But, you've had the episodes in the cave at Patmos and at other times than when broadcasting," she said.

"Whatever they are, I can't just have them anytime. I can't just perform like a trained monkey."

She stifled a laugh. "I guess that's what most believe, though. That you cause these things to happen."

"Yeah… Like that's what I want! The whole world turned upside down. This is all so much fun!"

"Well, I'm having fun," Marial said, pressing close to him, her face against his arm while they walked.

He stopped and turned to face her, pulling her gently

to him. "Me too...I definitely like this part."

He kissed her as they embraced, before beginning to walk slowly toward the building where the night's broadcast awaited.

\* \* \*

THEY WERE GREETED by a broadcast technician a few minutes later.

"Everything is ready, Mr. Greyson," the man in his twenties said. "Mr. Gesh wants to speak with you."

The young Israeli guided them toward the room just off the studio.

"We will have only about a hundred thousand viewers," Yendle Gesh said, pouring himself a cup of coffee from the large, stainless, commercial coffee maker.

"May I offer you coffee?" he said, holding a Styrofoam cup in their direction.

"No thanks," Greyson responded. Marial shook her head no.

"This isn't much more than a closed-circuit broadcast," Gesh said after sipping gingerly on the steaming coffee.

"Do you sense any...anything unusual before these...visions?"

"Not until the moment they begin. Everything just starts growing dark, and my thoughts start...swirling...I guess you would say."

"We want you in a broadcast situation, not a taping or cable networking situation. That's been your history. They happen only during live broadcasts. We thought that the exposure...the risk of their seeing the broadcast, would be much less by keeping it closed circuit, rather than over the air where it might be picked up."

It was ludicrous, Tyce thought. The Israeli's were supposed to be among the most proficient, the best intelligence entities on the planet. How did they conclude that such a sophisticated intelligence community as themselves—and the United States—wouldn't be able to detect the broadcast to find him? They would eventually!

"All of this is just to see if you can get out of me some sort of fortune telling? So, you can achieve military advantage?"

"To be frank, yes."

Ghesh's answer surprised him. The Israeli spoke again before he could respond.

"The world is forever changed, Tyce."

Gesh moved toward the door that led into the studio.

"You, my friend, seem to be at the heart of that change. We are surrounded by religious fanatics who are blood-vowed to push every Jew into the Mediterranean. We will investigate every possible advantage. Our very survival as a nation...as a race...depends upon staying ahead of our enemies."

The Israeli stepped aside to let Tyce and Marial pass through the doorway.

"Some force...an unknown force...has chosen you to foretell catastrophes before they happen. If we can harness that force...whatever it is...we just might survive as a nation...as Jews."

Tyce and Marial followed the Israeli deeper into the studio. Greyson wasn't ready to cut the conversation short.

"I've been told that your people; most Jews are totally secular, particularly those who run things, like the government. Why are you interested in such a *force* that you say you don't believe exists?"

"That's a very good question, Tyce. We shall pursue it

at a more opportune time," Gesh said, looking around the studio to determine the state of readiness for the broadcast.

Tyce glanced over at Marial. He still had to reassure himself she was nearby. He could never let them be separated again. He needed to know she was there.

He had no idea what the line of questioning would be. Yendle Gesh had said only that it would be a discussion about what had happened to the world in the vanishings. Mainly, the program was hastily arranged for the purpose of putting him to the test. To try and bring about, to induce another episode, another vision...

"We will begin in two minutes," the broadcast engineer said for all to hear.

A commotion just outside the studio doors drew his attention. Voices of men, speaking in Hebrew, became louder while the men approached then entered the room.

Yendle Gesh, obviously excited by something spoke, motioning to Tyce.

"Come, Tyce. Something has developed that is not good. We must go."

Within minutes they rode toward Sde Dov Airport at a high rate of speed.

"They got word of our location for the broadcast. We've been told to move to a more secure location," Gesh said from the seat in front of Tyce and Marial.

"Who are *they?*" Tyce said, loud enough to be heard over the vehicle's road noise.

"We are certain it is a select group of clandestine operatives. Probably from within the U.S. government."

Maybe Marial should not be with me! His thoughts leaped ahead. What would they do with her...to her... Use her as leverage to make him do their bidding?

"We have things under control, Tyce. Do not worry," the Israeli said. "We have contingency plans at many levels."

He turned to Marial. "You didn't sign up for this," he said, squeezing her hand.

"It must be something more than just wanting to investigate you," she said, ignoring his lightly-put question. "Israel is a strong ally. Why would they work against one another?"

"*Were*... is the operative word. America and Israel *were* allies before whatever happened with the disappearance phenomenon. The dynamics of relationships of every sort, have apparently changed."

Light was sparse once the headlights of the big van were switched off. The shape of a large, hulking object in the near distance made him understand the means of their next conveyance.

Within moments they climbed the few steps into the big helicopter.

"Where are we going?" Greyson asked while sitting where he was directed by one of the crew and buckling the safety harness.

"It's a short flight," the crewman said. "Sorry, but I am not allowed to discuss mission details."

The rotors began whirring and within several seconds the blades thumping sounds grew in volume and they felt the chopper lift with a jerk.

THE COPTER RIDE had been a short one. Their surroundings were even darker than when they left Tel Aviv. There were now no lights that he could discern. Obviously, the people who escorted them intended their arrival to be covert to the maximum degree possible.

"Where are we," Marial said, stumbling along beside a black-clad operative who held her by her arm.

"It's okay," he said. "We can see everything.

Tyce knew stories of the Israeli IDF—of their most secretive special forces. They had the most advanced equipment of, probably, any military on earth. These who escorted them in hurried fashion after leaving the copter no doubt had night vision capabilities that made the blackness as bright as daylight.

"Duck your head," the man who held Tyce's arm said. He did so and momentarily found himself, along with Marial and three men in black military jumpsuits inside a dimly lit enclosure.

Tyce recognized it as a corridor, with walls of concrete, framed by steel beams.

They moved further downward by a metal ramp, then stood before doors recessed in the wall.

When the doors slid apart, the party entered through the opening. The elevator hummed as it conveyed them to what, Tyce estimated, was three floors below.

Tyce realized the Israeli was missing. "Where is Yendle Gesh?"

"He will join you in due course," the uniformed man leading the way said.

"Where are we?"

Marial's question went unanswered. The man ahead of Tyce unlocked a steel door, allowing all to enter. The area smelled of dirt...of fresh, recently dug earth.

When the man pushed a button on the concrete wall, a large steel plate to the buttons right slid upward.

The reason for the odor of freshly dug earth became instantly apparent. They walked into a large, cavernous area that appeared to be an expanse of excavation in progress.

Several people in blue cover-alls stopped their work on their respective areas of digging to look at the newly arrived party.

A woman approached them, smiling and offering her right hand to Greyson.

"My name is Grishna, Mr. Greyson. Grishna Lanskye."

"What's this about?" he asked after introductions were completed.

The woman waved a hand in the direction of those who had gone back to digging.

"We are involved here in the search of antiquities...our people's artifacts...."

She looked into Tyce's eyes with understanding on her face. A lovely face that looked to be of middle age. A lovely, pleasant, face, he thought.

"We are well beneath the streets of East Jerusalem. These digs are undertaken in secrecy. The authorities have forbidden the exploration of our heritage in this area."

Her matter-of-fact forthrightness surprised him.

"Jerusalem... Why would you be forbidden? Who can forbid the Israeli government to dig anywhere in your nation?"

Grishna looked in a quick glance at the man who had led them from the helicopter.

"You didn't tell them we are of the Israeli government, did you, Joel?"

The man shook his head. "No, I told them nothing."

She looked back to Tyce then to Marial. "We are not associated with the official Israeli government. I say *official* because there are many within our...movement...who are also in government. Some in IDF, some within the ruling party of government."

"Not government? We were told...I was told that the Israeli government wanted to investigate my so-called, *gift*. They believe I can give Israel some sort of advantage, if they can find out the source and purpose of my ability to see things before they happen."

She studied him intensely before speaking. "The people who put you on Captain Kosner's submarine are not part of the official government, Tyce. May I call you Tyce?"

"Yes...of course...Who are they then?"

"They are part of those of us who desire to keep Israel in the *shadow of God*. We call our organization by the Hebrew term, Bezalel. B equals tzal equals **shadow,** el equals God."

"Israel's *shadow government*," Tyce said as if speaking only to himself.

"Exactly. The secularists within Knesset and government at all levels, know of us. Like the *Christian right* in your own country, we are marginalized...pushed aside as unimportant. But, in the case of *Bezalel* we carry on not only faith-based efforts to change government but involve ourselves actively in covert actions whenever possible. Thus, the reason for your being brought to us."

"So, your government, at the highest levels, wouldn't like my being here... Don't know about my being here?"

"Oh, no. that is not at all the case with this prime minister. He is...*covertly*...one of us. In spirit, if not actively; not openly," Grishna Lansky said.

"Then, there's nothing to worry about with our being here?" Marial said.

"I didn't say that," Grishna said. "Those who adamantly oppose the prime minister oppose us. They work to bring his government down, just as there those who fight to bring down your president at every turn."

The reminder jarred Tyce. The president was no longer in control of America's executive branch of government. Everything was changed for the world...including the United States.

"Your prime minister, he's still...this organization didn't take him?"

"No. He is very much in charge during this...strange crisis. We lost only a very few officials, I'm told," Grishna said. "He is still an ally. But, there are those of our government and of your...America's...government who will do anything to find you and extract anything your...gift...might harbor."

Tyce said, after a few seconds of reflection. "Is that not what your people... *Bezalel...* intend? To get from me whatever will benefit your organization?"

Grishna smiled a frown of mild amusement.

"It is indeed. But, we hope you will see that our...desires...are on the side of good, not evil."

* * *

"EVERYONE HAS GONE CRAZY!"

The television screen filled with mobs of people rioting. The scenes switched in five second intervals in quick succession to New York, Chicago, Los Angeles in the U.S., then to London, Paris, Rome, and other cities in Europe and beyond.

The Israeli who had shown them into the small lounge watched with Tyce and Marial while they awaited the arrival of Yendle Gesh.

He continued to watch the screen while he asked the question. "What is happening to people?"

A car in London exploded in flame when a bottle filled with gasoline was thrown into its interior through an open window. Police, armed with Billy clubs and shields were overwhelmed when rioters charged them, knocking them to the pavement, kicking and stomping their bodies even after they were unconscious or dead.

"The scenes are the same everywhere," the reporter's voice announced from the TV speakers. "Collapse of economies around the world are almost certainly the catalyst for a mass psychological hysteria, authorities are reporting."

The screen changed to a man dressed in a suit and tie standing behind a set of microphones. Tyce recognized him as the speaker of the U.S. House of Representatives.

"With the cities under siege we have no choice but to declare a national state of emergency. Therefore, under the authority granted me by the laws of succession under the Constitution, I am invoking Martial Law, effective now and for an indefinite time forward."

The president and Vice president, both missing...the speaker, next in line...

Tyce's thoughts and Marial's words came at the same time.

"The president and vice president really aren't there," she said in a tone of disbelief. "I thought maybe they were just staying out of public view until they figured things out," she said.

The scene soon switched from the recorded declaration of the speaker of the House to the violent street scenes.

"Martial Law...or the equivalent has been declared in most all nations of the west," the reporter said excitedly.

"It's as if people no longer have any control over their conduct," their Israeli companion said.

"Developing food shortages across the world are, apparently, the most pressing problem and the primary cause for the rioting," the reporter's voice continued from the television speakers.

When the lounge door opened, Yendle Gesh, followed by two men, entered.

"Please come with me," he said, continuing to walk to another door. Tyce and Marial followed the three men deeper into the building.

"Grishna has made a decision about how best to bring you into our orbit," Gesh said when they reached an exit leading to the back of the warehouse where they had spent the night.

"We have it on good authority that a newly formed U.S. and EU clandestine operative group is able to follow your movements. We thought we had our tracks covered. But, that's obviously not the case."

"Grishna made the decision? To do what?" Tyce said, surprised that the woman he found digging in the earth beneath an ancient Jerusalem street had such authority.

"She is second only to..."Gesh caught himself and pulled back from divulging too much. "Grishna is a highly placed leader within Bezalel," he said, leading the way to the dark blue van while he talked.

Tyce pressed the Israeli when they were seated in the vehicle. "What *decision* has Grishna made?"

"She is the one who is authorized to tell you. You will soon learn the details."

\* \* \*

MEN AND WOMEN in Israeli military uniforms stood at the ready at every check point in Jerusalem. The soldiers held their automatic weapons at arms when the van approached each of the stations.

Each time they were stopped, there seemed to be recognition on the faces of the troops charged with security. The soldiers would step aside in each case and nod to the van's driver, while motioning for the vehicle to proceed with a wave of their right arms.

One thing most noticeable to Tyce as they rolled over street after street—the scenes were entirely different from those in the other cities he had seen on television. Jerusalem was a city that might be, at this moment, the safest on the planet.

A distinct sense was conveyed by the van's quick approval for passing through the checkpoints. The Israeli military...all with whom they came in contact...seemed to be on board with Yendle Gesh's mission.

Tyce recognized that they must be near the digs. The underground excavation for ancient Jewish artifacts. Freshly turned earth, brought to the surface by conveyor belt lay in small piles alongside the roadway. The area was isolated from the main streets, just as he remembered in the scant light when leaving the area, the previous night.

"We are just arrived."

Yendle Gesh's words were spoken into a satellite phone, while the van was pulled to a stop by the uniformed driver.

"Yes. All is clear, they assure me."

Gesh listened for several second to the voice on the other end of the transmission.

"Very well. We will wait for your word to proceed," Gesh said, then folded the instrument.

He turned to be heard by Tyce and Marial. "There is

some question about the clearance according to their source," he said. "We will remain in the van until the okay is given."

"What...Who are they suspecting that might cause a problem?" Marial asked, after glancing nervously at Tyce.

"Believe me, the sophistication of these technologies allows us to know things that were impossible to know just a few, short, months ago. There appears to be signals of our movement being monitored from somewhere in Europe. That's about all I can tell you for now," Gesh said.

"They can monitor our movement, but they haven't located where we're going? That is, the place we are to meet with..."

Gesh interrupted Tyce's question. "We must...that is, our people must... through our own, masking technology, blind them to our whereabouts. Then we can enter the chambers."

In less than 10 minutes they moved into the familiar corridor encapsulated by concrete, then into the chamber where the digs were underway.

"Tyce, Marial, come! Come! We have been anxiously awaiting your joining us."

Grishna Lansky greeted them with a smile, clapping her hands together then bidding them to come with her in an inviting *follow me* wave. She led them to an area that had until now been hidden from view.

"This is our most secure place," she said after activating a metal door that slid open with a whirring sound. "Here, we are surrounded by the most advanced security devices imaginable. I, myself, marvel at the irony of it all..."

She gesticulated with a wave of her extended arm and hand.

"All of this, right in the center of some of the most ancient chambers on the earth."

Walls of non-descript material held back tons of dirt. The odor was of dank, dark, underground places, even though the chamber in which they stood appeared to be one equipped with highly advanced electronics.

"There is a person you must meet, Tyce...Marial..."

She punched a series of buttons on a small, control console. The material slid apart on one wall.

"Tyce heard shuffling and turned to see that a number of people had entered the room. They were wearing the type of blue cover-alls he remembered from the night before.

"These, Tyce...Marial," she said with a motion toward the 10 people, "are the counsel members of the Covenant of Bezalel."

She stood with her back to the big screen on the wall, to face Tyce, Marial, and the people who had just entered the chamber.

"And, now, you will meet our spiritual leader."

Grishna, without turning to face the console table, reached with her left hand to manipulate a button. The screen behind her instantly lit up with an image of a man in dark, Judaic, religious attire.

Tyce's eyes met those of the Rabbi. The man's intense gaze seemed to instantaneously pierce his thought process. Vision-dazzling shards of light fractured the cerebral veil of conscious thought. The veil parted. Effulgence burst forth in unprecedented understanding.

He heard the words. They echoed in thunderous, cavernous decibels that caromed within his cranium.

*"Israel is the sign of the end."*

# CHAPTER 10

Tyce Greyson's reeling, pulsing, cerebral turbulence made him sense that his brain was on fire. All thought rushed through his sub consciousness in a crushing flood.

The visions...his *prophesies...* given to the world through broadcasts...re-played, expanded one at a time then dissipated to the familiar, dark veil separating him from the conscious world.

His inner-eyesight—his mind's eye—strained to pierce the veil. The struggle to see through the blackness caused a sense of hopelessness—of futility, while a profound sense of sadness engulfed his core being. He could not break through the sheet separating him from what he must know...What lay on the other side?

A spark, a flicker of lightning-like brightness, appeared at the center of the veil. A more violent shard of brilliance shattered the fabric and the blackness burst open, causing the veil to disappear.

The mouth within the bearded face of the Jewish Rabbi began to speak in lecture-like fashion. His probing glare streamed into the core of Tyce's neuron to neuron synapses. Greyson was held captive within the trance, unable to do anything other than stare, transfixed while hearing the mesmerizing words.

*"You are chosen, Tycus Levi. Prophesy as you must."*

The Rabbi's countenance within the vision-scene changed, transforming into that of a snow-white lamb's face and body. It's eyes seemingly melded with his own. He fought the almost uncontrollable urge to weep, so great was the soul-rending compassion within those indescribably alluring orbs of infinite empathy.

\* \* \*

"YOU WENT INTO A TRANS-LIKE STATE," Grishna Lansky said, mopping his forehead with a cold, wet cloth. She looked into his eyes, seeing the pupils shrink from covering most of the iris to near normal size.

"Are you again with us?" Her question was asked in comforting tone.

"I... I guess so," Tyce said, his consciousness returning slowly.

"Do you remember anything of the episode?"

Yendle Gesh's question was to the point, probing.

"Shush!"

Grishna admonished Gesh.

"He must be allowed time to recover, Yendle."

The Israeli turned to meet with the others in the room.

"I saw the Rabbi. He was the one...the one who I saw years ago near the Wailing Wall."

"Are you sure you want to...feel like talking right now, Tyce?"

"Seems my name isn't *Tyce*, he said. "The Rabbi called me *Tycus...Tycus Levi.*"

"You became paralyzed in a trans-like state the moment Rabbi Elias began to speak," Grishna said, continuing to mop his forehead.

"This...*Elias...* he is the same man that came to me at the Temple Mount several years ago. He's the man who said *Israel is the sign of the end.*"

"He is spiritual leader of the *Covenant Bezalel.* Elias Coahn. He, like you, manifests... *unusual* abilities."

"All I heard him say was that I am chosen and to prophesy as I must. He called me Tycus Levi."

Grishna, after a look of thinking on the matter, said, "All Rabbi Elias said was your name. He said 'Tyce Greyson'"

Tyce sat up and took the cloth from Grishna's hand and began applying it to is throbbing temples.

"He changed, from the bearded face to a lamb. A lamb of the whitest wool I've ever seen," Tyce said.

"Did...I... say anything?"

His question was asked in a tone of apprehensiveness.

"Oh... You certainly did, Tyce...or Tycus Levi," Grishna said.

"Another ...*prophecy?*" His question was laced with *I hope not* exasperation.

"We were taping you while you were face to face with Elias," she said.

The realization his episode was taped made him want Marial by his side to review what might be on the recording. "Where's Marial?" he said, suddenly aware of her absence.

"Please ask Marial to step in," Grishna said.

"She had to go to the lady's facility, she just left moments before you began coming around."

The man in the blue jumpsuit, after speaking, left and came back in the room.

"We can't find her," he said. "They haven't seen her since she went into the latrine."

Another of the blue-clad group rushed into the room. He announced in a panic, "Grishna! They've found us. We must leave immediately!"

* * *

CLOUDS BOILED above the ancient city, dark, rolling billows that threatened severe weather. They sped toward a location Tyce was not privy to, having been told about the armed unit that wanted to abduct him. It was, they said, a secure place where the would-be abductors couldn't find them.

"Is Marial with us?" he asked for the third time, this time in a demanding tone.

"Tyce, I'm sorry, but we couldn't locate her," Grishna Lansky said.

"Couldn't find her?!"

His question, laced with profanity, caused Grishna, sitting next to him, to touch his arm consolingly.

"We won't stop until we find her," she assured.

"What...Where did she go?"

His irritation was gone and in its place was pleading to know.

"We don't know. The unit that was reported as assaulting us wasn't around the digs when we got the word of the attack. They were at least ten minutes from us. Marial was missing well before that time," Grishna said, still in a consoling tone, while patting his arm.

"We have very proficient people, Tyce. We will find her."

Rain pelted from the turbulent sky, many flickers of lightning creating tremendous thunder claps while they moved toward the hills outside Jerusalem.

"The Judean wilderness," Grishna instructed, waving a hand toward the window beside him. "Many ancient battles were waged in these mountains. We will soon arrive at our safe place."

\* \* \*

"Do you think they've got her?"

Tyce paced from the window, where he had been looking into the raging storm, to the table where Grishna sat with two members of the *Covenant of Bezalel.*

They studied a device they had brought with them from the electronic bunker within the digs. They each were attached to the device through thin wires that ran from the instrument to their ears.

"What are you looking at?"

His impatience and anxiety were growing, as he looked at the screen they were watching.

"Drones are following the movement of their people," Grishna said while listening intently to the device's audio.

"Who? What people?"

"The force that tried to take you from us," Grishna said, trying to both listen to Tyce and the audio. "The drones are following their movement...Reporting their whereabouts and their every action."

Tyce stared at the screen, seeing only rain-obscured video of the stark, desert-like landscape.

"I can't see any...action," he said caustically.

TERRY JAMES

"The drones are capturing it all, I assure you," Grishna said. "They see things we cannot and record it in great detail."

"What are they up to? Do you think we can learn about Marial through...these...drones?"

"If they have her, we can most likely determine her location with drones that have much greater capability than these tracking instruments. When the weather clears we will move the more sophisticated drones into position."

"Can't these people see the drones? Shoot them down or something?"

"No. The cloaking capability of these flying instruments make them undetectable, so far as we know. Only we Israelis possess this capability," Grishna said with almost a tone of pride in her voice.

"Cloaking? You mean it makes them invisible?"

"Well, of course, there is no such reality as invisibility," she said. "But, the technology can certainly fool the human eye—the human *senses* ... even the most advanced detection instrumentalities into being unable to detect the drones."

For the moment, Greyson's reporter's curiosity overrode his anxiety about finding Marial's whereabouts.

"Can you apply the technology to other things? make other applications?"

"Ah, well, Tyce, that is all under the auspices of Israeli military secrets," she said with amusement over his curiosity.

The three at the table continued to study the screen. Tyce again paced between the one small window and the table.

Finally, he stopped again to stare at the screen, seeing

nothing he could discern that might indicate where the force being follows might be doing.

"They must have some sophisticated technology, too. I thought Gesh said your...digs...couldn't be found by these people," Tyce said.

"Yes. The technologies are greatly advanced over even a year ago. And, most all advanced western nations have them. But, still, we are perplexed as to how we were located so quickly."

"Maybe it was an inside job," Tyce said. "Maybe somebody betrayed your location from within your organization..."

"That is precisely our thought," Grishna said, looking deeply into Tyce's eyes, then returning her attention to the screen.

* * *

CHURNING in his stomach caused by his depressed appetite due to his anxiety gnawed at him. He had to find a way to put worries about Marial out of his thoughts. His secondary concern was to find out what he had said upon seeing the Rabbi on the screen and going into the vision episode.

He sensed that they were deliberately keeping from him what he had said while in the trans-like state. Grishna had told him... at the time after coming out of the episode... that he had said things she indicated were profound in nature. The rush to leave the concrete bunker of electronic paraphernalia preempted his learning of exactly what he had said. He remembered only the man's face...the face that transformed into that of a lamb, whose compelling eyes he couldn't get out of his thoughts.

"It has begun."

Grishna Lansky's declaration startled him out of his thoughts. He turned from his laptop to see her as she entered the small room.

"India and Pakistan have had a nuclear exchange. They are saying more than two hundred thousand are dead."

"What do you think it means?" He said.

"It means you were right. Your...prophecy...came true."

"What?!" He stood and faced her.

"My *prophecy?* What prophecy?"

"We haven't yet discussed what you said during the time of your...vision. When talking to Rabbi Coahn."

"What did I predict?"

"Your words were, '*India will use atomic weapons. Hundreds of thousands will die.*'"

Stunned into silence, he could only stare at her.

"This could be the start of World War Three," she said. "We thought it would likely be Iran that started it. But this is even more dangerous in some respects."

He said nothing, but she saw he wanted to know her meaning.

"China might get involved. It affects them...That is, their hegemony and so forth. Iran's enemy list includes only, basically, us and America.""

"Where does it go from here?" He finally managed to form his question.

"There was more to your prophecy, Tyce...Much more."

Again, he was numbed into silence by her revelation.

"Your second prophecy was, '*A young man of unprecedented power and authority will bring peace.*'"

He spoke again after absorbing her words.

"And, has such a man come forward?"

She shook her head. "No... No such man is on the geopolitical scene."

"And, What else? Did I say anything else during the episode?"

"Tyce...It is something I didn't want to have to say...to tell you."

"What...Please...What else did I say?"

She hesitated, searching for the words.

"It's about Marial..."

"What about Marial?" His words came in desperation to know.

"Tyce, you said it might have been an inside operative who gave away our position to those wanting to capture you..."

"Yes...What about it?"

She said nothing, but Grishna's facial expression of compassion told him what she didn't want to verbally express.

* * *

SLEEP CAME GRUDGINGLY while he lay on the military cot beside the table where his laptop sat. he had been trying to make sense of what had happened to so disrupt his existence.

Marial...His betrayer? Why? Was it true it was her who was in league with...With who? Who wanted him? Why?

Were the globalists so worried about his...abilities. whatever they involved? Were they afraid that Tyce Greyson would interfere, somehow, with their plans for instituting their one world order? Their new world order?

Was he set up from the very beginning...When he first met her? At what point did their plan to take him into their blueprint for control include Marial?

It couldn't have been when they first met. He had not yet had the...visions. They couldn't have known at that time that he would begin to...prophesy.... to predict.

He shook his head in a moment of bemusement. Tyce Greyson...a prophet! Or was it Tycus Levi?... who made the predictions? Who gave the prophecies?...

Marial...a traitor, his betrayer... Marial, in league with...with whom? With something dark and evil...something beastly...

His emotions wrenched and exacerbated by lack of sleep, Tyce tried yet again to put out of his mind thoughts of her treachery. Beautiful Marial...her loving, caring touch he would never again know.

But, her conspiring with those who wanted him held in their clutches...The loving, caring, all a self-serving ruse...

Still, her face, her lovely, beautiful, face was there— indelibly etched upon his mind's eye... Perfection of feminine essence burning into his conscious thought process...a process that began to fade, moving him from the real world—through the gravity produced by sleep— into the darkening landscape of the surreal.

* * *

MAYBE THIS TIME getting into writing the book would clear his mind. Would help him think of things other than Marial.

He looked at the book manuscript's title on the laptop screen for the thousandth time.

*Israel the Sign*

Sleep had finally come. It was troubled with dreams —nightmares he couldn't remember. Unlike the vivid recollections when remembering the vision episodes.

Only the face of the man who transformed from the sea beast came into his memory when he tried to recall the dream world he left an hour earlier. A face that exuded strength of resolve, confidence—that commanded attention.

He typed in the document of notes begun at the book's inception.

*"Young leader awaiting his time. Somehow tied inextricably to Israel. A powerful force for good or for evil?"*

Knocking at the door caused him to turn.

"We will need you to accompany us, Mr. Greyson," a man dressed in a blue uniform said.

"To where?"

"Grishna will inform you, sir. Please come with me."

Grishna Lansky busily shuffled file folders into a brief bag. She looked up only with a glance at Tyce, then back at the task before her.

"Tyce, we must hurry to Tel Aviv. The prime minister awaits us there. We have important things to accomplish."

"What....Things?"

"There is no time now. We must leave. I'll tell you what I can on the way to see Bibi."

Five minutes into the helicopter flight to Tel Aviv, Grishna turned from studying the papers held in her hands to look at Greyson.

"Tyce, the prime minister asked to talk with you personally, and he requested that meeting immediately."

"Me? Why?"

"We will let you know specifically once we are there. We must have everything discussed in the most thoroughly secure place possible. The prime minister's location is that place."

"Why Tel Aviv? His office is in Jerusalem."

"He uses the Jerusalem offices for formal matters of state. Strategic planning and operational details are most often dealt with at Tel Aviv."

The copter suddenly tilted violently to the left, then to the right. The pilot began yelling in Hebrew into his helmet microphone.

"He says we are under attack. Make sure your harness is secure!"

Tyce craned to look in every direction. "I don't see anything."

"Our pilot does. On radar. He is taking evasive action," Grishna said, searching the sky.

""There! I see them!" Tyce pointed to the rear and to his left.

"There are a number of them," Grishna said.

The chasing birds of prey were closing fast, black specks that grew large quickly. When they drew near enough he realized that he had seen the type copters before. The latest, deadliest generation of flying, war machines.

Three of them! They had no chance! Despite the pilot's best efforts to maneuver so that the pursuers' weapons couldn't get a fix on their target.

The middle of the three attackers fired a missile. It streaked straight at them from behind.

Tyce and Grishna Lansky watched as the missile, fire blowing white-hot from it's rear, rocketed overhead and harmlessly into the desert ahead.

Tyce's heart raced with anticipation of instant death that would come at the next moment. The pilot put the chopper in a quick dive toward the desert floor. The pursuing copters flew above them, and the pilot of their bird pulled the helicopter hard to the right and downward.

Tyce and Grishna watched the more powerful, faster, black choppers rage past them.

The three-aircraft seemed to vibrate violently and rock from side to side. In the next instant they collided, as if an unseen hand had swept them together in an enormous burst of light. The exploded copters fell in pieces, flaming smoke trailing their plunge to earth.

Stunned, the pilot and passengers could but stare, watching the debris' descent to the desert floor.

The pilot spoke in Hebrew, in a barely audible tone.

"What did he say?" Tyce said.

"He said *'I think we have seen a miracle this day.'*"

# CHAPTER 11

"The prime minister will be with you momentarily," the assistant to the leader of Israel said.

Tyce Greyson peered through the window to his left. The tranquil scene of Israeli citizens moving about as pedestrian and vehicular traffic gave impression that belied truth. The world was at this moment in unprecedented turmoil. Yet Everything he could see from his vantage appeared tranquil, peaceful.

They had escaped being blown apart only thirty minutes earlier. Here they sat, in the office waiting room of one of the world's most important leaders. It was all moving too fast, in too many directions at once for him to grasp meanings and ultimate outcomes.

"Have you met the prime minister?"

Grishna's question pulled his thoughts from the window scene outside.

"I've been among reporters interviewing him. Always in a large gaggle."

"Never personally interviewed him, though?"

"No."

"He is among the most gracious, as among the most brilliant of the leaders I have personally dealt with.," She said.

"You will find him so, I am confident."

Tyce said nothing, thinking that this prime minister and Grishna Lansky were on the same political ideological page. Of course, she would think he was both gracious and brilliant.

He agreed with the brilliant part. There was no one more able to deal with the problems his nation faced than was this man. But, the gracious part depended upon with whom he dealt at any particular time.

His sharp-toned speeches, castigating Israel's enemies before the U.N. General Assembly were not always...*gracious*...

"Please...Come," the Israeli assistant said, beckoning them with a finger to enter the door where he stood.

"The prime minister will see you now."

They walked through a small anteroom and through an open door, one of two doors that, together, formed one large entranceway when both doors were opened.

Israel's leader walked to Tyce after greeting Grishna with a handshake and a hug.

"Mr. Greyson, I've certainly heard much about you," he said almost in a light-hearted tone.

"And, I, about you, Sir," Tyce said.

"Yes...Well, don't believe everything you hear, my friend," the prime minister continued the banter. "I'm not all bad..."

"I'm a great admirer," Tyce said. He was sorry he had said it. It was trite, fawning...

The prime minister smiled, accepting Greyson's words at face value.

"You were attacked, it is my understanding."

"Yes, Sir. I still can't believe what happened," Tyce said.

"These were sent from those who are fearful of your...your gift of prophecy," the Israeli leader said. "We must make sure that you are not so vulnerable ever again." The prime minister turned to Grishna.

"Have you told him the purpose of our meeting today?"

"No, Bibi. That is for you to do," she said in a polite but firm tone.

"So, it is," he said, turning again to Tyce.

"Let us begin by saying we have...somewhat intruded into your privacy, Tyce. I hope you will both forgive and understand."

He watched Tyce's facial expression to get his reaction. When Tyce said nothing, he continued.

"We...that is our science experts; doctors and psychologists or psychiatrists, primarily, determined to put a certain, newly developed...*sedative*...for lack of a better description, into your beverage last evening."

He studied Greyson's face again. Seeing only curiosity in his expression, the prime minister continued.

"Please understand, this is, they assure me, harmless. It will produce no after-effects. No future health problems. I would have never agreed to this, otherwise."

When two men entered through a side door, the prime minister bid them to come and place the two pieces of machinery on a table near where he stood.

"These," he said, pointing to the black boxes, "are a newly-developed technology. They have the capability of inducing, shall we say...stimulation that can bring forth spoken thoughts of a brain that is the state of sleep."

"And, you used that on me?"

Tyce's question was asked in a calm manner.

"Yes. To have first asked your permission...our scientists...our doctors say, would perhaps contaminate the process. Your subconscious would have pre-programmed your brain to resist, or to interact in unwanted ways, with the technology. We had to introduce the stimulation in this manner to bring out your subconscious sleep-thoughts as you spoke them."

"Well, Sir. I can't say that that makes me happy," Tyce said, controlling his building anger. "That's a lot like what we've always accused totalitarian states of doing."

"Agreed...I am not happy that it had to be done. But, Israel's very existence is on the brink. This...world-wide vanishing matter and all the collateral problems it created... And, you are the person...chosen by someone, somewhere...to predict all this... I had no choice."

Bibi's words were not stern, nor were they apologetic, rather matter-of-fact.

"Okay, Sir. I'll have to accept that. So, what were the results?"

The prime minister looked deeply into Tyce's eyes and paused several seconds before answering.

"Profound, Tyce. The results are profound. We will show you the result of what was revealed."

WATCHING his image on the screens of the advanced Israeli brain wave machinery caused him, at the same time, a sick feeling in the pit of his stomach, deep resentment, and a building fever of curiosity.

His image lay on the military cot beside the table with the laptop. thin, white wires ran from a black box on the floor to his temples and forehead, where they were attached by small, square electrode pads.

He looked to be sleeping soundly. There didn't appear to be any of the fitfulness he remembered before drifting off to sleep.

The time, in 24-hour mode, appeared in white, electronically etched numbers at the bottom of the screen. the time changed in 10-minute increments. His image began speaking at the 22:10 minute mark.

His voice was clear, each word pronounced with precision. but the words were not conversational. Like in the visions during the TV broadcasts, his words were robotic, given without a moment's hesitation where punctuation would normally cause pauses.

*"A man will proclaim peace. It is done. Israel is recipient."*

His image didn't move during the speaking of the words. The time at the bottom changed to 01:30.

Again, his image began speaking.

*"Nuclear arms are removed. Peace is achieved. Deceiver in process."*

Again, the time changed when his image finished speaking. The bottom of the screen read 02:10.

Again, he spoke within the new time frame on the screen.

*"Mecca is destroyed. All of Islam in foment. Israel endangered."*

The screen went black when a technician pressed a button on the unit. Tyce sat in a state of numbed silence.

"And, this, Tyce, is why we did what we did," the Israeli prime minister said. "With the entire world of Islam about to descend upon our small state, we must try for any and every advantage. We felt strongly that you might have answers within...within your obviously... visionary... subconscious mind."

Tyce didn't know what to say in response. If true, the world was in for war to be sure. Islam would explode along with its most holy place. But, what about his speaking about a *man of peace*?...

"We can now make contingency plans," Bibi said, putting his hand on Tyce's shoulder. "You have done Israel a great service, and we are appreciative."

"But, these...things I said...They might not be the same... They might not come to pass. This was in a dream state, Sir. The other things...the episodes...they were while broadcasting...visions while in an awakened state."

"Our intelligence service informs us that there are plans among the powers that be...those who would establish a new order in the world...to create a firestorm among the Islamist, the Arab world. This...prediction of yours...just might be what they plan as a catalyst for bringing the Muslim world together against Israel. They could, in some way, use the destruction of Mecca...blaming our nation to bring the world against Israel."

"But, how could that benefit them?" Tyce said after a moment's reflection.

"With Israel no longer on the scene, there could, they think, be brought about a peace in the region. They fear Israel- Jerusalem and Moriah in particular, as the number one danger for being the ignition point for global war. No Israel....no reason for war."

The prime minister walked to the door of the room, stopped, then turned again to face Tyce.

"You...your revelation might just have given us the heads-up; the time we need to prepare for this eventuality, should it come about."

* * *

THE NETWORK ANCHOR read the news, while video from around the globe rolled across Tyce Greyson's television screen.

"Food riots are the norm rather than the aberration. Violence breaks out anytime the food trucks show up."

Video of a large mob in Chicago dragging a driver out of a semi-tractor rig's cab, while others broke into the trailer remained on the screen for several seconds. The scene changed to one in Paris where enraged looters broke plate glass windows. The newscast cut to yet another scene of rioting, armed guards firing into an on-rushing crowd intent on breaking into a food warehouse in Spain.

"Even Martial Law has little effect," the anchor continued. "People within the mobs seem to have lost all reason."

Looters carrying sacks and boxes of food were, themselves, assaulted. Some were bludgeoned, the attackers then hurriedly picking up food from the ground, putting it into the boxes and running to avoid being attacked by other people.

"The global economic system has collapsed. There seems no answer to the crisis, according to Senator Charles Dodson of Maryland."

The senator stood before a reporter with the United States capital building behind him.

"Our global monetary system has crashed. We are calling for immediate emergency meetings to cobble together at least a temporary, stop-gap system. Until a more permanent system can be developed. Be assured, though. This crisis will pass. A new way will be developed. A new method of bringing the world's economy back into order will be achieved."

The reporter speaking with the senator asked, "And, another crisis compounding the one involving the economy,

Senator, the disappearance of millions and, particularly, the apparent vanishing of every baby, of every small child. What is the government's response? Or, what will be your response?"

The senator didn't hesitate, his calm tone unchanged.

"This whole disappearance thing. We are almost certain it has something to do with these lights, these large spheres of lights in the atmosphere that were observed right after the vanishings took place. Our scientists and so forth believe this might be part of some astral-phenomenon that might take place on earth every so many millions of years. Of course, in the past there were no human beings to vanish...or to report such phenomena. These are all guesses at this point, but we are confident we will have the answers."

"And what about the children, the babies that are no longer there, even those that were in the wombs of women around the world?"

"Well, that's a real crisis to be sure. There is massive hysteria. We are doing all we can to try to calm the populations, particularly those who have lost these babies."

His attention was diverted from the television screen when the door to the room opened, following a light knock.

"We plan to leave for Jerusalem within 2 hours," Yendle Gesh said. "Grishna asks that you join us."

"Okay...Sure. What's the purpose of the trip?"

"Rabbi Coahn has asked for a face to face meeting with you."

* * *

TWO HEAVILY ARMED, military helicopters accompanied the larger, passenger chopper as it whirred toward Jerusalem. They would not take a chance on having to depend upon anomaly to intervene, supernatural or otherwise, in case of attack. The Israeli prime minister had personally ordered the escort.

"It's a strange matter," Grishna said in her Israeli-accented English. "Jerusalem, probably the most volatile place on earth, so far as on-going conflicts are concerned...Jerusalem is probably the one place that is calm at this moment."

"What makes you mention that?" Tyce said, his reporter's need to know sparking the question.

"We always must know exact conditions of the areas into which we next move," she said. "We have learned that conditions must be determined because there are those constantly plotting to cause disruptions, especially in Jerusalem. We must be aware of these activities."

"And what's so unusual about conditions in Jerusalem at present?"

"There's not a single demonstration, not any protests or stone-throwing at police around the Temple Mount. Very unusual. Yet all around the world these riots are growing. It's just strange..."

"What do you think? Calm before the storm?" Tyce said.

"Hummm...Yes, that's probably a way to say it. It's as if something is pending...Something about to disrupt the tranquility."

"Any guesses as to what that might be?"

"To be frank with you, Tyce...Your words while under the influence of our technology- We are all a bit on edge. We know your track record, as they say."

"Oh, the thing about Mecca being destroyed?"

"Yes. This is a matter of concern. But, also your words about the man and the peace you mentioned..."

"Why does that concern you?"

"You will recall the words you spoke. About the *deception* in the process. This is what disturbs. You predicted that peace would be forthcoming. Then you indicated there would be deception in the process. We Jews have lived with deception all our existence. We must be wary. The world wants us eliminated. That is obvious from the lessons of history."

Tyce took in her words, glancing at the raw desert mountains that appeared to whisk by below.

"And, you think there is a plot in the making... to, somehow, through a peace process, do away with Jews?"

"Isaiah the prophet foretold such a peace."

"Oh? I thought most within the government of Israel were secular in their outlook."

"You forget, Tyce. Rabbi Elias Coahn is our leader...that is the leader of Covenant Bezalel. We are an organization... an unofficial organ of the Israeli government... which does believe in a higher power."

"In God?"

"It is difficult to believe in the God of ancient Israel. We have suffered horrendously. The holocaust took more than six million of us. It is difficult to believe in a hands-on God who cares. Such a deity certainly wasn't with the Jew during the Nazi years."

"But this prophecy...by Isaiah, you apparently believe

in what that prophet has to say? And what does he say that concerns you?"

"He says that in the future Israel will make a covenant of peace. But it will be a covenant made with death and with hell."

"Do you believe this will happen? That Israel will make such a peace covenant?"

"I believe that prophecy, if it has value, is to provide a way to avert the evil outcome that potentially exists."

"You mean that it...that is prophecy...is there to warn what will happen if caution isn't maintained...if preventative or preemptive steps aren't taken?"

"Exactly," Grishna said, after understanding his question fully. "Prophecy is not something destined to happen no matter what. It is to serve as a warning...given to provide a way to escape what will otherwise take place."

"You think it's a *higher power*...whatever it is, or whoever it is... that's using me to give these warnings?"

"It is all beyond the natural. There can be no doubt of that," Grishna said. "It remains to be seen to what end is the purpose of whatever, or whoever is working through you."

\* \* \*

DANK ODORS of disturbed earth like those of the digs where he met Grishna filled his nostrils. excavation of an area much more ancient than that of the earlier he visited lay before them while they descended. This was, he considered, seeing the earthen walls, somewhere beneath the oldest streets of Jerusalem.

"He spends much of his time here," Grishna said, shining a powerful flashlight beam ahead while leading the way down steps that had been in place for more than 2000 years. "He comes up only for our meetings or to meet with the Temple Mount Faithful."

"Temple Mount Faithful?" Tyce's question begged an answer.

"Those dedicated to putting the third Temple on Moriah," she said, turning to descend even farther down steps that lay at a right angle from the previous set.

"Do you think that's possible?"

"Rabbi Elias believes so. He is certain of it," she said, moving down the final stone step. She turned abruptly to her right and passed through an entranceway that was framed by heavy, wooden beams.

Three men dressed in black religious attire milled about in the cavern lit by large lanterns. Another, smaller man in the Jewish religious garb bent over a table with his back to the new arrivals.

"Rabbi, we are here," Grishna said in an almost reverent tone.

Elias Coahn turned slowly from his work to squint at them. He arose from the chair and shuffled their way.

"It is good to see you, Elias," Grishna said, reaching to touch the Rabbi's slightly moved forward hand.

"This is Tyce Greyson," she said, urging Tyce to move nearer the man.

The old man said nothing, but squinted at Greyson, as if trying to focus.

"Rabbi Coahn," Tyce said with a nod of his head. "Nice to finally meet you."

Coahn took Greyson's offered hand, pinching only the ends of the fingers with a brief squeeze. He said something in Hebrew, looking into Tyce's eyes.

Grishna interpreted. "He said *You are chosen!*"

"Chosen? How so?" Tyce said with a fleeting smile of not understanding.

Before Grishna could say anything, Coahn spoke in heavily accented English.

"Chosen to fulfill what must be hereafter, Tycus Levi."

Tyce started to respond, but the Rabbi turned his bearded face upward so that he looked to the ceiling. His eyes rolled beneath the lids so that mostly their white portion could be seen. He chanted something in Hebrew.

"He prays to Yahweh," Grishna said in a whisper, glancing at Tyce.

When Coahn next looked into Tyce's eyes, the discomfiting words from the Rabbi caromed within his mind.

"There is something for you, Tycus Levi," the Rabbi said. He turned to walk to the table at which he had been sitting when they entered. He returned with a rolled piece of what looked to be parchment or other material.

He unrolled the material and held it in both hands between himself and Greyson. He read in Hebrew what was written on the scroll.

Tyce looked to Grishna.

She said, "It is from the prophet Joel. 'And it shall come to pass afterward, *that* I will pour out my spirit upon all flesh; and 'your sons and your daughters shall prophesy, your old men shall dream dreams, your young men shall see visions.'"

# CHAPTER 12

"Your leader, Rabbi Coahn, is a believer, but the rest of you aren't believers?"

Greyson's question elicited an expression of understanding from Grishna Lansky's pleasant face.

"Rabbi Coahn believes in an intimate, hands-on God, who rules in Heaven and intervenes on earth," she said while they rode in the van toward the helicopter.

"We who work with him, on the other hand, are realists...pragmatists. We can't see, feel or touch the God he believes in, so stay at arm's-length from his belief system. On the other hand, there are things that have happened...that are happening...that make us wonder..."

"Like?"

"Like your...visions...coming true. Like Rabbi Elias foretelling that you would one day appear to see into Israel's future."

"This is why I'm here?"

"Well, certainly Elias believes so. He predicted as much more than five years ago...when we formed Covenant Bezalel as a shadow government entity. He said there would be one who would come into our midst who would see things of Israel's future."

Upon arrival at the hulking helicopter, whose huge blades drooped to present an ominous specter in the semi-darkness, the telecommunications device carried by one of the uniformed men squawked. the announcement was urgently transmitted in Hebrew.

Grishna immediately replied in Hebrew, manipulating buttons on the device held by her assistant. When finished talking into the device, she stared, as if in a trance-like state.

She spoke words quietly to the assistant, who turned and hurried to the vehicle that had accompanied the van in which she and Tyce had ridden.

"What's wrong?" Tyce saw tears glistening in Grishna's eyes.

She looked at him, still as if in a daze, the tears spilling in thin streams over her cheeks.

"Rabbi Elias has been killed in an attack. It happened just now."

"The attack was carried out by those who are determined to put you under their domination."

Yendle Gesh's stern tone made Tyce sense the Israeli was condemning him for the Rabbi's death. He fought the urge to tell him, tell them all, that he didn't ask to be brought into their clandestine cabal.

Grishna's words disrupted his thought. "They are allowed to locate and murder our spiritual leader. But not allowed to get to you, Tyce. We must find out what this means. Israel's very life depends upon learning their designs...their purpose. And their methodology."

"They've introduced some sort of technology to infiltrate...to locate our most protected sanctuaries," Gesh said in the continuing tone of pent-up anger. "

We must have our people sweep our every crevice for electronic breeches of security," Grishna said. "We shall begin this day to complete that sweep."

* * *

"THE UNITED STATES and the European Union today conjoined all military operations."

The news anchor in New York gave the news. Video rolled of uniformed, U.S. and EU top echelon officers sitting around a large, round, conference table.

"Reports from top American officials have it that the U.S. is so adversely affected by loss of people in key positions that the move is essential to America's national security. European military top brass now holds key leadership roles in the newly amalgamated force. The EU now is possessor of America's nuclear stockpile and the means to deliver nuclear warheads. While Russia has more nuclear weapons in its inventory, the United States weaponry is said to be superior in technological capability."

A quick cut filled the television screen with a man in military uniform standing at a podium before a battery of microphones. He spoke in French. The translator spoke in English.

"Today we form the most powerful and proficient military force in the history of mankind. We do so to secure world peace, not to enforce our will on the world."

The anchor's face again returned to the screen while he read.

"Meantime, the India-Pakistan movement toward all-out nuclear conflict is heating up. To add to the rumors of war, Chinese leadership declares that nation will now consider all of Asia under its hegemony. The reason given is that the mass disappearance of so many around the world has altered the existing order. The Chinese communiqué announced today that they must assert China's dominance to assure the security of its people."

Tyce Greyson's thoughts returned to the laptop screen when he used the remote to mute the television.

He stared again at the book title at the top of the monitor screen.

*Israel the Sign*

All the world's nations were in turmoil. Nuclear conflict threatened at many points around the globe. America, the apex nation of history...no longer the superpower, but a subservient addition to the now more powerful EU. Yet tiny Israel was, for the moment, relatively calm. Except for the attack on Israel's most secretive national security cabal. On its spiritual leader, Rabbi Elias Coahn.

And, somehow, he knew that he, Tyce Greyson, was complicit...even if unwittingly...in the Rabbi's death at the hands of...of those who were determined to hunt him down.

\* \* \*

GRISHNA LANSKY WAS UNUSUALLY SUBDUED. She wanted to ask him something, but was, for some reason, hesitant, almost to the point of seeming in pain at having to ask.

"Just say what you have to say," Tyce said, seeing the angst in the expression of this usually totally confident woman.

"Yes. That is best," she said with seriousness in her voice. "Were you and Marial...ever... intimate?"

The question took him aback, but none-the-less brought a brief, wistful smile.

"You mean, did we have sex?"

"Well...Yes. were you together like that?"

"Why? What are you getting at?"

She again was hesitant, but her expression was one of resignation to what had to be said.

"We suspect, Tyce, that you have been implanted with some device...A chip that gives them the ability to know your location."

"And, you think Marial implanted me with this.... chip?"

"We fear so. Yes."

"Is there a way of checking?"

"Yes, we have technology that can scan for such...devices. If you were...intimate...you could have been easily implanted while you were asleep."

But, that would have woken me up."

"Not if you were given a sedative. And the devices are so small and can be injected by a very fine needle. The *chip* can actually be injected as a liquid. It then turns into a silicone and metallic object once under the skin."

"Well, you attached electronic wires to me while I slept. I guess your theory isn't out of the question," he said.

"Likely it would be at the back of the head, just beneath the epidermis within the scalp," Grishna said. ""Let's see if there's one there."

His emotions ran the gamut. From the anger of possibly having been implanted by the...whosoever they were, to the maddening, depressing probability that the only person he had ever truly felt such passion for could betray him.

"The procedure...the scan...will take only a few

minutes," Grishna said, then called for the matter to be done.

* * *

AN HOUR after the technicians scanned his body, the results were handed to Grishna. Tyce turned from the laptop to watch her enter the room and approach. She held a sheet of paper.

"Just as we thought, there was a device...actually two devices implanted. One just under the hairline at the back of the scalp and another beneath the arm...the right arm pit."

Tyce shuddered inwardly, knowing that the things had been with him...for how long. When did she inject him? Just before their making love? Was that what it was, making love? To inject your lover with a device that would lead to the death of someone? That would make it possible for them to track him down?...

"We can remove them by very small slits in the top layer of skin," she said. "Not much more trouble than removing a splinter."

Grishna's words were assuring, meant to remove anxiety from the extraction procedure. He saw on her face, then, the same look as before. The need to address something about which she was reluctant to talk about.

"What else?" he said, seeing her now familiar hesitant manner reappear.

"Tyce...the prime minister requests that you...that you undergo another of the vision-inducing sessions."

He said nothing, his expression unchanged.

"It is imperative that, if possible, we stay ahead of these...these enemies of Israel. The world has turned against us since...since the vanishings. it's as if they want to take it all out on the Jew. We must take every advantage. You might just provide that advantage."

He digested her words before speaking.

"Well, you Jews aren't the only one they hold responsible, apparently. They are determined to be rid of me as well," he said in a half-joking tone.

"Oh, no. They want you alive. They want the...miracles...you can provide them through the...prophecies."

"Well, they tried to take me out as well as the rest of you with that helicopter attack."

"They could have hit us with their missile. Those type armaments do not miss once locked on their targets. They purposely set it to fire past us. They wanted to force us down...to land. But, they were...supernaturally...prevented."

It was true. There could be no other explanation that made sense. It was a supernatural act that prevented the copters from destroying them...or forcing them to land. He listened while she continued.

"This same...*supernatural*...influence, we feel, has determined to use you to provide information regarding our future. To preserve us...to protect us from those who would destroy us."

She awaited a response, which he felt compelled to give.

"I guess we should have another go at it, then," he said, not knowing what else to say.

"Aren't you afraid that my knowing about undergoing the... induced vision...might, as the prime minister said, *contaminate* the process?" Tyce swallowed the liquid from the vial after asking the question.

"We don't think that will be the case," the doctor who had handed him the vial said. "You volunteered, seemingly without anxiety. So, there should be no problem...no interference by your cerebral condition...that should act as an inhibitor."

"Let's hope it works," Tyce said, lying on his back on the bed.

The doctor attached the wires to his temple and forehead while a technician fidgeted with the black boxes on a table nearby.

"We will record your every word, Tyce," Grishna said, standing at the end of the bed. "We are grateful for your doing this for our people."

His senses, already in the throes of the drug's affect, began to darken. Thoughts of Marial, her pretty face smiling and welcoming, fading, then to be replaced by storm clouds alive with fractured lightning. A storm of immense magnitude, rolling and boiling above Mount Moriah, the golden globe of the Dome of the Rock reflecting each flash.

Again, the beast in the turbulent sea slogged on its four, leopard-like legs onto the sands of the beach. Now there were seven heads at the end of its dragon-like neck. Upon the heads were ten horns.

The massive beast began transforming, metamorphosing into a smaller and smaller form. The form of a man. It possessed the face of which he was familiar.

The scene before him exploded, sparking bursting splinters of light. When he next could make out the vista that was in front of him, the figure of a man lay in repose upon a funeral pyre. The face of the corpse was the bearded countenance of Rabbi Elias Coahn.

The transformed beast-man entered the scene before

his astonished gaze. The man stood over the pyre, his arms outstretched over the corpse.

"Tyce...Tyce... Wake up," the female voice called to him through the veil of opaque grey. His sense of reality came into focus, feeling the cold, damp compress upon his forehead.

"It is Grishna," she said, wiping his forehead and face with the cloth.

"How did it go?" he asked, finally able to fully comprehend his circumstance.

"The things you told us will be invaluable," Grishna said. "We will fully inform you when you are rested."

HIS IMAGE on the screen spoke clearly, in undisrupted, instructive pace and tone. Seeing his own body, lying as still and corpse-like as had been the Rabbi in the vision, brought shivers of realization. His was a strange, troubling commission to be sure. From *what*, from *whom* ...he knew not. But the words came without apparent effort— a stream of conscious declaration that was rendered while in the unconscious state.

Tyce listened intently as did the others in the room who viewed the video.

*"The prince that will come will harbor miracles. The dead will be resurrected to life. The chief friend of Bezalel will arise before the power of the prince."*

A pause of 10 minutes became apparent when the time marker at the bottom right of the screen display changed from *10:00* to 10:10, at which time Greyson's image spoke again.

*"Israel will believe. The prince will prevail. Beware the prince who causes the dead to rise. Israel, beware."*

Ten minutes more elapsed and Greyson's image on the screen spoke yet again.

"The two are one in the covenant of peace that war threatens. Mecca is destroyed. Danger to Israel brings deception by first and second beast through peace that will destroy the unwary."

The screen went black and Grishna spoke.

"What do you make of it? Do you remember any of it?"

"Only a small part. The same man that I first saw transform from the gigantic sea-beast. He stood over your rabbi...Elias Coahn."

"Elias?!"

"Yes, it was Rabbi Coahn."

"Could it be? Could it be that Elias will yet live?"

Her question was spoken with joy in her voice.

## CHAPTER 13

Yendle Gesh was becoming more exercised by the minute. He paced upon the carpet just outside the prime minister's office, stopping only to peer out the large window onto the plaza milling with people, then pacing again.

Tyce watched Gesh from an overstuffed chair nearest to the large, double doors to the office.

"Any detail you can think of to give Bibi will be most helpful," Grishna, sitting in an identical chair next to Tyce, said.

One of the double doors opened and a woman bid them to enter.

The prime minister spoke in Hebrew and low volume to the woman who had opened the door. She then took some papers he handed her and left the office through another door.

"Tyce," the Israeli leader said, holding out his right hand. "Thank you for coming. We consider your input essential. Particularly at this time."

"Whatever I can do, Sir..."

Tyce shook the Israeli's hand.

"Yendle..." the prime minister said. "Is there any news from our people on who was responsible for the attack on Bezalel?"

"It was not Hamas as was first thought, they are sure," Gesh said. "It was almost certainly a black ops group from somewhere within EU."

"What does this assault portend?"

"We don't know at this point," Gesh said. "All we can determine is that Israel's most secretive security ranks have been breached. The extra dimensional ranks."

The prime minister seemed to calculate Gesh's words, then turned to Tyce.

"You haven't heard the term, *Extra Dimensional,* Tyce?"

"No, Sir."

"We've decided to bring you into our confidence in this most clandestine of our services. We do so because your...gift for foretelling...whatsoever it entails, is in alignment with this...esoteric realm. this force that has developed."

"Tell him about how it began, Bibi," Grishna said, her tone somewhat filled with excitement.

"Bibi, I don't think it wise to divulge to...an outsider...about *Extra Dimension,*" Yendle Gesh said, frowning and raising his voice.

"And why not, Yendle?"

"Because he is susceptible to being taken by the European cabal. his...female...associate...has been complicit, we believe..."

"We have a handle on all of that, Yendle," the prime minister interrupted. "We have brought him into our ...intrigues. It is only right and fitting that he be made privy to what is entailed if we expect him to use his...special talents...to help Israel."

"Tell him all about it, Bibi," Grishna said again, in a firm tone.

The Israeli prime minister took time to gather his thoughts before beginning.

"Tyce, it involves you right from its very beginning."

Greyson said nothing, but his curiosity piqued to the maximum.

"When we first heard you talk of the vanishing...predict in the broadcast the disappearance that was to take place. This was the beginning of this matter we've come to term *Extra Dimension.*"

"It was as if we were pointed the way of Israel's future course of movement," Grishna said, excitedly, interrupting the prime minister's words.

"It was as if in days of old, when Israel's great men were given direction from other worldly powers," the prime minister said. "Call it *God,* or whatever... We, within days of your prediction about the vanishings that would take place coming to pass, these...extra dimensional spheres of brilliant light began appearing to us."

Grishna Lansky begin to speak. "So, it was you that we knew we had to bring into our orbit...."

"We knew that you held the key to learning about what this extra dimensional interdiction involved," Bibi said, interrupting Grishna's excited insertion into the prime minister's explanation.

"The orbs of light," Tyce said, as if to himself.

"Exactly. It was the orbs of light that made us know we had to bring you...as Grishna put it...into our orbit."

Grishna again spoke. "Tyce, these orbs of light, they have enlightened us in ways that can only be described as supernatural."

"*Extra Dimension* is the term we use to encapsulate all

TERRY JAMES

of the things we have learned...are learning from these spheres," the prime minister said.

"We believe it was these spheres that swept the pursuing helicopters from the sky when we flew toward Tel Aviv," Grishna said.

"But, they didn't protect Rabbi Coahn," Yendle Gesh said with cynicism in his declaration.

"Ah, but the final chapter isn't written in the matter of Rabbi Elias," Grishna said. "Not according to Tyce's most recent prophecy."

"And, this is what I most want to know, Tyce," the prime minister said. "What do you think this portends...this vision you have been given? Do you believe these...light orbs...these spheres...might be involved in your having the ability to predict, to prophesy?"

Tyce felt overwhelmed with the disclosures of the preceding minutes. His senses were in overload.

"Sir, I think they *must* have something to do with these visions, based upon what I'm learning today."

"My thinking, too," the prime minister said. "These...orbs...don't tell us the future in any sense. But, they hover over our scientists, our military leaders, over me. They, through unspoken process of some sort, tell us things that produce profound technological and strategic ways to conduct, for example, military planning."

"And, they say nothing, only influence through thought?"

"Yes," the Israeli prime minister agreed. "They have been doing so since the day of the vanishings of people around the world."

"What do you think it all might mean?" Grishna's question was put to Tyce.

He didn't answer, but the convoluting thoughts gushed through his mind, one on top of another.

For him, it started with the Rabbi's words. The strangeness then took on exponentially-increasing influence over his life within the Patmos cave. The snake's bite and all that ensued.

The first vision...the huge sea beast that he somehow knew had symbolic meaning beyond his ability to discern. The beast, throughout subsequent visions, transforming into human form. The form of a man. The man who would have powers to raise the dead.

"I don't know any more than you do, Grishna. But, I have a feeling we will all learn more about all of this at some point," he said finally.

"We must do so," the prime minister said. "Our very existence as a nation...as a people, I believe, somehow depends upon our knowing more about this strange matter."

* * *

HE THOUGHT of the scripture for the hundredth time. His eyes blurred from lack of sleep. The words of the prophet Joel, given him by Rabbi Elias Coahn, played in his fatigue-plagued brain. He could repeat it verbatim.

*And it shall come to pass afterward, that I will pour out my spirit upon all flesh; and your sons and your daughters shall prophesy, your old men shall dream dreams, your young men shall see visions.*

"You must go to Marial."

Tyce looked around from his sitting position in bed. The voice still lingered in his senses. Had it been an audible voice?

Scant light poured in the small window of the room.

The room the Israeli's provided. Light from somewhere outside in the public square that bordered the government building.

Had he *really* heard the voice? Or was it just the trick of a tired mind? A mind-trick while drifting into sleep...

*"You must go to her,"* he heard the voice say again. It was clear and familiar. It was the voice of Elias Coahn.

"Where are you?"

Tyce's own words reverberated within the room. "You aren't alive," he said, searching the semi-darkness for the source of the Rabbi's voice.

"Go find Marial. She is in great distress. You must free her."

"Rabbi? What is this? You are dead. Killed by..."

"Find Marial," the voice interrupted.

The darkness coalesced with the room's temperature to impose an oppressive, ambient chill. Diffused illumination at first grew in influence upon the darkness until a globe of light appeared somewhere at the room's center.

At its center appeared the one who personified his most ardent obsession. Marial's image, sat somewhere within a dwelling place as dimly lit as his own. her pretty face was creased by streamlets of tears that ran over her cheeks while she stood and moved to a window and peered into the night.

*"You must go to her, Tycus Levi,"* the voice of Elias Coahn said once again.

"But how," Tyce responded in a pleading way. "I don't know where she is...how to begin looking..."

"You will be shown," the Rabbi's voice affirmed.

Violent pounding at the door caused him to lurch upward in the bed. He blinked, trying to clear his mind from the deep sleep...from the dream-state that had held him within its emotion-wrenching grip.

Yendle Gesh burst through the door opening. His words shattered the early morning quietude.

"Your presence is requested by the prime minister. There has been a most distressing development."

\* \* \*

SEVENTEEN MINUTES later the Israeli prime minister's conference room was abuzz with muted chatter. Tyce stood near the Israeli flag as it draped in one corner of the enormous chamber.

"What's this about?" his question was directed to Grishna Lansky, who had just broken off conversation with one of the nation's top generals.

"We will know the full details momentarily. Bibi is meeting with his advisors," Grishna said, her eyes on the many people in the conference room.

Within moments the big doors opened and a contingent, led by the prime minister, hurried into the room. The leader's expression as he moved to the area with microphones was grim, deeply etched in concentration.

There was no introduction. He took a folded page of white paper from his suit coat pocket and unfolded it. He glanced at it, but didn't read from the paper, when he spoke.

"We have learned that Mecca has been partly destroyed by several missile strikes. The Kabba was completely destroyed, we are told."

The prime minister hesitated to form his thoughts into words in precisely the way he wanted the world to receive them.

"I make it clear here and now that the Israeli forces,

either overtly or clandestinely, had nothing whatsoever to do with this attack. Such an action would certainly not be in the best interest of Israel."

Again, he paused to get the words exactly as he wanted them presented to the world press, the gaggle of reporters gathered just in front of the battery of microphones.

"Already, we get word of those accusing us of this action. We absolutely disavow any association, in any way, with what has happened."

Tyce Greyson's thoughts were many. The prime minister's words undulated with almost painful resonance within his brain, weary from fitful sleep.

What did it mean? His...*prophecy*... had come to pass. What next? What revelation of future events did the *higher powers,* or whatever was the source of his cerebral torture, have in store?

Grishna leaned to pull at his shirtsleeve to make him bend so she could speak with low volume into his ear.

"We are prepared for this...Thanks to you."

* * *

"You see, now," Yendle Gesh said, standing beside Tyce, who watched the members of the *IDF* move about, "why it is vital that we have you in this with us."

Someone handed the Israeli a piece of paper which he quickly perused then folded it and put it in his suit pocket.

"The prime minister will be ready for us in about five minutes," he said to Tyce, then walked to speak to several uniformed officers a few yards away.

"What does the prime minister want of me?"

Greyson's words caused Grishna to reflect on the question for a few seconds.

"He almost certainly will want to go over the precise details of the vision you had regarding the matter of the destruction at Mecca."

"How serious is the threat to Israel that this has caused?"

"According to the very scant information I've gotten, the war councils of the Arab world are meeting now. All of Islam is in an uproar. But, this, too, you predicted. And, thanks to your...*prophecy*... we are as prepared as it is possible to be prepared..."

"We can see the prime minister now," Gesh said. The three of them moved through the crowded waiting room and were ushered into the office.

The prime minister was huddled with two of his top advisors near the big desk. Gesh, Grishna and Tyce waited patiently for the men to finish their hushed conversation.

When the leader looked in their direction, he said something quietly in Hebrew to the men then came, smiling, toward the latest arrivals.

"Tyce, you are a God-send to us. Thank you for your friendship and cooperation. You have been invaluable in helping to lessen this crisis."

He shook Greyson's hand vigorously, then led him by the elbow, urging him to be seated. The Israeli leader took a chair directly across from that of Greyson.

Grishna and Yendle Gesh sat a few feet away on a sofa.

The prime minister didn't hesitate to issue his thoughts.

"Tyce, your prophecy came true to the letter. At least the part about Mecca being assaulted and the world of

Islam going into a rage. We must assume that the rest of the prophecies you gave on the evening we induced the sleep-state will also come to pass."

Bibi awaited reaction from his guest but saw and heard none.

"This...*man of peace*...you spoke of while in the state of suspension of consciousness...what do you think that might have to do with this...attack...this destruction at the heart of Islam?"

"Mr. prime minister, I really have no idea what ever. You know as much as I do in that regard."

Bibi's face tightened in an expression that said he thought as much. He nodded understanding.

"Very well. We shall learn together what it portends," he said, before turning to Gesh and Grishna.

"What are the plans for Elias?"

"His body lies in repose in Jerusalem," Gesh said.

"Bibi, as you know, Tyce's foretelling is that Elias will be raised," Grishna said.

"No offense," the prime minister said in a serious tone, turning to Tyce. "But if *that* prediction comes to pass, we will be at a crossroads experience, the likes for which it is impossible to prepare."

He turned back to Grishna. "When is the SHIVNA?"

"Tomorrow."

"The body is under constant attendance until burial, of course," Bibi said.

"Of course, as is our custom," Grishna responded.

The prime minister stood and checked his watch. "I must go now to a meeting." He turned again to Tyce.

"Tyce, we will know tomorrow, perhaps, more about this...*gift*...that you have had bestowed upon you."

\* \* \*

HE AWOKE EARLY. The trip to Jerusalem was one he didn't want to make. The Rabbi's funeral and SHIVA awaited, and they expected him there.

The SHIVA, the seven-day period of mourning, he knew was the Jewish way of honoring the dead after the funeral. It was something he had witnessed. He didn't want to go, only to be treated as a curiosity. He had said the man would be resurrected. All eyes belonging to those who knew of the prophecy would be upon him.

The dream kept running through his thinking. The Rabbi's telling him to go to Marial. Her image within the orb of light. her forlorn peering out the window. As if looking for someone... for him.

The television screen filled with Mount Moriah. the golden dome glistened in the early morning sun. The news narrator's words described the scene when the screen showed a quick cut to several men in business suits entering a building.

"The delegation from the European Union represents the EU *Council for Peace.* They hastily assembled following the destruction of the Kabba and much of Mecca. The council is made up of members of Europe's diplomatic corps. They have been commissioned to oversee the peace effort to resolve the most urgent issues that threaten war. The United States has acquiesced to the EU in the present crisis because of the continuing work on restoring American government following the disappearance of Americans, including some key governmental figures."

Another quick cut displayed the Israeli prime minister hurriedly walking from a limo and into the building, accompanied by a number of security men and Israeli government officials.

The narrator continued. "Israel's prime minister will

meet with the Council for Peace. He will lay out Israel's position in working to prevent war that looms."

Several quicker cut shots of the European delegation ended with interviews of several individuals. When a reporter spoke with the delegate that was third in line for interviews, Tyce stiffened to attention, his eyes zeroing in on the subject.

He didn't listen carefully to the conversation. He did, however, study the face intensely. It was a face burned into his cognition. The unforgettable countenance of the transformed sea-beast to man that had haunted his existence for months.

* * *

"YOU HAVE HAD A CHANGE OF HEART," Grishna said lightly shortly after they touched down at Ben Gurion. "You were rather glum, before, about our request that you accompany us to Elias' funeral."

"Yes. Well, I'm not so reluctant now," he said, glancing at Grishna then out the window of the SUV that whisked them toward the synagogue.

"Why the change?"

"Just need a change of scenery, I guess," he said, not wanting to talk about his real reason.

"We must be prepared for any eventuality. And you are key to our being able to plan...ahead of our enemies...through use of your prophetic ability."

"How is my going to Rabbi Coahn's funeral—to his SHIVNA...going to help Israel's planners?" his question was put with mild irritation in his tone.

She smiled a tolerant smile before answering.

"We want to have instant access to your gift when you employ it. We Jews want to take every advantage over our opponents," she said with humor. "That includes the timing factors involved in our dealing with them."

Tyce made no response. Instead he watched the other government vehicles ahead of them as they turned into the inner city and toward the small synagogue where lay Rabbi Elias Coahn.

They saw ahead a crowd of people, preventing their vehicle and the others from proceeding. Tyce thought at first it was a mob—rioters who were disrupting traffic.

No, he decided, it was a large group of people, and they were excited. But, they weren't acting in a destructive way. They looked to be—at least those on the outside of the mass of people—looked to be trying to see past the mob to look at something of great interest.

"What is this?"

Grishna strained to look past the driver and Israeli security agent in the front seats.

"They are all looking at something," Tyce said, trying himself to see beyond their own vehicle and those ahead.

"The security agent opened his passenger-side door.

"I'll find out what it is about," he said, before walking to near the crowd.

They watched him question some on the outside of the crowd of people that pressed forward to see something at or near the building's front doors.

The agent returned to the SUV within 3 minutes.

"They are saying somebody who died was just raised from the dead."

\* \* \*

WITH THE CROWD gone 45 minutes later, they entered the building next to the small synagogue. The security agent, instructed by Grishna Lansky to do so, came to them with 2 people in tow.

He introduced the man and woman, then said, "They were at the front of the mass of people. They know the reason for the excitement."

"Thank you for agreeing to come to us," Grishna said with a smile. "Will you please inform us?"

The woman, obviously still excited about what they saw, spoke.

"The Rabbi is alive! The man took his hand where he lay and..." She gestured with her right hand, indicated a lifting motion. "The Rabbi opened his eyes and sat up!"

"Yes! He then moved off the table on which he had lain," the man said with equal excitement, in heavily accented English.

Grishna and Tyce remained silent, not thinking of further questions to ask. The couple continued their excited explanation of events.

"The man in the suit and tie, they say he is part of the group from EU," the woman said, then was interrupted by the man.

"He raised the Rabbi from the dead! He then left with the others...the Europeans who came with him to view Rabbi Coahn's body."

Grishna turned to Tyce, holding his forearm and squeezing it. "It seems your ability to prophesy remains one hundred percent intact," she said.

\* \* \*

"All of Israel has heard of this miracle," Yendle Gesh said. "Many are saying this man is the Messiah...Ridiculous!"

Gesh plopped down a couple of newspapers on the table. He seated himself next to the table.

"The Rabbi is nowhere to be found," he continued. "They say he left with the one who...*raised*...him from the dead."

His words were said with irritable skepticism in his voice.

"We will locate the Rabbi soon enough," Grishna said, turning to Tyce after speaking to Gesh's statement.

"What do you think this means, if true, Tyce?"

"You know as much as I, Grishna. But, I believe it must mean something about the peace process we've talked about."

"The peace mentioned by Isaiah the prophet? The peace covenant made with *death and hell?"*

"According to the words I spoke, there will be deception in the peace process," Tyce said.

"But how does this...*resurrection*... if true...How can it be part of the efforts to make peace?"

Her words were, he took it, almost dismissive of Tyce believing such a miracle could be part of something so evil as perpetrating deception upon Israel.

"Maybe it's not the case. Maybe the two statements I made are mutually exclusive. I don't know. But, the...prophecies...were made in exact proximity to each other."

"All I know is that if Rabbi Elias is indeed still with us, I am ecstatic and can see only wonderful results from this...this *miracle."*

Was she expressing just her own happiness over the report of the Rabbi's being raised from the dead? Or was it a prophesied blindness that she and all of Israel would suffer as things played out? All citizens of the nation were observably, to his way of thinking, now caught up in the...*miracle*... of the Rabbi's being raised from the dead.

People didn't come back to life. It just didn't happen. Yet his own words had predicted it...*prophesied* it.

His purpose for being brought to their country by the Israelis, according to them, was to serve to give the leaders of the Jewish state a heads-up on future matters. To help them get a head start on problems that would pop up because of Israel's many blood-vowed enemies.

Grishna Lansky, at least, would take his forewarnings at face value, only if they didn't stand in the way of her own perception of things. Was it blindness to a coming deception, or...

"Rabbi Elias is returning to synagogue," one of the security agents announced after entering the room. "he will speak on things that have transpired."

* * *

PEOPLE PACKED the small sanctuary. hundreds stood outside trying to get a glimpse of, to hear the words of the Jewish holy man, now raised from the dead.

Tyce sat beside Grishna Lansky while a group of men in Jewish religious garb moved from somewhere in the synagogue's rear portion. The Rabbi that was the object of attention, shorter than most of the others accompanying him, could at first not be seen.

When several of the religious men moved aside, Rabbi Elias Coahn came fully into view. he then shuffled to the podium, placed there especially for this moment.

"I am speaking in English rather than in Hebrew because many here have English as a second language. My beloved friends of the European delegation, for example, speak the English language as well as their native tongues. I would like to especially address them."

All were hushed. A man...dead and now alive! Nothing like it had been experienced. Yet they all believed it, Tyce thought, looking around at the rapt expression of attention on every face. They all believed totally that this man had, genuinely, come back from the dead.

Grishna, too, believed. He studied her face from his position to her left. The glistening eyes, filled with tears and emotion that said...she believed, absolutely...

"Today, I return to you for a divine purpose," the Rabbi said, speaking slowly in the familiar voice.

"I come to address what has transpired in these past hours. But, more than that, in these past weeks."

Coahn lifted his face toward the ceiling, appearing to be summoning assistance from somewhere above. He again leveled his gaze toward the many eyes that were fastened intently on him.

"My death...my arising... is tethered, to, is linked inexorably to, the phenomenon that has so affected, so mesmerized the peoples of Planet Earth."

Camera shutters whirred and clicked, their flashes lighting the chamber almost blindingly while the Rabbi spoke.

Was he, Tyce Greyson, the only one among those gathered before the holy man who doubted? Were there none others who had serious issues with, had questions about...about someone being raised from the dead?

For now, the questions would have to languish beneath the overwhelming gush of emotion. A man stood before the world...raised from death. Time for his questions would have to await opportunity.

"You have seen this day the beginning of the time of

the miraculous. He who brings answers to mankind's mounting problems is among us."

The Rabbi's words raised one question. Tyce Greyson was determined to explore. Who was this miracle worker who could raise the dead?

CHAPTER 14

I t had been impossible to get to the Rabbi following his brief statement. He was whisked away through the back of the synagogue by the other Rabbis.

Tyce looked through the old Bible he had been given by a preacher long ago. The book was marked with underlines and notes in red ballpoint the pastor had made in the margins.

He searched until he found chapter 28 of the Old Testament book of Isaiah. He had first searched on internet, using the words *covenant made with death, Isaiah.*

He copied the passage when he found it then pasted it into his documents of notes.

28:14*Wherefore hear the word of the LORD, ye scornful men, that rule this people which is in Jerusalem.* 28:15*Because ye have said, We have made a covenant with death, and with hell are we at agreement; when the overflowing scourge shall pass through, it shall not come unto us: for we have made lies our refuge, and under falsehood have we hid ourselves:*

28:16*Therefore thus saith the Lord GOD, Behold, I lay in Zion for a foundation a stone, a tried stone, a precious corner* *stone, a sure foundation: he that believeth shall not make haste. ²⁸·¹⁷Judgment also will I lay to the line, and righteousness to the plummet: and the hail shall sweep away the refuge of lies, and the waters shall overflow the hiding place.*

*²⁸:¹⁸And your covenant with death shall be disannulled, and your agreement with hell shall not stand; when the overflowing scourge shall pass through, then ye shall be trodden down by it.*

Sleep tugged at him. He had been awake since 4 a.m., and his eyes no longer were faithful to the task before him. The scriptures ran together, and his vision blurred when trying to make sense of his notes.

The passage was concerning Israel's end of days. A prophecy about a covenant of peace that would go terribly wrong, according to the prophet Isaiah.

But where to go next in his attempt to make sense of it all, he knew not.

He switched off the light by the bed and drifted soon into sleep.

Marial, beautiful, sensuous Marial... The love of his every conscious thought. Now she traversed his dream-world. Elusive, chiffon-like, wind-blown... Unattainable.

Her face, turned to the window. Tears flowing while she looked too lonely to see beyond her own confinement. Beautiful Marial...

Dream-visions moving, ever moving. The bearded face of the Rabbi. His eyes wide and glistening in the Jerusalem sun. His whispered words..."*Israel is the sign...*" Repeated, "*Israel is the sign of the end...*"

The European. The man in the business suit. Reaching his hand to take that of the Rabbi's corpse. Lifting the dead, Jewish holy man to life...

The burning debris of the destroyed Kabba...The angry, screaming faces of millions upon millions of worshippers of Islam. The cries: *"Death to Israel...Death to the Jew!"*...

The European delegation, walking toward the building somewhere in Jerusalem. Neville Chamberlain's words while he waved the piece of paper. The black and white film... the shouts of many voices *"Peace for our time!"*

The EU peace-seekers, moving toward the Israeli prime minister; a young leader among them. The face...the same as on the beach at Patmos. The pages of the old Bible, opening, pages turning as if blown by a strange wind. A cold, mysterious wind.

The pages settle into an open book configuration. The book title- *Daniel.* The chapter burned into his memory... *Daniel, chapter 9...*Verses *26* and *27*...

Morning's first rays of light warmed his face and painfully pierced into his eyes. Tyce struggled from his lying position on the bed. He turned to sit on its side, trying to focus on the sites of the early hours of the day.

The dreams had all but faded. He tried to remember them, but they fled from his memory. Except for the scripture...The scripture that still was etched upon his sleep-recovering brain.

He reached to the table, retrieved the Bible and began thumbing through its pages.

He found, finally, the object of his search. the Book of Daniel. now to the chapters and verses. Daniel, chapter 9, verses 26 and 27.

He read them silently.

*9:26And after threescore and two weeks shall Messiah be cut off, but not for himself: and the people of the prince that shall come shall destroy the city and the sanctuary; and the end thereof shall be with a flood, and unto the end of the war desolations are determined. 9:27And he shall confirm the*

*covenant with many for one week: and in the midst of the
week he shall cause the sacrifice and the oblation to cease, and
for the overspreading of abominations he shall make it desolate, even until the consummation, and that determined shall
be poured upon the desolate.*

\* \* \*

HE COULDN'T SHAKE his thoughts of how the scripture
from Daniel were at the center of the intrigues. The
intrigues of the assault on Mecca, of the destruction of
the Kabba.

Daniel, who somehow knew, had looked down
through the many centuries to this moment in time. The
scripture was speaking to all these strange things in his
own life.

But how was he involved, why had he been chosen to
witness...to be a part of the unfolding of history long ago
prophesied by Daniel? What did it all mean...his being
betrayed by the one person he cared about most...the
person he loved? How was it destined to end?

"The Arabs are going crazy," Grishna Lansky said.
"The rest of the world, too. even America is blaming us
for things that happened in Mecca."

She talked while they rode quickly toward the Tel
Aviv government offices.

"Our satellites and other intelligence informs us that
they are preparing a Nasser-type attack."

Tyce remembered the lessons of Israel's history.
Gamul Abdul Nasser, president of Egypt, led the 1956
war against the Jewish state. Arab nations, with few
exceptions, joined in the attack. He remembered, too, the
result. Israel defeated and won territory from the
aggressors.

"It is just a matter of time. I believe that this time Bibi will use our atomic weapons," Grishna said.

"Nuclear? Why? You've always won against over-whelming odds," Tyce said.

"It is true. We have always won. However, as is repeated many times, we must win every time. They must win only once. With their sophisticated weapons now, supplied by Russia and others, we cannot take a chance on losing that one time."

"So, war is almost a certainty?"

"No. I would say it is *definitely* a certainty," she said adamantly.

"What is this meeting with the prime minister about?"

She took a moment to think about how forthcoming she should be before answering.

"Partly, it is about your ability to...predict...the future of any future war with our enemies," she said.

When she explained no further, he said, "And, what about the other thing or things he wants me there for?"

"I'm not altogether sure, Tyce," she said. "We shall see, together, what Bibi has in mind."

Military activity was inescapable. Transports carrying supplies and machinery of war moved along the streets of Tel Aviv as their SUV carried them toward Israeli headquarters.

Jet fighters roared overhead, while mobile, armored weaponry rumbled in all directions. When they arrived at their destination, several armed IDF soldiers examined the exterior and interior of their SUV before waving them through the checkpoint.

Once inside the building, other, uniformed personnel checked them carefully before allowing them to move further toward the prime minister's suite of offices.

"This is the highest of alerts," Grishna said, acknowl-edging unprecedented security for this building.

Several IDF officers and men dressed in civilian suits and ties moved through the halls, each seeming to be headed for specific destinations as quickly as possible. When they were allowed to enter the inner-most areas of the offices, familiar faces of his most intimate assis-tants bid them to enter the prime minister's office.

He had a phone to his ear, listening to his caller. He bid them to come in with a come-hither movement of his finger.

He spoke softly in Hebrew into the phone and momentarily was finished with the call.

"Tyce. It is good of you to come, my friend," he said, coming to shake the journalist's hand.

"There is much activity today, as you can see."

"Yes, Sir. I see that for sure," Tyce said with a quick smile.

"Grishna, you haven't been informed of develop-ments of the past couple of hours."

"No, Bibi. What has ...developed," she said, returning his brief hug.

"It is almost as miraculous as Elias being resurrected," he said in a light tone. "And, it involves Elias, so maybe the two miracles are part of the one."

"What is this riddle, Bibi?"

Her question was offered with genuine perplexity. She had not heard such talk from her friend of many years.

"Rabbi Elias and the Muslim's top religious leader-ship have worked out some sort of peace arrangement. The Arab leadership of all their council has agreed to step back from this insane rant against Israel over the Mecca and Kabba destruction."

"Peace?"

Tyce's interjection into the prime minister's just divulged information made the leader look at Tyce with an expression of curiosity.

"I'm sorry, Sir. But, hasn't these peace gestures always failed, ultimately?"

"There are no conditions whatsoever on what the Rabbi and the ruling Imams have decreed," the prime minister said.

"But, the religious elements can't make peace unless the government people are involved in the process," Tyce said in questioning tone.

"In most of the Mid-East...the Arab nations...the Islamist leaders, hold the true power. This has always been the hold-up to the peace process," the prime minister said.

"Elias and the Imams? Rabbi Elias was able to accomplish the impossible?"

Grishna's words verbalized Tyce's own question. Such a think seemed to fly in the face of Arab-Israeli history.

"Miraculous is the word," the prime minister said. "If what I've been told is true, we do have a miracle in the making," Bibi said.

"I know you, Bibi...You are being facetious. You don't believe this *peace-making* by the Imams...by the leaders of the Arabs for a second."

Grishna's words made the prime minister smile, before reaching to grip her arms and pull her to himself.

He said, while hugging her, "You do indeed know me well, my dear friend!"

He turned to Tyce.

"Your words still ring in my ears, Tyce. You predicted

Elias' resurrection. Then you said the thing that my mind will not dismiss."

He went to his desk and took a sheet of paper from a drawer.

"I have the transcription of your words. they haunt me. Here is the first of your prophecies."

*'The prince that will come will harbor miracles. The dead will be resurrected to life. The chief friend of Bezalel will arise before the power of the prince.'*

And, here is the second.

*'Israel will believe. The prince will prevail. Beware the prince who causes the dead to rise. Israel, beware.'*

And here is the third.

*'The two are one in the covenant of peace that war threatens. Mecca is destroyed. Danger to Israel brings deception by first and second beast through peace that will destroy the unwary.'"*

The prime minister glanced at Grishna then looked into Tyce's eyes, an expression of concentration on his face.

"Tyce, it is obvious to me...to my people that things are not as they seem. This sudden joy over Rabbi Elias suddenly coming back to life. Raised by this European diplomat. It is something we can't and won't buy. The people, though, are ecstatic. There seems no governor on their sensibility.

He paused for a moment, and then continued, "Why do I bring you into these *strange* developments? It is obvious that the *revelations you've* been commissioned to give...by *someone, somewhere...* are meant to help guide us. Guide *Israel* through these very strange times."

Tyce took in his words and considered them before speaking.

"Of course, I'll do anything I can...But what can I do?"

"Bibi, do you think Elias would be party to putting Israel in any sort of danger," Grishna said.

"Do you not see the *strange* times we are in, Grishna? The disappearance of millions all over the world...Every baby and small child vanished. The orbs of light. The raising of the Rabbi. By a European, from the EU, an entity that has sided with the U.N.'s condemnation of our country on many occasions. Now, this European comes forth to bring apparent peace where there have been hatreds, animosities, for centuries. These Imams, across most of the Arab world...the Islamists...suddenly agreeing to make peace. Dropping their refusal to recognize Israel as a legitimate state. Do these things not seem strange to you?"

She said nothing in response, seeing resolve in the prime minister's eyes.

"Tyce, getting back to the reason I have determined to bring you into these intrigues," Bibi said, turning to Greyson. "How can you help, was your question...

We have kept you from the public for your safety's sake. And, admittedly, for selfish purposes. To help us try to stay ahead of those who want to destroy our country...to completely do away with the Jewish race."

The Israeli leader paused, as if to collect the best way to approach what would come next.

"People all around the world know you, and your face, Tyce," he continued. "We have had to keep you out of the public eye, here, in Israel. The prophecies have made you quite well-recognizable. Those in the U.S., in your government and your former employers at the network- They want to grab you from us!" The prime minister glared. "Because you are well-known; because people will be fascinated by what you have to say, I'm going to have to ask you to allow us to expose you to the danger of being located by those who are desperate to find you."

The prime minister looked at Tyce for response. Seeing none, he continued.

"The danger to Israel is even greater than the danger is to you, Tyce. If the people demand that we fall for this false peace overture, our nation might be lost. This EU attempt to bring us into a peace covenant, I'm convinced, is a ruse. But, our people...the Israeli citizens, are in a state of euphoria, seeing this *miracle worker* among us. And, the Rabbi, joining in the peace effort? We haven't been able to find or talk with him. It is troubling and very treacherous for our nation."

"What can I do?"

"We want you to go on television. To tell of the prophecy. We will air the video of your...your vision while under the effects of our scientists' devices. The people will watch this program in record numbers. We hope they will be convinced not to fall for this EU peace ruse."

"But, Sir, Isaiah the prophet has said Israel will fall to this end of days peace process. Daniel prophesied that a coming prince would make a covenant that would bring about world calamity. If these prophesies are truly fore-telling, given by a higher power... it is destined to come true! So, nothing I could say would change the outcome. The prophecy would be fulfilled."

"But, if the prophecies are as I believe them to be, they are given to do things which will preempt the adverse things predicted...We can prevent them from coming to pass by taking appropriate actions."

Tyce said nothing in response. The thought, however, ran quickly through his mind. Bible prophets were either one-hundred percent accurate, according to his research, or they were stoned to death.

* * *

VIDEO of light orbs above Jerusalem played upon the large screen recessed into the wall. Tyce Greyson sat in the chair, being dabbed with make-up to take the oily shine from his skin. His thoughts were, as always, on Marial.

The remembered image of her within the encapsulation of light played in his thoughts while he awaited the interview for Israeli TV.

The Rabbi's words, "You *must go to her,*" were words that he didn't want to shake from his memory. They, somehow, kept him moving—in his mind, at least— toward a reunion with Marial… sweet beautiful Marial.

"You are on in ten minutes," the technician said from the doorway of the make-up room. Tyce nodded understanding and the female applying the make-up finished her work then removed the covering from around his neck.

The TV news anchor's voice spoke in Hebrew. Tyce read the text that scrolled along the bottom of the screen in English.

*"The globes of light are becoming more in numbers. They are also spread to most major cities across the world. Some leaders are saying they are soon to reveal what, or who, these orbs of light might represent. Meantime they seem harmless enough, according to the mayor of Chicago in the United States."*

The scene changed to the mayor being interviewed by a female reporter.

*"They actually put on quite a spectacular light show in the night skies. People, I think, are getting use to these visitors."*

Tyce took his gaze away from the television screen and looked toward the doorway. The broadcast technician awaited to escort him to his chair upon the raised platform that housed the set where the interview would take place.

"I have not seen such security at our station," the technician said in accented English while escorting him to the set. "The armed IDF are everywhere."

Tyce said nothing in response, except to thank the man for getting him seated. After affixing the microphone to Tyce's tie by an alligator clip, the man said, "Mr. Greyson, might you sign an autograph for me?"

It was a first for him. "Sure," he said, taking the pen and note pad the technician handed him.

The news anchor who would do the interview introduced himself then moved to the chair nearby.

When the red light came on one of the cameras, the anchor introduced his guest. The program, from the studio in Tel Aviv, would be joined by many broadcast and cable affiliates by satellite.

"Mr. Greyson, you are being interviewed at the personal request of Israel's prime minister. What is the reason for this unusual step by the Israeli government?"

Tyce shifted slightly and looked in the camera lens he knew was trained on him.

"To let the people of Israel, learn about the vision I had about the destruction in Mecca. And, things that have happened surrounding that event."

"This...*vision*...was video recorded by government people, is that right?"

"Yes. It was recorded two days, rather two nights, before the assault in Saudi on Mecca," Tyce affirmed.

"We are going to show our audience that vision and the predictions you made, with the dates time-stamped at the bottom of the screen."

The video ran for seven minutes, showing only the minutes that he spoke during his vision-induced state.

"Well, as we know, Mecca was indeed attacked and the Kabba...Islam's most holy place, destroyed. Israel has been accused of being responsible. Some might question; was this prophecy, as some are calling it, self-fulfilling? That is, did it inspire the attack? Since the only ones who viewed these predictions prior to the attack was the Israeli government. Some are saying it was the government that took these as a prompt to actually carry out the attack!"

Irritated by the anchor's assertion, Tyce responded. "It seems to me that's an asinine assertion by whomever made it. Why would anyone in their right mind want to risk bringing the entire Muslim world down on them by such an act? What would be gained by such action?"

The anchor seemed taken aback by the response. He cleared his throat slightly and continued. "And then, an even more profound set of predictions. You *prophesied* that Rabbi Elias Coahn would be killed-which he was. Then you said, he would be raised to life by a European. That *all* happened. And, you said that there would be a peace made from all this. But, you predicted, it would be a deadly peace for Israel. So, what is the bottom line we are to take from all this?"

"I believe this peace that is being offered and apparently accepted by so many as a good faith effort is...in actuality... a long-ago prophesied matter now unfolding."

"Oh? Can you tell us about it, please… the ancient prophecy?"

"It's from the prophet Isaiah. It's found in Chapter 28

of the Christian Bible. Verses sixteen and eighteen. It says there is coming a peace that will cause great trouble for... aand great harm to Israel. It will be a covenant made with death and hell!" The King James Bible version says this."

"And this is what the Israeli government wants you to tell the Israeli public...That this is not a so-called peace that they should desire?"

"That's what I, Tyce Greyson, want to tell the citizens of Israel. I believe this is what my vision means."

"The people of Israel are almost in one accord, it seems," the news anchor said in a tone of confrontation. "They believe in this miracle worker from the European Union."

Tyce started to respond to the man's words. His senses began to darken when he looked into the camera lenses of the studio camera that came alive with the red *on-air* light.

He tried to catch his cerebral fall into the midst of the veil before him. He could do nothing but follow its alluring tug into its depths.

Again, when the veil rent, the beast upon the sands of the beach stood, it's seven heads swinging wildly upon it's serpent-like neck. Upon the seven heads were ten horns, the center-most horn looked to be the face of a man. He saw the human mouth moving, as if talking. Above the mouth were eyes that pierced into his soul.

He next felt himself being lifted by strong arms. They carried him along while he was unable to respond, to move in any direction.

Then he was lying still on his back, someone attending to him with a cold, wet compress of some sort.

"Mr. Greyson! You must awaken," the voice of a man said. "You must wake up."

When his senses began to clear he saw the face of the man. A beret sat atop the soldier's head. An IDF soldier.

"What did I say?"

"There will be time for answers," the soldier said, continuing to work on his face and forehead with the cold, wet cloth.

Momentarily, Grishna Lansky bent above him, taking over the duty of mopping his brow.

"You've given us another prophecy, my dear Tyce," she said "A most stunning prophecy."

CHAPTER 15

"Tyce Greyson, known as the man who can predict the future, has surfaced. He was interviewed on Israeli television, at a local Tel Aviv station. It's his first appearance since he was believed kidnapped more than a month ago."

The TV anchor read the news while Tyce spoke during the interview. Greyson sat watching the screen with Grishna and several Israeli security agents. His image transformed, while they watched, into the familiar, strangely glowing countenance like in the other times.

"Greyson went into the same sort of trance-state as in his previous predictions made on television. Predictions that came to pass in each case."

The eerie pallor appeared to alter his facial features. His eyes looked to be black, the pupils expanding to their maximum dilation. When he spoke, the voice was deep, guttural and staccato in delivery of the foretelling.

*"A sign in the heavens is harbinger of the messiah. The*

*Moon will reel. The body from the heavens strikes. Seas rush, tides crush."*

He saw his own image look upward, his eyes wide, staring. His TV image looked into the camera and muttered words he couldn't understand. The video cut back to the news anchor.

"The last words were in Hebrew. They were: *'The messiah comes forth to make peace that destroys many.'"*

Video file footage showed a shot of a full Moon, while the anchor continued.

"Astro-scientists say there is no asteroid within striking distance of the Moon that has thus far been spotted."

Grishna used the TV remote to turn the set off when the anchor went on to other news.

She turned to Tyce. "You remember none of this, just like the other times?"

"Not one second of it. All I saw was that same beast-the sea monster. It had ten horns on seven heads. One of the horns had the face of a man, it's mouth talking. It was part of the horn. It appeared to be smaller than the other horns.

"How do you interpret that?"

"It is in a prophecy...a Bible prophecy. I've read it somewhere."

The Messiah? That's exciting. Believing Jews have been expecting him throughout all our history," she said.

"Do they expect this Messiah to bring peace?"

"He will be king of all Israel, they say."

"Well, this Messiah, according to yours truly- Tycus Levi- and the seven heads and ten horns, will bring a peace that destroys." Tyce said.

* * *

LEAFING through the pages of the old Bible, he came finally to the concordance passage he desired.

He found the words *ten horns,* then looked at the scripture book and verse he needed.

When he arrived at the scripture in the Book of Revelation he ran his index finger down the page. He whispered the words as he read.

"¹³:¹And I stood upon the sand of the sea, and saw a beast rise up out of the sea, having seven heads and ten horns, and upon his horns ten crowns, and upon his heads the name of blasphemy.

he read the references in the margins then quickly turned forward in the same Book. Again, he read.

¹⁷:⁹And here *is* the mind which hath wisdom. The seven heads are seven mountains, on which the woman sitteth. ¹⁷:¹⁰And there are seven kings: five are fallen, and one is, *and* the other is not yet come; and when he cometh, he must continue a short space. ¹⁷:¹¹And the beast that was, and is not, even he is the eighth, and is of the seven, and goeth into perdition. ¹⁷:¹²And the ten horns which thou sawest are ten kings, which have received no kingdom as yet; but receive power as kings one hour with the beast. ¹⁷:¹³These have one mind, and shall give their power and strength unto the beast."

Again, Tyce turned to the concordance to find the scripture he had not yet looked up. The Book of Daniel...

He found the scripture and read silently.

⁷:⁷*After this I saw in the night visions, and behold a fourth beast, dreadful and terrible, and strong exceedingly; and it had great iron teeth: it devoured and brake in pieces, and stamped the residue with the feet of it: and it was diverse from all the beasts that were before it; and it had ten horns. ⁷:⁸I considered the horns, and, behold, there came up among them another little horn, before whom there were three of the first horns*

*plucked up by the roots: and, behold, in this horn were eyes*
*like the eyes of man, and a mouth speaking great things.*

It was overwhelming. Information overload, especially for someone who rarely looked into the scriptures.

Tyce opened the document on the laptop labeled, 'Addresses'. He would look for the pastor's phone number...The pastor in Texas whose sermons on Bible prophecy had kept him fascinated through their entirety.

He had called him on two occasions. He found the preacher in San Antonio to be down to earth, and very easy to approach.

He needed help in breaking through the complexities of the prophetic scriptures, and what they meant in view of the visions.

So much had changed in the short time since the vanishings. Technologies had been reconfigured, some re-invented or developed to cope with the technical difficulties produced by the disappearance event. There was no guarantee he could get through...that the Texas preacher's phone number remained the same.

After trying several times for a connection, he heard the phone on the other end ringing. He hoped it was the phone number he was trying to reach...

"Hello," the young, female, voice said after a number of rings.

Tyce introduced himself and the purpose of his call—to talk to the pastor. He had, he told the woman, spoken with the pastor on two other occasions.

"I'm sorry, Mr. Greyson," she said. "The pastor isn't here. He was taken in the Rapture."

Tyce was silent, trying to understand her meaning. "He was what?"

"My father, Pastor Hasting, was taken in the Rapture," she repeated.

The realization hit him hard. The term was one he had almost forgotten. The *Rapture*. The book series that was a big seller. The fiction series...what was it called?

"He is missing in the disappearance matter?"

"Yes. The Rapture of the church," the woman said with increasing irritation in her voice. He heard also sniffling, muffled sobbing.

"To whom am I speaking?" Tyce said, his mind still fighting to recall the name of the book series.

"I'm his daughter, Sarah," she said.

"Sarah...I'm sorry your father is missing," he said, not knowing how to console her.

"He's exactly where he wants to be," she said, letting her emotions go, breaking into unrestrained sobbing. "He is in Heaven. He tried to warn me...to warn everyone. He told everyone that we would be left behind if we didn't..." Her sobbing prevented the words from coming.

That was it! The name of the book series. The series of novels was called *Left Behind*.

* * *

"The UFOs, the light orbs, are becoming more in number. They are becoming more intrusive," Yendle Gesh said, putting a briefcase in the back seat of the sedan.

"And there is to be a meeting about this at the Tel Aviv offices," Grishna asked, climbing into the car's back seat.

"There is to be an announcement. Bibi wants you and I, and Tyce in attendance," Gesh said, sitting with the briefcase between himself and Grishna.

"Do you know the nature of the announcement?" Tyce questioned from the front, passenger seat.

"It has to do with these orbs, I'm told. Someone other than Bibi will be making the announcement, as I understand."

There was much speculation about the discs of light that now appeared as nightly visitors above most every major city across the globe. The consensus by news pundits around the world was that these were responsible for the mass vanishings.

Whatever they were, they had a mesmerizing, sedative effect, upon many within the populations. The rioting had calmed over the past days and the orbs were given credit for somehow soothing the fears.

The discs of light didn't intervene into human affairs...at least there were no reports of intervention, according to news reports. But Tyce remembered how the prime minister had described the spheres of light and the interaction with his associates and with the prime minister, himself.

The lights above the cities of the world might not intervene, however, they were intrusive, in that they now were seemingly absorbed into everyday life. rather into every night life.

Tyce contemplated what the announcement or announcements might entail while they drove toward the government complex.

"It is rumored that we will hear from the European who they say raised Elias. It should be interesting," Gesh said from the back seat.

Upon their arrival, Tyce noticed there were no people crowded into the square where protests usually were held. Whatever the announcement was about, it apparently was one that would be meant for a limited audience. There had been no alert that the announcement would be made.

In the large room, where normally was arranged dining configuration for special visits from world dignitaries, there were chairs facing a podium with a battery of microphones.

Many government and diplomatic types engaged in noisy conversation. A uniformed IDF colonel emerged from the crowd and came to Yendle Gesh.

"The prime minister wishes to see you. Please follow me," he said and led the three of them into the crowd.

The ever present, three-man, Israeli security detail shadowed them closely. When the milling group crowded too closely to them the men rushed ahead and physically formed a barrier between Grishna, Yendle Gesh and Tyce.

Tyce had almost gotten used to the security arrangements. It was all for him. He was, he was told, under constant threat of being grabbed by those whom were never specified.

He never sensed that he was in danger. Maybe it was the burly agents that made him feel impervious to being grabbed.

The thoughts of the security that cleared the path abruptly changed when he saw the Israeli leader's worried expression. The prime minister dispensed with the usually smiling greeting, instead instructing the colonel to usher them into a room nearby.

Bibi lingered outside the room for five minutes, speaking to assistants before entering the room and shutting the door behind him.

His somber expression had not changed. He got right to the business at hand. "Tyce, Israel is facing its greatest crisis since Nasser invaded in nineteen fifty-six," he began.

He moved to a small desk and retrieved a few sheets

of paper from a drawer. He held them up for the three of them to see.

"These are reports from around our country. They are analyses of our population, our people. They are accurate. I trust the reports implicitly."

He plopped them on the desk's top and turned again to them.

"The people are insisting, in great numbers, that we follow Rabbi Elias Coahn's directive."

"What directive," Grishna said, in a tone of exasperation.

"That we, the government, accede to the Rabbi's call to accept the peace proposed by the European Union's Council for peace. This meeting was called by the majority of Knesset. I could not refuse to allow it. The people of Israel are as if in a collective state of delusion. They believe they can depend upon this peace overture to secure peace and safety for the nation. Rabbi Coahn's supposed resurrection from the dead is apparently responsible for at least part of the delusion they are suffering."

"There are TV cameras directed at the podium. It will be broadcast...to what extent?"

Yendle Gesh's question caused the prime minister a moment of considered reflection. The look on his face became even more somber.

"Yes. They insisted that it be beamed by satellite. It will go to every point on the globe."

* * *

THE LARGE MEETING hall was alive with conversation, with speculation about the purpose of the calling together of diplomats and governmental leaders. They had flown, overnight, from many parts of the world, to Tel Aviv.

Rumor had it That they would get a look at the member of the EU Council for peace who had performed the miracle. Had raised the Jewish Rabbi from death.

Tyce gathered from the few he heard in conversation nearest him that they doubted the *miracle* had taken place. Most seem lightly amused at the thought of such a thing.

But, they did believe what they were given as proof of how both the Israeli people and the Arabs would accept a peace that before was impossible to achieve. The belief that peace was now not only possible, but probable was at the heart of the optimism. Whatsoever had made that peace a possibility, a probability, was acceptable to those in attendance, so far as Tyce Greyson could tell.

If the people on all sides believed there was a miracle worker among them...a Messiah...then so be it...

Momentarily, the crowd raised a collective volume of chatter, then the noise lessened. People began settling into the chairs when a delegation entered the platform from somewhere in the rear of the building. An Israeli Knesset member stepped to the podium, put a few pages of white paper on its top and waited for the crowd to become quiet.

He spoke in English, the most commonly understood language of those in the audience.

"Today there is a call for peace...for safety and security for all peoples."

The audience applauded, some rising to their feet. He waited for them to again settle.

"The great crisis that has befallen every nation...for we are all affected...makes it imperative that we seek solutions to the deadly possibilities that threaten all of humanity."

The Israeli paused to again let the applause subside.

"Now, we who have worked within human government must step aside to allow providence opportunity to join in the effort to bring the peace and security for which the people of Planet Earth are calling.

Proof that providential assistance is available to bring that long-sought peace is the one I present to you. He is one raised from death itself. I give you Israel's own holy representative...Rabbi Elias Coahn!"

All delegates rose to their feet as one, applauding, while the small Jewish Rabbi moved to the podium.

Tyce looked at the expressions on the gathering of governmental leaders and of those dressed in religious robes. They looked to be of one mind-set, their eyes affixed upon this man who apparently was recipient of miraculous resurrection.

Rabbi Coahn spoke when the audience was again seated.

"Peace, as of this day, is becoming reality for Israel, for the Palestinians, for the world."

The audience jumped to their feet again, their collective roar of approval at deafening decibel.

"The father of lights chooses to impose peace on our fragile planet. That peace begins here, in the most sacred geography on earth...the Holy Land."

After those in attendance had again exploded into applause then settled, the Rabbi continued.

"You have been witness to a miracle. I was raised back to life following death by an act of terror. With the miracle comes the additional miracle of the end of such terror. I give to you the son of lights...representative of the father of miracles."

Through the applause and shouts drowning out the Jewish Rabbi's words, the young man in a navy-blue suit stepped into the light illuminating the lectern. His smile was bright, but fleeting.

It was the same face. The face he had seen in the visions.

Tyce stood with the rest when the young European came before the microphones. He stood, however, not to show adoration, but to get a better look at the face that had haunted his thoughts since he first saw it following the Patmos beast when it trudged on shore.

\* \* \*

THE EUROPEAN indeed had a mouth speaking great things. Those words of the prophet Daniel about one who would come speaking great things continued to reverberate within his mind while he remembered the man's words to the congregants—to the world via satellite.

The young, European diplomat was one who had risen through the ranks, but swiftly so. Tyce knew nothing of him—of his geopolitical ideological view of things.

He came out of obscurity. At least, so far as Tyce could tell. Yet here he was...holding the world in the palm of his hand. He was able to raise the dead...That was the belief of a vast number of those left on earth in the wake of the vanishings.

Word quickly spread among the audience that he was partly Jewish. The holy men, the religiously-garbed ones, agreed that this fact made him eligible to become the much longed for Messiah. There seemed consensus among the Jewish clergy of every stripe. This man was a miracle worker...exactly the required credential for the Messiah when he would make his appearance.

The European spoke of the time for healing, for bringing the brotherhood of mankind together. He talked of how Israel must be allowed to build its third Temple on Moriah. The declaration had drawn an enormous response among the Jewish representation. Strangely, Tyce thought, there were no angry protests from the many Arabs, the Muslims in the chamber.

The European declared in the next breath, when the cheers for the Temple rebuilding had subsided, that the Palestinians must be given their own state. They must share in the holiest city's prosperity...the newly found oil and natural gas deposits throughout the region.

The cheer coming from the Arabs in the room were almost as great as had been the cheers from the Jews. Again, Tyce noticed that there was no opposition protest from the traditional, enemy side.

Clearly—by the very fact that many Arab leaders were in attendance—there had been groundwork laid well before this time of announcements.

Then came the truly stunning declaration. The young European had said in perfectly spoken Hebrew, Arabic, and then English that agreement had been reached on an already existing document of peace. The covenant would be further announced, the time of it's signing by all parties involved, within seven days.

The man spoke with amazingly few words. Each, however, seemed to have resounding impact upon listeners in the chamber. What would be the reaction across the world, Tyce wondered, while looking at the laptop screen.

Rabbi Elias Coahn...What about this little Jewish religious zealot he first had contact with on Moriah? What part did he play in all this?

The Rabbi, leader of the religious force within Israel's shadow government...suddenly a force that galvanized all of Israel into accepting this young man from Europe as their possible Messiah?

Tyce Greyson...who the Rabbi called *Tycus Levi*... What part did he play in all this surreal intrigue? Why did the Rabbi start all of this by coming to him at the Wailing Wall...by declaring three times that Israel is the signal? The sign of the end?

The cave at Patmos, the snake bite and the subsequent visions...What did it all mean?

Certainly, it had to do with prophecies from the Christian Bible. That was obvious beyond all question.

Where would it end? What was the conclusion of the whole matter? Would the European man make it more understandable in seven days? He promised, while speaking his almost hypnotic words in Tel Aviv, to do so...

Marial...What was her part in all of this that had so changed his life? Why the vision...Rabbi Elias Coahn commanding him to go to her...

"Tyce, it has happened!"

Grishna Lansky burst through the door, her hands flailing in gesticulation while she excitedly gave the news.

"The Moon has been struck by an asteroid!"

* * *

"THE STRIKE actually caused the Moon to wobble a bit on its axis. We are seeing great disturbances in oceanic tidal patterns because of the gravitational dynamics.

Also, the so-called *Ring of Fire* is active. There is some fear that the great Yellow Stone caldera could be induced to blow because of tectonic plate shifts that might occur."

The scientist spoke from the TV screen while Tyce, Grishna and the several security agents watched.

"Overall, however, the steroidal strike seems to have left no permanent after-effects. The Moon apparently as resumed a normal rotation. Its revolving path seems unchanged."

"Your prediction ..."

Grishna couldn't finish her intended, spoken thought. She listened intently to the scientist's words.

Tyce's thoughts turned to the singular most pressing thing constantly at the back of his mind. It all had to do with Bible prophecy in some way. Everything was going according to a Divine schedule.

\* \* \*

SITTING AGAIN in front of his laptop, he reached for the old Bible to his right. He found the concordance and thumbed through the worn pages until he found the word of his search.

He ran his index finger down until he located description that most likely fit his desired, scriptural explanation.

He next found the book of Luke.

He read silently the words in red letters—marking that they were the words of Christ.

[21:25]And there shall be signs in the sun, and in the moon, and in the stars; and upon the earth distress of nations, with perplexity; the sea and the waves roaring; [21:26]Men's hearts failing them for fear, and for looking after those things which are coming on the earth: for the powers of heaven shall be shaken.

Signs in the sun, Moon, and stars... Along with all the other things that had taken place... His own ability to...prophecy...

He, Tyce Greyson, was part of some grand, prophetic unfolding that was put into a blueprint, millennia ago. What was he to do with his...his gift, if that was what this thing that now ruled his life could be called.

*Israel...*Also at the center of that grand blueprint. *Israel...the sign of the end...*

The words of Daniel the prophet..."*A king of fierce countenance, and understanding dark sentences, shall stand up. And his power shall be mighty, but not by his own power: and he shall destroy wonderfully, and shall prosper, and practice, and shall destroy the mighty and the holy people. And through his policy also he shall cause craft to prosper in his hand; and he shall magnify himself in his heart, and by peace shall destroy many...*"

Epiphany struck. The word *peace*... The sort of *peace* that would destroy...

He found the word *Peace* in the concordance and again ran his index finger down to the scriptural reference he sought.

When he found the Book of First Thessalonians he quickly located the verse he wanted.

*5:2For yourselves know perfectly that the day of the Lord so cometh as a thief in the night. 5:3For when they shall say, Peace and safety; then sudden destruction cometh upon them, as travail upon a woman with child; and they shall not escape.*

Tyce looked at the laptop screen and the title of the book.

*Israel The Sign*

All of Israel was now saying *Peace and Safety*....

* * *

"IT IS ASTONISHING!"

Yendle Gesh spoke in an incredulous tone, while the prime minister listened.

"The Knesset is in total agreement. It has never happened."

Tyce and Grishna listened to Gesh's words while he paced up and down in front of Bibi, who sat, calmly listening to his unofficial advisor.

"They believe everything this European upstart says. It is beyond belief!"

Bibi spoke in a calm tone. "I think it is nearer to the truth that they believe everything Rabbi Elias Coahn has to say. They believe he has been raised from the dead. Therefore, it is a sign from Yahweh."

Gesh stopped pacing, considered the prime minister's words, and spoke angrily in Hebrew.

Grishna turned to Tyce and translated. "He said that Israel is full of fools, especially in leadership."

The prime minister answered, "But, that is how it is, Yendle. We are on the outside looking in. There is no choice..."

"You will resign?" Grishna said.

"No choice," Bibi repeated. "I cannot govern against the people's overwhelming consensus. And, I cannot change my way of thinking."

Tyce was overwhelmed with thoughts of the history he was witnessing. Still, he knew there were considerations much deeper...much greater than living through the historic moment of this long-time prime minister of Israel resigning.

"They want peace, and this man...validated by Elias...offers them peace. The Temple guarantee is something I cannot fight against...Nor, I think, do I want to fight against it. It's the dream of every Jew, whether believing Jews or not."

"But, Sir, it is a peace that is going to destroy the nation...the people."

Tyce surprised even himself by blurting the declaration.

Bibi looked surprised at the American's insertion into the discussion. He frowned in an expression of trying to understand more fully Tyce's meaning.

Greyson explained without being asked.

"Sir, I am convinced with all that is within me, that this whole matter is from your Old Testament prophets. The prophet Isaiah said there will come a peace that will be a covenant made with death and hell.

Daniel the prophet said that there will come a peace that will destroy many. That there will come a covenant of peace that a great prince will sign. It will begin the end of all human history. Daniel said, specifically, that this...prince...will come from the same people that would destroy the city and the sanctuary...Jerusalem and the Temple."

"Yes. I have heard all that before," Bibi said. "Some believe that the prophecy Daniel gave was by another man named Daniel *after* the AD 70 destruction of the Temple and Jerusalem by Titus and the Romans."

"Yes," Grishna put in. "It is said by other scholars that it was impossible for a man to be that accurate in his predictions. So, it had to be another, after the fact, who said the words attributed by some to the Daniel of antiquity."

"Impossible?" Tyce's words cut through the air with a tone of irritation. "Why am I here in Israel with you, Grishna? Is it possible that I, a mere journalist, certainly no Old Testament prophet, can prophesy with one-hundred percent accuracy? Yet the prophet Daniel, thousands of years ago could not prophesy with one-hundred percent accuracy?"

After a brief pause, the prime minister spoke. "Yes. Certainly, your case is proof that the Daniel as attributed could have given the prophecy."

Bibi arose from behind his desk and walked to where the others sat.

"Whether real peace, or false, it looks as if Isaiah's and Daniel's prophesied *peace will become a reality.*"

"THERE ARE few of us who realize the danger we are in. All the people see, listening to the promises of their representatives in Knesset, is peace and prosperity. There is talk of beginning to dismantle our military, so the cost of defense can be put into Israel's economy. They are anticipating an economic boom."

"It is insanity," Grishna said, agreeing with Yendle Gesh's analysis. "I, too, was at first made to believe this was a God-send to our nation. now...thanks to you, Tyce, I've come to believe it's from the other end of the religious spectrum from Satan; if indeed such a creature exists."

"He does," Tyce said while they took yet another short helicopter flight from the Tel Aviv airport to Jerusalem.

"They believe all this...this peace and prosperity talk and there have been no guarantees of any sort. All there has been is a proposed peace plan and glowing words by this European. This thirty-something year-old European, low-level diplomat."

TERRY JAMES

"Yes, Yendle, but this 30-year-old European *did* raise our Rabbi Coahn from the dead."

\* \* \*

SIGHTS IN JERUSALEM'S night's sky was spectacular. Tyce, along with hundreds of gawkers stood outside the building where Israel's history was to take a profound turn, whether for the better or for the worse.

Tyce knew the answer. There could no good come from the turn of events.

The crowd of onlookers audibly gasped in unison while brilliant discs of light hovered high in the blackness, or suddenly, shot at sharp angles in every direction. They grew in size and effulgence to look as if they were huge, radiant globes, only to shoot off to great heights to become just pin-points of star-like objects.

"They seem to be engaged in some sort of dance choreography with their movement," one woman near Tyce and Grishna exclaimed, transfixed on the orbs while they moved about.

"There seems to be a mood of delight among them," she said with elation in her own descriptive of the light show.

The doors to the building opened and the crowd began moving into the main room that would seat more than 1,000 people.

Tyce, upon seeing the lights go through their antics in the night sky, considered the changes over the time since the disappearance...The disappearance he had predicted in the broadcast. Before the orbs of light...the UFOs...would have panicked people. There would have been psychological maladies that would have to have been dealt with. Terror of invasion would have in past times wrought unimaginable fear.

Now, people smiled and took delight in these bright disks that danced against the black, velvet backdrop. As if it was all a show specifically intended to entertain those below.

The European would speak tonight. He would present the European Union's and associated nations' peace plan that was to forever make life on earth, heaven on earth.

Whatever the plan involved, he knew...was inalterably certain...that it would not lead to the betterment of or for mankind.

THE PRIME MINISTER had held off on resigning. He first wanted to get full understanding of what the young European—the consortium of western nations proposed.

Now, he knew, and he read the statement before the cameras that lined up in the large studio.

Less than 150 people stood around the room while he read the brief statement. Bright, studio lights spot-lighted the free-standing microphones and Bibi while he spoke.

"While my concern for my nation is great, for I know beyond any doubt that my people, that my colleagues in Knesset have chosen a deadly path, I none-the-less step aside as prime minister of Israel. I implore the leaders who govern the nation in the future to reconsider this pathway down which they have thus far determined to go. I cannot express with adequate emphasis the trepidation I sense as I turn the reins of government over to you who will now be responsible for this miracle called Israel."

There was no applause when he finished. There were tears on the faces of many within the studio. Grishna's were particularly profuse.

"I love you, Bibi," she said, hugging the now former leader. "We shall never look upon your likes again," she said, wiping her eyes with a tissue someone handed her.

\* \* \*

TYCE, back in Tel Aviv, sat in the dimly lit room in front of his laptop. He thought on the past 24 hours—of things that had transpired. Things of such profound nature as to question the reality of his circumstance.

It was real enough, he thought with an inner smile, taking a drink from the diet tea. His aching head made him sure it was all *real* enough. He swallowed some Advil then got back to the monitor screen, his weary eyes studying the document he had opened forty minutes earlier.

He had determined to do it, from the time they left for Jerusalem before the European's speech. He would sit down at first opportunity and detail every point, analyze everything going on that lined up with things he researched. Things of Bible prophecy.

The book could wait. *Israel the Sign*.

But, it was all part of the book he wanted to write. All of it involved Israel, just like Rabbi Elias Coahn first told him that day at the Wailing Wall.

Everything pointed to Israel as the signal of how near the end was.

To the end of what?

To the end of...

He remembered the words of Jesus Christ. The so-called *Olivet Discourse.*

Christ had said, in answer to his Disciples question: *"What shall be the sign of thy coming, and of the end of the age?"*

The end of the age... The word *age* he had researched and found that it wasn't the end of the world as some thought. It was the end of the *age...* A specific dispensation, some believed.

His research confirmed for him, although many would disagree, that Christ was talking about a specific time called the *age of grace.*

The sign of the end, then, would be the sign of the end of the age of grace...

He sat back in the chair and studied the notes he had scribbled while listening to the EU diplomat speak.

The times were strange to be sure. But, the European's words were even stranger. They stretched credulity. None-the-less, everyone in attendance, Tyce noted on the yellow legal pad, had seemed to be in rapt attention to every word.

He checked the legal pad for anything he might have missed, then studied the monitor screen for the information he had earlier transferred to the electronic document.

Things that were said astounded him now while he remembered the eloquent explanations and promises.

The vanishing from the planet was, the European said, not extraterrestrial in nature, but inter-dimensional. The orbs of lights seen for throughout the centuries The UFOs were entities far advanced, and beyond the limitations of humans.

He gave the analogy of the orbs being like Klaatu,

who came to earth in the film *The Day the Earth Stood Still.*

The planet had become a danger to other worlds and Klaatu and Gort, his powerful robot, came to offer both threat and hope. Threat of destruction if peace was not achieved and great hope if it was accepted and implemented fully.

Some who vanished were taken for re-learning how to assimilate within such peace. Others were incorrigible and... The European had let the thought drop there.

Babies in the wombs and small children were removed to make sure everyone on earth understood the seriousness of the message; that everyone paid attention to what had taken place. The children, he said, would be returned at some point when peace had been sufficiently achieved.

He offered an economic plan based upon electronic currency units. A computer monetary funds transfer system in which all the world's various monetary disparities would be corrected and reconfigured under a single standard. The total world's wealth would, by computer selection that harbored no biases, be redistributed fairly.

Israel would be guaranteed protection by the newly formed western world alliance. The Jewish state would give up its military capability except for a small force for enforcing laws within its own national borders. All its nuclear stockpile would be taken into the western alliance's arsenals.

Islamist nations would give up their nuclear program developments as would those of those within the orbit of the western alliance.

Jerusalem would be divided and the Jews would be allowed to rebuild their Temple and worship atop Mount Moriah.

There was no mention of what would be required of Russia, China or the countries under their hegemony.

Tyce stood, picked up the glass of tea and sipped, still looking at the monitor's screen.

The young European and his reference to Klaatu, to Gort, to *The Day the Earth Stood Still...*

The resurrection of the Rabbi... It wasn't unlike that movie he remembered watching years ago.

The visitor to earth, Klaatu—shot by the U.S. military because of misunderstanding. The robot, Gort—picking Klaatu up from the ground and going into the saucer that was their spaceship...Then Klaatu being alive again, before warning the people of earth to conform to what the people of other worlds wanted or become a cinder... It was all similar. Like a prototype scenario people would understand and accept.

"They want to talk to you, Tyce."

Grishna Lansky's words pulled him from his thoughts.

"Who wants to see me?"

"The leadership of the Knesset. They want your input now that Bibi is no longer part of government."

"Why? They have rejected my telling them that this is a false peace. That this will end in their destruction."

"None-the-less, they want you to come to them...to speak with you," she said.

"And if I don't?"

"We must placate them, Tyce. Your safety -your continued security is dependent upon how those in charge of our government views your value to them."

Tyce put the empty glass on the table beside the laptop.

"I guess I have no choice, then," he said with resignation.

CHAPTER 16

Orbs of light now appeared by day as well as by night. They looked to be more like large discs of gleaming metal during daylight hours as they danced above Israel. Gigantic, flashing silver objects that Tyce witnessed now while climbing the steps leading to the building to which he had been summoned.

People seemed more and more oblivious to the orbs. Those accompanying him up the many steps appeared not to notice the one flying disc that suddenly hovered one thousand feet directly above them.

Desensitization to the changes taking place in Israel and around the world had set in, he considered while going through the door at the top of the steps. It was as if what was happening around the world was simply the new norm, as the popular term for changes that couldn't be avoided would have it.

One of the changes was that governments everywhere were using violent force on their populations. The methodology for control of rioting was no different in middle America than for rioting in New York City or

London. There was no tolerance for the anarchy that strained at the tether of civility. People had lost the ability to cope with the growing hardships. Governments allowed no quarter in employing draconian restraint against any movement toward even the slightest protests.

He wondered now, while walking with the several Israeli government officials toward their meeting whether *Covenant Bezalel* was now an organization that must be dealt with in the draconian way. He was, no doubt, considered part of that organization...

"Mr. Greyson," a Knesset member greeted him when the contingent entered the chamber. "We have been looking forward to this meeting with you."

The man's smile seemed genuine, his handshake warm and inviting.

"We have much to discuss with you. Thank you for agreeing to meet with us."

After meeting with several other members of the governing body, the man who initially greeted him spoke.

"We, of course, are aware of your fame as one who looks into the future. However, we have learned much more from our friend Yendle Gesh and from the former prime minister about the service you have truly rendered to our nation. We hope you will continue to help us as we move into this new era of peace."

Tyce wasn't sure how to respond. He had forewarned time and time again of the peace that would, according to Israel's own prophets, lead to great trouble.

"Well, Sir, I will of course do whatever I can that might help."

"Then, let us proceed," the Israeli said, leading Tyce and the others into yet another, smaller room.

He recognized the set-up instantly. The black boxes, the monitor screens. The set-up for inducing and recording the visions they hoped they could extract from him.

The feeling, the sensation was not the same. Different from the times he underwent such intrusion into his inner-most thoughts for the prime minister and his people. He felt genuinely assaulted and insulted by having his brain invaded by these governmental entities. These, who had already fallen for the lies that were being perpetrated. There could nothing good come from his collaborating with them.

None-the-less, he gave in rather than resisted. Perhaps, he thought, while they handed him the vial to drink, he, too, wanted to look into the future. The future, about which they, and he, had such differing expectation.

His first sensation was of drifting into dark, viscous, liquid. He floated, deeper, ever deeper into the thick, liquid darkness.

He next seemed to straighten and, the warm, liquid around him dissipating, his feet came to a soft landing on sandy soil.

Like in other times the sea, as far as he could look in the distance, began to boil and froth.

Again, the massive, greenish hump of shimmering scales raised from the heaving waves. The sea monster emerged from the raging billows.

Suddenly, the entire scene before his astonished inner-vision changed to one of a vast, desert landscape.

Gone was the frothing sea. In its place was desert, with a huge cloud of dust beginning to raise on the far most horizon.

Soon was heard the grinding, the roaring of noise he could not at first make out. It became clear, then.

It was the sound of machinery...Mechanized weapons of war...rolling swiftly toward him. Battle machinery of every sort, accompanied by hundreds of thousands of marching soldiers, weapons at the ready.

"It is time to awaken, Mr. Greyson."

The voice was of a female, he determined. Why was a female voice calling to him from within the tremendous dust storm...the assault force about to overrun where he stood?...

"Please awaken," the pleasant voice said again.

He saw the face of the woman, looking at him with concern.

She wore a white smock...a scientist or doctor, he surmised through his drug-affected eyes.

"Do you recall your vision?"

The man wearing a double-breasted suit asked his question in a clinical tone.

"I never remember details while having the episodes," Tyce said, trying to deal with the throbbing headache.

"You made troubling assertions," the man said. "We would like you to review the videos of those assertions."

He sat with the men while they watched the video, thirty plus minutes during which he spoke while under the drug that induced the vision.

Again, the image of his face took on an eerie glow, a pallor that seemed to change his features. The time markers at the bottom of the screen indicated his words came at ten-minute intervals.

The first statement, like all other times, were spoken with deep, guttural, staccato delivery.

*"They attack from the north. They have no fear of battle. Israel is without defense."*

Tyce watched his own image that seemed to be strug-

239

gling for breath, before settling into what looked to be
peaceful sleep.

When the next ten-minute marker appeared at the
bottom of the screen, his image again spoke.

*"Russians come to take plunder. Arab world wants only the
death of every Jew. It is the peace that will destroy."*

With the video at its end, the Israeli in the double-
breasted suit looked to Tyce. He spoke in a soft, but
serious tone.

"Mr. Greyson. These sorts of predictions are counter-
productive to our purposes. We must ask you to refrain
making them in the future. Our citizenry is depending
on a time of peace and prosperity. The first in our
history since nineteen forty-eight."

Tyce studied the man's face before replying.

"I have no control over what I report from these...vi-
sions. I have no idea of what I'm saying when giving
them in these...episodes."

The Israeli glanced at the two men with him and then
back at Tyce.

"We have no choice but to exercise control in the
matter of seeing to it that nothing interferes with the
making of this peace."

* * *

"THEY WOULD NOT ALLOW Yendle or myself to sit in on
the sessions," Grishna Lansky said. "We are no longer
part of the inner-circle of Israeli government."

"Did they threaten you?" Yendle Gesh questioned,
while the three of them talked, sitting in a *safe room* that
had been checked for electronic eavesdropping.

"They said they have to *control* what is given to the
Israeli public. They said that what I have been

saying...what I said during the episode they recorded was *counter-productive* to their purpose. I inferred they were going to have this peace, no matter what."

"And you said in the prophecy the same thing you've foretold before? That this peace was prophesied by our...by Israel's...prophets in the scriptures?"

Tyce considered Grishna's question and nodded affirmatively.

"We didn't discuss the prophecy made by Ezekiel, but I told them the same thing I've been foretelling from the first time I was given the...prophecy."

"And you say there is an attack coming from the Russian coalition from the north," Gesh asked.

"That is what I said in the recorded session. That is also what I read from Ezekiel the prophet."

"This...peace... It will include Israel's giving up it's IDF. We will give our nuclear stockpile to the European-American consortium," Gesh said in questioning tone.

"The western *Alliance*," Tyce said. "Israel will keep only a military sufficient to control domestic uprisings. And, even this, according to the European's speech, will be carefully monitored and controlled by the western alliance, which they are beginning to term *European*."

"And, this is prophesied, specifically? I mean prophesied by Ezekiel the prophet," Grishna said.

"Ezekiel, in the prophecy, said that the leader of the coalition force, which I indicate in my episode as the leader of Russia, will think an *evil thought.* That leader will think to, as it is put in the King James version of the Christian Bible; to go into Israel. The prophecy says that Israel will be a nation of *unwalled villages.*"

"Without defenses," Gesh said.

"Yes," Tyce continued. "The nation will have no military defense."

Grishna said, after a pause for reflection, "And there-fore this is the peace *that will destroy many,* as you have said?"

"And this is as far as you've gone with this prophecy? That is, this is as far as you discussed with the government now in control of Israel," Gesh said.

"Yes. At that point they indicated I had better shut up."

"And, what else does Ezekiel's prophecy say?"

Grishna's question surprised him. He was shocked that Israelis, so steeped in Jewishness...in the history of the people and all it entailed, wouldn't know the end of the old prophet's foretelling."

"God, Himself, will destroy all but one-sixth of the invading army."

* * *

SLEEP TUGGED AT HIM. He had run out of allegiances. Israel, he thought, was his last, best hope within which to plan and work his way back into some semblance of sanity.

They had not yet come for him, to shackle him liter-ally. But the words of the Knesset officials had shackled him with their threats. He knew in the deepest reaches of his being that time for moving into a non-threatening place was running out.

He had agreed with the Israeli who, in effect, told him to *prophesy* no further. He agreed that he would comply. how long they would feel they could depend upon his pledge was the unknown factor.

He knew he had told them only what they wanted to hear. That was always the thing to do when real threat loomed. Just tell them what they want to hear. But, did they really believe him, or did they, too, know that he was only complying to turn their thoughts away from further shackling him?

One thing was sure—he was driven. Driven to take this...this whatever it was... out to its conclusion. Call it a commission from God, or from an unknown master, he had to know where the revelations he had been commissioned to present would take him.

His mind drifted while he lay on the pillow, face up toward the ceiling. Darkness descended upon his conscious senses. He again traversed the dream-world that harbored his deepest desires, ever present in his subconscious.

Marial...Again there was beautiful Marial. She was again at the window, looking into the darkness, a single stream of tear on her cheek.

He must find her. Must find her and take her from her place of confinement.

Again, the Rabbi's bearded face replaced the scene of the love of his life. The Jewish religious man was mouthing the familiar words..."*Go to her. You must go to Marial.*"

But how to find her, to get to her, to escape with her to a safe place...

Again, Rabbi Elias Coahn looked into the eyes of his dream-sub consciousness. The Rabbi... The one who had started the journey into this nightmare from which there seemed no logical exit.

"*Israel is the sign of the end,*" the old Rabbi said. His words burned into Tyce's mind like at the time in the visit to the Wailing Wall.

*The dream vision image of the Rabbi spoke." I, Rabbi Elias Coahn, am the answer to finding her... Find me and you find Marial...*"

\* \* \*

GRISHNA LANSKY LISTENED to his account of the previous night's dream. She frowned herself in disagreement when she heard his conclusion to what must be done.

"I've got to move from here. They will come for me at any moment. I can sense it."

"But, there is no place safer for you than here in Israel. We still have a degree of sanity...of good will left among our people," she said in an almost pleading tone.

"Grishna, there is a dwindling amount of sanity, even in your nation. They are falling for this peace that is going to destroy them, according to their own prophets."

"But, God will defend against that assault, the Ezekiel prophecy says."

"But, this phony peace goes far beyond that attack. The peace will become a bludgeon this European will use against your people...Against all of humanity."

"This is only how *you* interpret the prophecy," she said, disagreeing in her tone that his assertion was the correct interpretation.

"Even you, Grishna. You, too, believe this peace is something other than that Ezekiel prophesied."

His words were gentle, not accusatory. He reached to pull her to himself.

"You are unable to believe otherwise. I believe the Jewish people...all of Israel...is destined to fall for these peace overtures. Even your beloved Bibi."

"Then, if I cannot dissuade you... If you must go, I shall see to it that you have the very best assistance and means to travel. At least, Yendle and I still have a network of operatives throughout Europe and most of the Middle East."

# CHAPTER 17

Tyce embraced Yendle, then turned to hug Grishna. There were tears in her eyes but resolve in her words.

"Whatever is the outcome of this strangeness," she said, "may Yahweh direct and protect you, Tyce Greyson."

There were tears in his own eyes. He thought how until this moment he didn't know the depth of his feelings for her. She had become, during the short time he knew her, as close to a family member as he had known —in his heart, at least. Just old enough to be his mother. A mother he never knew, being adopted following his mother's death shortly after his birth. She and his father, he was told, killed in a plane crash.

She spoke something to him in Hebrew and stretched upward to kiss him on the cheek.

"I said *you take my heart with you wherever you go.*"

"I can't speak Hebrew, or anything other than American English. But, it's directly from my heart. I love you, Grishna."

\* \* \*

THERE WAS no place on the planet he could hide. Not if they really were determined to locate him.

It was foolish, if he truly expected to escape those who were forming the changed world order. Foolish to keep his smart phone device with him. To keep the laptop.

The book, the information, however were all important to him. It overruled the inner-urge that screamed at him to part with them. He rationalized—or maybe it was that he deluded himself—that the higher power that set him on this course in the first place would see to it that he escape them.

Familiar fish-smells filled his nostrils. He was near the Mediterranean and the submarine.

Darkness obscured all but faint light in the distance. Again, the operatives who were loyal to Grishna and Yendle Gesh could see their surroundings with daylight clarity. The night-vision equipment was unexcelled by any military in the world.

Within minutes he stepped in a small row boat and shortly was climbing the iron ladder welded on the hull of the black sub. He was guided into the hatchway and stepped onto another iron ladder leading down the conning tower and into the interior of the ship.

Yorbi Kosner grabbed him and, after embracing him, pumped his hand vigorously with both of his.

"Welcome, my friend! It is so good to have you aboard again."

"This is beyond anything I was thinking. Yorbi, I can't tell you what it means..."

"Ah, my friend," the Israeli captain said, interrupting Tyce's words. "We will move heaven and earth if necessary. Your mission is from above. I am honored...we of the Rahav are honored to have you aboard."

Momentarily, Yorbi issued Tyce into the small, sparsely-appointed captain's quarters.

"Our course is plotted. We will have you there by tomorrow evening," the captain said, reaching for a tall bottle within a cabinet above the compact desk area.

"Let us have a small bit of wine to celebrate your being with us," he said, taking two small glasses from the cabinet and beginning to pour.

"You do like wine, don't you?"

"Sure. Thanks."

Yorbi watched for his expression after he allowed the American to take the first sip.

Tyce lifted the glass in the Israeli's direction. "Very, very good!"

"Ah! I thought you would like it." He described the wine's name and year, replaced the cork and returned the bottle to the cabinet.

"Our plans are to place you off the toe of the Italian boot. That is the best I can tell you. Some of Yendle Gesh's operatives will be awaiting if our plans hold."

"Are you aware of what the plans entail?" Tyce said.

"Yes. Our people will meet you just off a small cove. You will be transported further inland, and eventually to Rome."

"I've not been told details. Just that Marial is some-where in Rome. She is being held there."

"That is my understanding, also," the Israeli said.

"How did you find out?" Tyce questioned.

"It is my understanding that Rabbi Elias Coahn provided the information through an Italian emissary with whom he is dealing on behalf of Israel."

"Dealing with on behalf of Israel?" Tyce was surprised at the revelation.

"Yes. Rabbi Coahn has been instrumental in the peace that has been negotiated. The European leaders made him the key contact between themselves and Israel in the process, as I understand it. Rabbi Coahn also is acting as key negotiator on behalf of Israel with the Palestinian leaders and other of the Arab government and religious leaders."

The news stunned him. He was being led to Marial by the resurrected Jewish religious leader. The man who was leading Israel into a covenant made with death and hell as the prophet Isaiah would have it. A peace that would eventuate in an attack from the north of Jerusalem...

"You look shocked," Yorbi said. "Does this news surprise you?"

"Yes. Very much so. Have you been told anything about my vision-episodes?"

"You are famous, Tyce. Of course, I know about the visions...*Prophecies,* as they are called by our people."

"I mean about the most recent."

"Not specifically," Yorbi said. "Tell me."

Tyce spent the next minutes explaining about the sessions that revealed the peace proceedings and what he saw in the visions. How the peace would lead to destruction for Israel and the world. How there would be the attack from the Russian coalition according to Ezekiel, Israel's prophet.

He then told him that God, Himself, told through Ezekiel that He would personally destroy all but one-sixth of the Russian force when they invaded, because Israel would no longer have a military to defend itself.

"This is certainly news to me," Yorbi said, a frown of

disbelief on his face. "As part of Israel's primary deterrent force, that is most troubling, if it is to come to pass."

The Israeli and Greyson silently considered what each other's next words might be, then the Israeli spoke.

"Tyce, if God, Himself, is to intervene...to destroy the invading force, then maybe the Rabbi isn't a force for evil, but for good."

"How so," Tyce said.

"Perhaps this is all being brought about. This peace covenant. Taking away Israel's defense so that the evil ones...the Russians and the Islamists, will come down into their place of destruction."

Again, he was amazed. This hardened military man, responsible for Israel's prime deterrence, was so trusting of a higher power watching out for his nation. He was a believer like none he had found in all of Israel.

\* \* \*

THE TRIP aboard the Rahav had been uneventful. If the enemy was alerted to his being aboard they had not acted on it.

Captain Yorbi Kosner seemed confident it was next to impossible to follow the sub's movement. Israeli technology was advanced far beyond even the U.S. submarine tracking and cloaking technology. They would slip into the waters near Italy without being detected, the Israeli had no doubt.

While Tyce appreciated his friend's confidence, he none-the-less went over many concerns in his silent thoughts while they glided toward their destination.

The Rabbi had given them the heads-up on where Marial was being held. This confirmed the vision. The vision of Rabbi Elias Coahn telling him that he...Rabbi

Coahn...had the answer to where she was waiting for Tyce...longing for him to come to her.

If it was in the vision, then the higher power that provided the vision was in control. He wasn't warned not to heed the Rabbi's allurement. Everything seemed predestined, preordained.

Even now, while thinking on the dangers, there was no gnawing fear of what might await him at the end of this quest...the effort to find...to be reunited with Marial.

Not even the fact that she seemed to have betrayed him any longer troubled him. Her complicity had to in some way been pre-ordained, predestined. By the higher power that had brought him this far.

"Until we meet again, my friend," Captain Yorbi Kosner said, firmly holding Tyce by his arms, then embracing him. "May Yahweh be with you."

"And you as well, Yorbi," Tyce said. He then departed the sub by stepping into the small rowboat which met him, manned by two operatives.

"Believe it or not," one of the men said while they rode in darkness, toward Rome in a small truck. "We will be going to beneath the city. Actually, will meet in the ancient catacombs with those assigned to this mission."

"Catacombs! Really?"

"Yes, after all the centuries and the history involved," the man said, "the catacombs still provide the greatest degree of safety."

\* \* \*

ROME'S NIGHT-SKY was dotted with light orbs that pulsed, grew larger and smaller and moved at unbeliev-able speed. Like in all other places, people went about business as usual—as if the orbs were now the norm. He considered how they had seemed to be instrumental in quelling the insanity to some extent. The rioting, especially in the huge cities, had settled into, not tranquility, but into controllable chaos.

He wondered if the European's address to the world from Tel Aviv had anything to do with the changed comportment. The words that compared the orbs to Klaatu, Gort and the movie scenario in *The Day the Earth Stood Still.*

The warning that Planet Earth must comply with the peace that was offered or be turned into a cinder.

What was *his* part in all this was the question that gnawed constantly at his psyche. What part was he to ultimately play in this obviously preordained, predestined plan for humanity?...

"We go by foot from here," the driver said, stopping the truck.

They exited the vehicle and the men hustled him forward, guiding him by both arms into a building.

They descended steps and walked across a concrete floor.

Two of his companions moved a large, wooden cabinet, then a large rug, exposing a trap door.

They quickly nudged him down steps and into the underground caverns that he knew must be the ancient catacombs of Rome.

After several minutes of walking quickly they arrived at a large chamber, into which the tunnel emerged. A man approached.

"My name is Yitssak Steyn," the man said, shaking Tyce's hand. "Welcome to our tomb-office."

His words were lightly offered with a broad smile.

"These are our accomplices," he said with equal levity, introducing each of several men and women.

"Who arranged all this? I mean, my only need...my mission is to try to find Marial Gunn. Is all this just for that purpose?"

He was genuinely puzzled. So much effort for such an insignificant matter, in the overall scheme of things?

"Oh, no, Mr. Greyson...Believe me there is much more involved here than your quest to have Miss Gunn returned to you."

The Israeli changed expression to one more serious.

"Your visionary abilities are vital to us beyond your understanding. You have been set on a course that we do not understand. Some force we don't pretend to understand is moving you- has been moving you since you first made public broadcasts and your prophecies came true.

That force, that higher power, has given you the vision that you are to find Miss Gunn....Marial. Our purpose- those of us in *Bezalel* who are in the *shadow of god*... our mission, is to see that this is done.

Things in the world are so drastically changed since you made the prediction...that the world's populations would disappear... we know things are beyond our own ability to control. We must find the purpose of this force and follow its directive."

The words were jolting. He could only ask, "And this is why all of the effort?"

"Can you think of a better course," Steyn said. "We have no understanding...no explanation for this craziness going on. Following someone who can tell the future...this is the only logical course in the totally illogical circumstances in which we find ourselves."

"I've tried to tell you and tried to tell Israel's leaders that this is a deadly peace, according to your own prophets. My own visions confirm it. What do you hope to learn from me beyond that?"

Tyce's question harbored no malice or anger. He was genuinely perplexed.

Steyn thought on his words before answering.

"There are those among us who have no pre-conceived notions. We are not deluded into believing that everything this European We are convicted that following closely your thoughts and your movement through this strange circumstance in which we find ourselves is wise. It is in Israel's best interest. We believe something from Israel's God must be involved. Not all, but some among us believe this."

"You mean within *Covenant Bezalel?*"

"Yes. There is a very minimal number who believe Yahweh uses you to show us...that is, this small number within Bezalel, the pathway to Israel's security."

\* \* \*

"WE ARE HERE in Rome because we, that is, our intelligence, indicates that this is where the power resides."

"What power?" Tyce asked, while again on the move, sitting beside Yitssak Steyn in the small sedan.

"The power that intends to establish a changed world order."

"You mean the globalist elite?"

"Yes, but it goes much, much, deeper," Steyn said. "We have become convinced that it is a supernatural element that commands the globalist cabal. Perhaps a supernatural, religious element that drives the matters involved."

"So, is that the purpose for my being sent in your direction?"

"I believe you will find what lies at the bottom of all

this of interest," Steyn said, while the car veered right and onto an off ramp under a large, overhead sign that read Entering European Rome."

They reached their destination within five minutes of leaving the highway. The driver maneuvered the car around and through several, orange barrels that marked a construction zone.

"Again, we must stay within the catacombs...a different section than under Rome proper," Styen said. "This construction area is not as it appears at first. The area has been contrived to give cover as we move in and out of these ancient, underground tomb sites. We believe this to be among the most secure locations to be found."

"Is this where I'm to meet with Rabbi Coahn?"

Tyce's question brought a startled response from the Israeli.

"Oh, my...no! Quite the contrary, my friend. But you will find the ones you will meet to be most fascinating, I assure you."

There were no buildings in the area. Tyce thought it out of place. It was a vast area with no signs of construction, except for a shed which sat up against a large boulder surrounded with vegetation. Yet, several construction cranes and pieces of earth-moving equipment were scattered about the area.

The Israeli who had ridden in the passenger side of the front seat hurried to the shed and unlocked the big door that slid upward. With the four men inside on the concrete floor, the same man manipulated something Tyce couldn't make out in the semi-darkened room.

"Come, quickly," Yitssak Steyn urged, pressing against Tyce's arm with his hand.

Steps led downward what Tyce thought to be more than twenty feet. Roughly-hewn tunnels went in three different directions from the central entranceway at the bottom of the steps.

Tyce and Steyn followed the other men into one of the openings.

"These are thought to be the most ancient of the catacombs," Steyn lectured while they walked. There was barely enough headroom in the tunnels they traversed. Occasionally they came to sections that the men had to bend over to negotiate their way through.

"Here we are," Yitssak said, while they stepped into a much larger tunnel.

They were met by a man wearing a military-type jumpsuit. An automatic weapon was affixed to his shoulder by a leather strap.

"Eli and Moshi await," the man said. He led the way deeper into the tunnel.

He stepped aside to allow the four others through an opening in one of the rock walls.

Several men dressed in the same type of military jumpsuits watched them as they approached.

Steyn introduced Tyce. There were no handshakes, no embraces. Just nods of the head acknowledging his existence.

He noticed, then, two other figures, who emerged from the shadows deeper within the catacomb recess.

"These are the men you must meet, Tyce." He introduced Tyce to them.

They wore robes. Not like the Jewish Rabbis, but like those worn by some he had seen at the Wailing Wall and other Middle Eastern places.

They were small men, with long beards and hair to the shoulders. Obviously, Tyce thought, from one sect or another within Judaism.

One was balding, the other, looking considerably

younger, with an indistinguishable expression, stepped forward, the scant light from the several military-style lamps lighting his face.

"I am Moshi," he said in a voice that was almost inaudible. "This is Eli," he said, gesturing with a slight hand movement toward the other man, who, it became obvious now in the light, was considerably older.

"We have come here to meet you, Tycus Levi."

Tyce felt as if he jumped inwardly, hearing the words. Stunned by the name being spoken, he said nothing.

"There are things...Many things...you must know," the older man said. The intense gaze seemed to X-ray his inner-most being.

"What things," was all he could mutter.

"Things of eternal consequence," Eli said. "You are chosen."

Tyce hesitated for several seconds, then said, "Chosen? You mean the...visions?"

"You are here as part of the great time of trouble the world will endure," Eli said.

The voice was strong, echoing within the cavern's rock-encapsulation.

"Revelations of many things to come are within your assigned message, Tycus Levi."

"Why do you call me *Tycus Levi*," Tyce said, becoming frustrated with the mystery of it all.

"You are of Jewish descent," the younger man said.

The older man continued, "Your father, your mother, Hebrews and priestly servants."

Tyce sensed his mind beginning the familiar convolution toward unconsciousness...toward the familiar vision-state.

"You must not go from us in your spirit at this

moment," Eli said, touching Tyce's forehead with fingertips.

His mind immediately cleared, the old man's bearded face coming into focus.

"There is much you must learn at this time. We are here to teach you all you must know."

* * *

TYCE STOOD in the room into which he had been ushered. He thought it to be somewhere within a hotel in a lesser populated section of the *Eternal City*. The part of the city indicated on the highway sign marked "European *Rome.*"

The four men who accompanied him were in surrounding rooms. They had left him around midnight after instructing him to open the door for no one and to immediately alert them if anyone tried to intrude.

He was handed an instrument he was told he must use to electronically beckon them in case of trouble.

The device was no larger than a cigarette lighter, he considered, exposing a single button when the lid was opened. He placed it on the table with his laptop and started to work on the book.

"Tycus Levi."

The voice made him jerk quickly to see the intruder. He reached for the device, but didn't summon help, instantly realizing the identities of his visitors.

Standing in the middle of the semi-darkened room were Eli and Moshi, gazing at him from five-feet away.

"How did you get in?"

They made no answer to his question. Instead, Moshi spoke.

"We are here that you learn of things to come."

He started to say it would be better time for learning when he was rested. They gave him no time to speak.

Eli stepped forward, his dark eyes focused intensely on Tyce's eyes.

He reached his hands to touch Tyce's head on either side. The old man said nothing, but shut his own eyes, then lifted his face in the direction of the room's ceiling.

Tyce sensed a slight chill run through his body, while Eli kept his hands in place for a matter of seconds. He then lowered his face, looking again into Tyce's eyes. He released his touch from Tyce's temples.

Greyson felt as if he had received a night's sleep in the few seconds the old man had touched him.

"What did you do?"

Eli said nothing.

Moshi spoke instead.

"You will receive what you are meant to know before you awake," he said.

Tyce's eyes closed momentarily—involuntarily—and when he opened them the men were gone.

* * *

"Who are they? Where do they come from? Are they of some sect in Judaism?"

Having pushed the button within the intruder-alert device he was given, Tyce questioned Yitssak Steyn in rapid fire fashion. There was something different about these two religious men...totally different.

"All in good time, my friend. I'll answer your questions to the best of my ability. The problem is, I haven't the answers you seek," the Israeli said.

"You mean you know nothing at all about these men?"

"I didn't say that. I simply mean that I, nor anyone of

us here, know exactly their origin or their purpose. We only know that they have mystical abilities."

"I know...I've seen them at work," Tyce said. "They have put thoughts in my mind with a touch of their hands. They disappeared right in front of me."

Steyn said nothing, a look of concentration on his face that said he was absorbed in Greyson's words.

"They taught me...not with a lecture, but by simply placing hands on each side of my head- my temples, and through some sort of thought process, I don't know what else to call it, they caused me to understand everything."

"Everything?" the Israeli questioned.

"Everything to do with what the EU, this *European*...the globalist cabal...is up to."

"You mean they made you understand your part in all of this?"

"I mean that they know the prophetic things involved. Where it will lead."

Again the Israeli awaited Tyce's explanation.

"The European. He is the man who will be history's final dictator. He will enslave most of the world. They said he is the *Antichrist*."

"And, did they tell you what your part in this involves?"

"They said I would know when the time was right," Tyce said in tone that indicated he was as unsure as was Yitssak Steyn about what lay ahead.

# CHAPTER 18

His sleep was fitful. He looked at the laptop's monitor screen, through sleep-deprived senses. The clock at the bottom right of the screen read *2:46 a.m.*

The words Israel the Sign headed the document. As always, he was drawn to all that the title entailed. So much had happened, and it all came rushing back now, in an early morning gush of what it all meant.

Everything that had happened, that was to come, had the nation Israel, its people, at its center. The nation, the people were on the verge of being led into the most destructive era of any in history.

The strange, robed men known as Eli and Moshi couldn't be brushed aside in his thoughts even for a moment. They burned deeply into his troubled thinking now, while staring at the monitor screen.

Eli, the older one, had given him knowledge in a matter of seconds that couldn't have been accumulated over months of study. He did so by holding his fingertips against Tyce's head at the temples.

At the time he felt only a slight chill. But, the manifestation of the learning he acquired in that few seconds grew more profound by the hour.

The knowledge manifested itself now, while he considered the words Eli had told him were key to understanding with what and with whom he, actually all of Israel was dealing. European... The young European who was at its nucleus...

He reached for the old, worn, Bible to the right of the laptop and thumbed until he found the scripture Eli had impressed so strongly upon his thoughts in those early morning hours. Hours when he and the other, younger man suddenly appeared, then just as suddenly disappeared.

The words were those of Jesus Christ. His words were the most important ever spoken, anytime, every time he spoke them, Eli had impressed upon his thoughts.

*John 5:43 - I have come in my Father's name, and you do not accept me; but if someone else comes in his own name, you will accept him.*

Thinking on the scripture unleashed other scriptures Eli inculcated within his memory during those early hours.

The prophet Daniel's words...That there would come a man understanding dark sentences. That he would speak *great, swelling words.* That the peace he would bring to Israel, to the world, would be a peace that would destroy many...

The peace now being offered was one that would be a key sign of the end, Eli had impressed the moment he touched Tyce. The scripture emblazoned across the forefront of his mind now.

*When they shall say peace and safety, then sudden destruc-*

*tion comes upon them as travail upon a woman with child. And, they shall not escape.*

All of Israel, except for this very few among those of *Covenant Bezalel* were saying *peace and safety.* The whole world was calling for peace and safety. The peace promised by this young, European.

What was his, Tyce's, part within these incomprehensible things? It would do no good to deny that he had been chosen, as Eli had said, to do whatever the great power that commands such things desires. His destiny was inalterably linked to whatsoever the future of Israel, of the world might hold.

He had been given the visions. He had become known world-wide because he could look into the future and... prophesy...with one-hundred percent accuracy. The requirement for Biblical prophets.

The name given him, first by Rabbi Elias Coahn. Repeated by Eli. The name *Tycus Levi.*

The revelation by Eli that his dead parents, parents he never knew, were Hebrews...Jews.

The words Eli then gave him...The same words Rabbi Coahn gave him on animal skin parchment...

*Your young men shall see visions and your old men shall dream dreams.*

The vision then fulfillment of the disappearance of millions across the planet. All small children and babies, even fetuses, vanished...

The orbs of lights that now moved above the planet, almost without notice or reaction by a world of people seemingly gone insane over developments since the disappearances.

The European's miracle-working, giving him world-wide validation. Giving him credence within Israel that his swelling words could be trusted, that peace for the beleaguered Jewish people was, at last, a reality. The man who explained the orbs, the lights in the sky as from other dimensions...other worlds... here, like Klaatu and Gort, to enforce the peace...

Again, Tyce heard the words of Jesus to the Jews of the time he walked the earth in flesh.

*I have come in my Father's name, and you do not accept me; but if someone else comes in his own name, you will accept him.*

Did the European cabal, those who would establish a changed world order, still want him...still want Tyce Greyson? Did they hold Marial? The thought was, thankfully, the last before drifting off to sleep.

* * *

"WE HAVE A PLAN."

Yitssak Steyn's words were matter-of-fact. As if inalterable.

"We want to get you into what is going on within *Europan,*" the Israeli said, walking hurriedly to sit across from Tyce at the small table while he ate.

"*Europan...* For what reason?"

Tyce's question was put equally matter-of-factly.

"As we discussed, you have been commissioned, for lack of a better term, to have these...this ability...to prophesy future things. We take it that you have been given these abilities to help Israel, to help the Jewish people."

The thought quickly came. The words *Tycus Levi,* spoken, or given him cerebrally, by Eli and Moshi. He said nothing, but chewed the bite taken from the sandwich held between his fingers, while awaiting Steyn's next words.

"We also have promised to help you find Marial. We keep our promises."

"What's your plan involve?"

"We are preparing your wardrobe for the role you will play," the Israeli said with a tight smile, before biting from the sandwich he held.

* * *

"YOU MUST SPEAK as little as possible, and when you do so, try to speak only to those who speak English," the Israeli said, smoothing the black material on the robe-like garment the man had just slipped over Tyce's head.

"How will I be able to avoid speaking to others?"

"Our main concern, of course, is that you don't fall into conversation with anyone who speaks Hebrew. You are supposed to know Hebrew, as the Hebrew Rabbi you will appear to be."

"And how do I avoid speaking to someone who speaks Hebrew?"

"When that happens, just say these words, on this paper." He handed him a small piece of paper. "Practice them. I will teach you how to pronounce them."

"What does it mean?"

"It just means that you are suddenly feeling nauseas and that you ask to please be excused for the moment. Then, just walk quickly away from the conversant."

"Clever," Tyce said, smiling.

"When you converse, do so in accented-English. You know...like we Israelis do," the man said, completing the smoothing of the material on the robe.

"I think I can handle that," Tyce said, looking at his robed-figure in the long mirror.

"But, won't I need a beard?"

"Certainly. We have some of the finest make-up prop people to be found," the Israeli said, admiring his work on helping Greyson look like a Rabbi.

* * *

"WE HAVE ARRANGED to have you introduced to those in Brussels. We have embassy people who are with us. They will carry out the ruse," Yitssak Steyn said, looking Tyce over.

"You will pass very nicely," he said, feeling the coarse beard by pinching it with thumb and index finger.

"I don't know if I can pull it off, Yitssak. Even if I must admit that I *do* look the part," he said, looking at himself in the mirror and running his hand over the black beard.

"Just act Jewish," Steyn said lightly. "Now that you know you're Jewish by birth that should be an easy thing."

"Well I don't yet feel fully Jewish," he said, turning to face the Israeli.

"We believe this is the way to get you close to this peace process...to learn the true nature of the things that are planned. We must find out their plans specifically for dealing with our nation...our people," Steyn said.

"We know that the scriptures foretell a future that's not pleasant. How do you expect to do anything that can alter what is prophesied by your own prophets?"

"All we know is that the holocaust must not be repeated. To do nothing in the face of obvious evil is to fall into the same foolish, deadly pattern our people always seem to adopt."

"I don't know what I can do, Yitssak, but we will

depend upon, maybe, that greater power that you and your people keep saying is in control."

* * *

THE BEARD PASTED to his face was driving him to the brink of insanity. His face and neck itched in a thousand places.

He was told that he would soon get used to the irritation, but the itching and tickling had not yet abated while he paced, awaiting the incognito trip to Brussels.

His task was daunting, he thought, while stopping to check his appearance in the full-length mirror. Best to try and just not think what lay ahead... Think only of the next step...one at a time.

Yitssak Steyn and other of his Israeli contingent had gone over anticipated things he might encounter. There were too many details, too much to remember.

He would be introduced by the people still loyal to *Covenant Bezalel* and to the former prime minister. they would say he was chief Rabbi Yehuda Levitt, representing the most orthodox sect that would participate in the peace negotiations. He was a legal scholar, sent to simply *observe* the goings-on, not to intervene, unless he saw an egregious religious-legal problem in the proceedings, from the sect's perspective.

He didn't have to interact was the main point. He could meet surreptitiously with those of *Covenant Bezalel* who had an inside track on how Europan operated.

His thoughts were on Rabbi Elias Coahn and the Rabbi's telling him in the dream-vision to find Marial. Was Rabbi Coahn really an insider within the cabal...within *Europan*? Would he, in some way, have the pathway cleared by the old Rabbi, leading to finding

Marial...to getting her away from the world order change agents?

Beyond that, why did they want him to go to Brussels, disguised as a Rabbi? To do what, exactly?

He would know when the time came, they told him. Just pay attention during every second of the trip, he had been told. He would know.

Yitssak had told him that the two, strange men in robes were at the center of the whole matter. He, for some reason he couldn't pinpoint, derived a certain comfort from knowing they were involved.

\* \* \*

HE THOUGHT the orbs of light over Jerusalem and Tel Aviv were plentiful. Those moving above Brussels now, however, appeared twice in number over the orbs above those cities. It was as if the UFOs, too, were to meet in some grand convention in the city of the European Union headquarters.

Still, people went about daily life, seemingly paying little attention to the disks that moved about, hovered, then streaked off at tremendous speeds to disappear somewhere in the velvet blackness of the night. It seemed that not even the spectacular light show, making them look to be glistening diamonds against the black backdrop, any longer held interest to the people on the streets of Brussels...of the world.

"Remember, Yehuda Levitt," Yitssak said while sitting beside him in the stretch-limousine. "Just say as little as possible. When asked what is your position or purpose, simply say...in accented-English... that you are just here to observe that your Judeo-constituency is represented in the peace arrangements that develop."

The Israeli glanced at him and handed him a brief-case. "Got it?" he said.

"Got it," Tyce said. "But, can I carry it off, I'm not sure."

"I mean the briefcase," Yitssak said with a quick laugh.

"Got that, too," Tyce said, taking the case and putting it at his feet.

The limo soon pulled in line with several other black limos awaiting their time under the large portico. The dignitaries stepped from the cars and were greeted personally by a few men in suits and ties. Obviously, Tyce thought, officials of *Europan* in one capacity or another.

He, too, stepped onto the carpeted portico drive when the limo driver brought it to a stop at the proper spot.

Steyn, acting as Yehuda Levitt's assistant, faithfully followed him through the line of officials, carrying several brief bags.

Tyce, as instructed in preparation for this moment, smiled only slightly and bowed his traditionally-garbed head in the direction of each of the men who, brightly smiling, shook his hand in welcome.

So far, so good, he thought, making no verbal response to each greeting. He thought that the more strangely he acted, the better. These men looked upon religious men of any stripe as strange...weird. So, he would act the part, validating their stereotypical belief. Maybe he could indeed get into this acting assignment...

They were soon in their elegantly-appointed suite, somewhere deeply within the huge building. They would have to maintain the facade of Jewish rabbi and assistant throughout the stay. They could only be themselves—

speak openly—when in places other than the quarters given them by *Europan.*

The electronic, eavesdropping bugs were no doubt there. Tyce was told, beforehand, not to speak unless necessary. They would be listening for the Hebrew they expected, and he spoke none of it. Anything he just had to say while in the accommodations should be said, he was told, in accented English.

There were locations they would go where their operatives had checked for bugs. there they could talk freely.

TWO DAYS INTO THE MEETINGS, Tyce was getting restless. He had heard all the talk of peace he wanted to hear...peace he knew was evil, designed to enslave...

Tonight, was the big night for the conference billed as *Planet for Peace. Europan's* young, charismatic star would speak to the attendees. There was euphoric anticipation on each of the faces as Tyce looked around the vast chamber. conversation was ablaze with expectation of what this man had to say. He could see it in their eyes...the same look as in the old black and white films of those who watched the Fuehrer perform on his rise to power.

The lights dimmed. Only the bright spotlights in the massive ceiling, much like the light orbs in the night sky outside, shone in spotlight fashion upon the audience. Several larger, brighter lights beamed upon the podium as one of the *Europan* leaders stepped to behind the microphones.

\* \* \*

THE EUROPEAN'S words still burned in his thoughts. One who heard him speak could never forget them. It was as if one's brain switched on a recorder, every sentence rebounding within the cranium, as if in an echo chamber.

Every eye within the chamber, every ear, was on, was attuned, to the man's promises. Promises of peace for the Jews, for the Arabs, for the whole world.

Daniel the prophet's words also caromed about in his head. *"He will speak great, swelling words...Through peace he shall destroy many..."*

"Do you see how all of them were hypnotized?"

Yitssak's question abruptly yanked him from his thoughts.

"Astonishing," was all Tyce could say in agreement.

One thing stood out most. His thought turned back to the European's speech. To the thing that most troubled him.

"He called for all religionists to come together in a session tomorrow," Tyce said.

"That is good. It will get us closer to understanding more about what is planned. What they plan to do with our opposition to any religious authority other than that of Yahweh."

"But, the other Jewish religious people will be there. They will want to know who I am, what I'm doing there."

Steyn reflected for several seconds on Tyce's words before replying. "Just remember what to do if they want to talk in Hebrew. Do you have it committed to memory?"

"Yes. That much Hebrew I can speak," Tyce said.

"Try to avoid talking with people in the time before the session begins. Don't allow yourself to be drawn into chatter before they get started," the Israeli said. "Get out of there immediately when the meeting concludes."

Tyce looked out the window of the SUV their operative drove through the Brussels streets. Under the guise of sight-seeing, they used the opportunity to speak freely. To go over things they were unable to discuss while under the scrutiny of the Europeans.

"He continues to perform miracles," Yitssak said, again pulling him from his thoughts.

"What?"

"I said, this man continues to perform miracles. There was a blind Imam there. Had no eyes whatever. Just empty sockets since birth.

I had to leave you for a few minutes, after the speech. The European was walking out of the chamber near where I was coming out of the men's room. The Imam was led to the European. He wanted to shake his hand. The man touched the Imam's eyelids, and the Imam, when he opened his eyelids, had eyes. He could see perfectly."

There was silence for a few seconds, while the Israeli stared out the window, as if thinking on his own words about the thing he witnessed.

"Why have you not said anything until now?" Tyce said, thinking that such a profound thing, Yitssak surely couldn't keep silent about.

"I guess I'm becoming desensitized like everyone else," he said.

Tyce said nothing but looked quizzically at Steyn.

"Like everyone in the world. These formerly unbelievable things are becoming commonplace," Yitssak said, again staring out the window at the sites of Brussels.

\* \* \*

He had been dreading this meeting. This would be a test of his ability to carry out the act, to be sure.

He had the line of Hebrew memorized, but hoped it would not need to be used. He checked the note for what he thought was about the thousandth time. He silently mouthed the words in the way he was tutored.

If spoken to in Hebrew by a fellow "Rabbi," he would utter the words as if sick at his stomach and hurry out of sight...

"You are new to our gathering."

The man spoke in English, smiling and bowing slightly in Tyce's direction.

"I am Krashni Harini," he said, again bowing slightly without offering his hand.

"And, I am Yehuda Levitt," Tyce said in the accented-English he had practiced diligently over the past days. He put his hands together and bowed as slightly as had the man, who, he thought, was likely a Hindu holy man.

The man's eyes were dark brown, soft, not threatening.

"I am new to this forum," Tyce said, gesturing with his right hand in a slight wave toward all in attendance. "I am just arrived from Jerusalem."

"Welcome, Yehuda. You will find this gathering filled with love for mankind," Krashna Harini said with a pleasant expression.

"Love is what is needed," Tyce replied.

"Yes. Mankind is at a juncture. We must move into a new era of acceptance and love. The ascended ones will help us to move toward the ascended order."

Tyce didn't know how to properly continue the

repartee. But, he thought how this wasn't a moment that called for using the Hebrew excuse he had memorized.

"They are here to enlighten," he said, pleased the words had come to him.

"We are all brothers. Brothers with each other. With those who come from other worlds," the Hindu holy man said, closing his eyes in a moment of epiphany, then opening them and smiling pleasantly.

"The brotherhood of mankind is all important at this juncture," Tyce said in accented-English, again pleased that he so easily engaged in the back and forth.

He had learned much from the brief meeting. He was glad he had ignored Yitssak's admonition to not engage in conversation prior to the session's beginning.

He knew now where the religious element of the Brussels', *Europan*-sponsored conference was aimed. At least, he believed he knew.

It all revolved around the orbs of light that moved and hovered above them now in the Brussels' night sky. It was all aimed at a coming together in a common faith of some sort.

When the Hindu broke off the conversation by seeing another robed religious man he went to greet after politely excusing himself, Tyce saw others approaching.

They were several Hasidic Jews, according to their dress. He could see that they had a bead drawn on him.

He turned quickly and mingled with a large group, distancing himself from the men. He was not yet prepared to use the memorized Hebrew as a means of escape.

Loudspeakers announced the session's beginning. He took a seat 15 rows back, directly in front of the lectern.

A bearded man, looking to be an orthodox Episcopal clergyman of some sort, stepped to the lectern.

He spoke in English, the chosen common language of the conference.

"My brothers of humanity's deity," he began, bringing all in attendance to attention.

"We witness today the dissolution of the hatreds that have beset the world for millennia. Here is proof of that dissolution and of the installation, truly, of the love we now embrace, one for another."

A large spotlight shown directly upon three men, each dressed in robes, but those that were distinctively different one from another.

One, Tyce recognized as a catholic cardinal, the second a Muslim Imam, and the third, a bearded man in the attire of Judaism.

The third man, when the light illuminated his face fully, he recognized instantly. his senses suddenly snapped to alertness, his cognitive processor searching for meaning.

It was Rabbi Elias Coahn!

* * *

EACH OF THE men had taken their time at the lectern, their words broadcast not only within the EU complex, but, via satellite, throughout the world.

The words that played again his mind now were those of Elias Coahn. It was Elias Coahn's oratory, in volume and strength unlike he had remembered when the Rabbi had spoken in previous times, that burned in his memory.

*"This day we announce a covenant of peace between all people of planet earth. It begins with the peace that has eluded mankind for millennia. The peace between the Arab people and the Jewish people."*

The audience had arisen to their feet in applause that continued for more than 5 minutes.

Coahn, chosen by the others to make the announcement, spoke eloquently about only one thing and one person. He gave praise for the peace covenant that was "confirmed"—as he had put it—by the European miracle worker.

* * *

"HE LOOKED RIGHT AT ME," Tyce said, while he walked with Yitssak Steyn at his side.

"He didn't recognize me. He just glanced my way and went on to others in conversation."

"Why does that surprise you," Steyn said.

"Because of the supernatural element in all this. The man has been my constant companion in my subconscious ever since that day on the Temple Mount. I just can't believe that this Judaic get up, with the beard, could fool him."

"Have you considered that possibly this involves a supernatural element...as you put it...greater than that surrounding Elias Coahn?"

Tyce's realization was shaken. It was as if suddenly being stung between his eyebrows by a wasp. His moving about incognito was almost certainly not possible simply because of a few props like clothing and the beard. Realization struck that he might be supernaturally *cloaked* for the task at hand...whatever that task might be.

He still didn't know what was the task that fate—the *supernatural element*—had placed before him.

"You handled the whole matter very well," Steyn said.

"What did you pick up from those around you? Was there anything special that you learned?"

"Only that this...this *miracle-working* European has the whole body of these religionists eating out of his hand. They have plans for some sort of amalgamation of religion. Some brand of religion...of belief system...that everyone on the planet is to embrace. All as part of this peace *covenant.* I heard over and over that the *brothers of the lights* have enlightened these religionists of the gathering."

"These disks of light?"

"Yes. They are to guide us all into the *ascended order...* into perfect peace and harmony, A *harmonic convergence,* they said, like it is where these things...these UFOs come from...Some other dimension."

They walked into the suite in the early morning hours. Snooping devices surrounded them. Their conversation would have to be curtailed. Sleep beckoned. There was no need to talk further.

* * *

IT WAS NO DREAM. His sleeping brain knew it instantly. The black veil that always preceded the clearly define, acutely-focused inner-visions began to scroll apart at the pinpoint of incendiary, white light.

Marial's sweet, lovely countenance projected from the scene. Her face turned toward the window, the thin stream of tear showing against her cheek.

She looked at the gray opaqueness that lay outside the window. She wanted something, someone to relieve her misery, her sadness.

He tried to reach out to her, but his thoughts had no arms, no hands with which to reach to her. He could do nothing but watch her weep while peering longingly out the ever-present window.

*"You must go to her,"* the voice said. The familiar voice. Not commanding and powerful like it was during the Europan religious cabal. Rather soft yet persuasive, like on the Temple Mount. Like the times within the archeological digs. Like in the several dream-episodes...

*"Israel is the sign of the end,"* the voice of Elias Coahn said again, *"Go to Marial to find your part in these end of days."*

The revelation shocked him into consciousness. As if prodded by a sharp object.

He sat up in bed, blinking and staring into the semi-darkness. He started to reach for the lamp that sat on the nightstand beside the bed.

"Tycus Levi," the voice said.

He looked around the room, the words interdicting his reach for the switch on the lamp.

"Eli?"

Tyce knew the voice the moment it cut through the darkness.

There began a yellow-glow somewhere at the center of the room. Momentarily, he could make out the figures of the two men.

"Eli, Moshi?"

"You must do as the dark prophet says," Eli said, his eyes seeming to pierce into those of Tyce.

"Dark prophet?"

His question came before he realized he was thinking about asking it.

"There is truth in the dark prophet's sentences. There elements of truth always. Follow his words in this matter," Moshe said from within the radiance at the center of the room.

"What...What should I do? I have no idea what it all means."

"You will know when the time has come. You are chosen," Eli said.

"But, what can I expect? What sign will there be telling me what I should do?"

Both robed men's voices blended into one as their images faded into blackness. "You will know when the time comes, Tycus Levi."

\* \* \*

"AND THEY TOLD you to do as Elias Coahn said?"

Yitssak carried the brief bags for the Rabbi he supposedly assisted. They approached the limo awaiting less than ten feet away.

"They called him the *dark prophet*," Tyce said. "They said I should follow... that is, do what he said. they said that there are elements of truth...There are *always* elements of truth in what the dark prophet says. What does that mean, Yitssak?"

Steyn had no answer by the time they entered the limo and moved through the old streets of Brussels toward the European Union headquarters building.

Yitssak had obviously been thinking on Tyce's question. he addressed it at the time they turned onto the boulevard leading to the EU building. Tyce saw the many flags come into view at the time the Israeli spoke.

"Elias has been turned totally by this cabal...by Europan. We understand the dark nature of this peace...arrangement. Elias has proven to be a prophet of Israel. So, the term dark prophet might have its basis in these facts."

"How, then, can he be relied on to ...to guide me, as Eli and Moshi suggest?"

"You said he didn't recognize you when he looked directly at you. We discussed how this might be super-natural cloaking...hiding your identity by the greater power. Maybe this means you will be able, as Rabbi Yehuda Levitt, of going places and doing things you could not do as Tyce Greyson. Maybe that's what it means to be *Tycus Levi*...your true name from birth."

Tyce listened to Yitssak's words without replying. He felt, none-the-less, fortified by them. The words of Eli again ran through his thoughts. *"You will know when the time has come. You are chosen."*

STEPPING onto the elevator brought a blush of panic to his senses. Four Rabbis entered the conveyance directly behind him. He returned the smile of the man who greeted him in Hebrew.

He couldn't say he was sick, then run off to the men's room. He was stuck for the next thirty seconds in this box, while it slid upward toward the twentieth floor. They were headed toward the same destination, he knew, as the meeting for the amalgamation of religious leaders was set for that floor.

The Rabbi looked at him again, after turning from his companions and talking to them in hushed tones.

"Are you of Haredi?"

The man asked the question in Hebrew. He hesitated after hearing the words. He understood them. The man had spoken Hebrew, and he understood the words!

"Yes. Jerusalem is my place of ministry."

He had given an answer...And, he did so in Hebrew!

The realization was overwhelming. The sudden ability to understand and speak Hebrew...What did it mean?...

Not only did he understand and speak in Hebrew. He somehow could now converse on things about Judaism he knew nothing of!

He decided to not question it. Just relax and go with the flow...

The transformation was mind-bending. He sensed almost as if he had become the Rabbi, Yehuda Levitt, from the moment he stepped into the elevator.

"Already, our leadership has agreed to transfer all nuclear weaponry to the arsenal of Europan," one of the Rabbis said, turning the man's attention from Tyce, back to the group.

Still, they spoke in Hebrew and he understood every word.

"This means the nation will prosper like never before," the man continued. "With no massive military to fund, the heavy taxation of our people can be brought to much lower levels. Revenues will now go for building our industry, toward raising our standard of living."

Hearing the words, spoken by an Israeli Rabbi...a *true* Israeli Rabbi...sent a chill over his body. The words from remembered scripture echoed in his thoughts.

*"When they shall say peace and safety, then destruction comes upon them like travail upon a woman with child. And they shall not escape."*

These holy men of Israel...fallen totally for the peace that will destroy many... It was if at the same time a veil was lifted from his own eyes...from his now, limited mind, a curtain that now blinded even Israel's most religious leaders from truth.

The world had changed in that instant millions vanished from the earth's surface. The vacuum created seemed to bring the filling of that vacuum with deception...Deception that was right in front of his face while they neared the 20th floor.

Again, words from his intensive study over the months sounded like a weather warning siren in his mind's ear. He didn't know why the scripture suddenly leaped from the darkest regions of his brain. He had not understood any of it when he had read it...tried to study it over several months. But there it was, resounding in his head as if spoken by the man named Paul, the apostle who had written it.

*For the mystery of iniquity doth already work: only he who now restrains will restrain, until he be taken out of the way. And then shall that Wicked be revealed, whom the Lord shall consume with the spirit of his mouth, and shall destroy with the brightness of his coming: Even him, whose coming is after the working of Satan with all power and signs and lying wonders, And with all deceivableness of unrighteousness in them that perish; because they received not the love of the truth, that they might be saved. And for this cause God shall send them strong delusion, that they should believe a lie: That they all might be damned who believed not the truth, but had pleasure in unrighteousness.*

He suddenly understood what had totally confounded him during those times when he read the scriptures. Read them over and over, then searched through volume after volume of those who had written about the verses...the scholars, from many backgrounds and perspectives.

He needed no volumes by prophecy teachers at this moment. Required no further study. Suddenly his understanding was clear, while the elevator doors slid open and they walked onto the 20th floor of the EU headquarters building in Brussels.

The delusion taking place that he was witnessing became blatantly clear...The blindness suffered by these religious Israelis...the acceptance of the deception suffered by the whole world at this Divinely-appointed moment, he now understood.

\* \* \*

HE MOVED about the many brands of religious clerics with complete freedom. Something...Someone, some-where, had imbued him with the knowledge, the free-dom, to move in these circles as if he was born to it.

He spoke Hebrew when with the Hebrews, but the language most spoken was English. He listened now to an Arab Muslim, explain the Islamist perspective.

"We now have Jerusalem promised as seat of our new nation. The Jews have agreed, under the leadership and authority of this body...under the power and ability of this man...to divide and share. At last, we have escaped the foot of oppression upon the Palestinian neck. This will all be enforced with absolute certainty. Therefore, we can live beside the Jew."

The man, his bearded face beneath the burnoose he wore contorted in thought while he considered his next words, said, finally, "Allah's will be done. Our people will no longer be murdered by Israel's militants. Europan will govern over the new, divided, Jerusalem."

The Arab saw that Yehuda Levitt, a Jew, was listening in. He glanced at him in a look of disapproval, then back at the men he held in conversation.

Tyce, after listening to the Muslim cleric explain Islam's position to several Catholic priests and other robed religionists from various nations and belief systems, moved further toward the center of the expansive chamber. He still had no idea of what his purpose was for his being among the gathering. However, he no longer felt unsure about the certainty that someone...something, somewhere wanted him to be part of this massive enclave of religionists.

He sensed the pathway to whatever was to be his inevitable destination being paved—being made smooth while he moved forward. He did, in fact, at last sense that he was indeed chosen for the mission.

Israel was now under great deception. The whole world was suffering delusion. It had everything to do with the disappearance of millions from every part of the world. His mission was somehow wrapped up in the vanishings...in Israel's rescue out of the great deception that had the nation, the people in its evil grip.

The enclave was called together for meeting and getting to know each other. They were to be the nucleus of the love that was to begin spreading to the world. The young European had promised that it would be not unlike an infection spreading throughout a dying biological entity. Only the religionist, in ecumenical unison, would create a miracle of love...An antidote to the hatred and division that was destroying *Mother Earth*.

*Brothers* from other worlds, from other dimensions, would carry the antidote to hate, would spread the infectious love instantaneously to all parts of the globe. The saturation would be total, with no culture, no society left untouched.

All religions...coming together...to, for the first time, unify the earth...truly make it the *Brotherhood of Man*.

Tyce Greyson, Yehuda Levitt, Tycus Levi... or whoever the higher power considered him, suddenly realized at this moment that there had to be a message spread across the globe, touching every nation, culture and society. But, it was not the message this European, that Europan, that the light orbs planned to carry.

Although he didn't yet know exactly what the message was, he knew that he, a mere journalist chosen for this moment, must be part of that dissemination of the higher power's message.

# CHAPTER 19

The sense of bravado had deserted him some moments after the receiving line was set up in the great hall. Each of the religious figures, representing their various areas of the world and their own faiths, lined up. They would each have opportunity to meet and greet Europan's top leadership.

His confidence had waned. One within the leadership particularly troubled his thoughts. The young miracle worker.

He saw, from his position in line, that the man was stationed at the very center of the lineup of perhaps 18 men.

The contrast was stark. The men in expensive, tailored, business suits and ties and the clerics of the diverse religions, many attired in their colorful robes of their various traditions.

That he would shortly be in front of the European troubled him while he moved in line with the others. The pleasantries between the greeters and those being greeted were going well. Most spent a few seconds making small talk in accented-English.

He, too, exchanged pleasantries with each of the leaders, but kept one eye on the line. Now only five to go...

He noticed that the young man had few people with whom he spent time in conversation. They seemed to glance into his eyes, then move along quickly to the next dignitary. The man made no effort to engage in idle chit-chat, he determined. The face to face should go quickly and without consequence...

The Hindu priest he had met when first coming to the chamber was ahead of him and bowed slightly to the European. The younger man acknowledged the Indian with a slight nod of his head and a faint smile.

He was next and moved to in front of the European. Tyce sensed the things surrounding the two of them growing dark. Only he and the young Europan leader seemed present while their hands met.

The surrounding that engulfed them was like that in which Eli and Moshi had appeared to him. An eerie, yellow-glow that created a misty ambience of diffused light.

The European's penetrating gaze tugged his own into its gravity. Something akin to electrostatic firing seemed to leap between their clasped hands.

It as if the two of them were in a time-warp, unable to break free.

When the handshake ended, everything surrounding them seemed normal. No more than a few seconds seemed to have passed.

"So good to meet you...Rabbi...Levitt," the European said with a smile that somehow expressed an overly effusive statement. "We shall...I prayerfully hope...talk again very soon."

Again, the European smiled brightly. It was not a smile that made one feel as if something warm and fuzzy had just taken place.

* * *

"Everything went well again," Yitssak said, hefting the brief bags into the limo. "Do you believe that they accept you as a Rabbi representing Israel?"

"I think the other Rabbis do," Tyce said. "But, I'm not at all sure about the miracle worker."

His use of the term was spoken with facetious inflection.

"Did he say something to make you suspicious?"

"No. He was quite pleasant. Overly so."

"Oh?"

"I watched him very closely the whole time I was going through the line. He didn't say anything except 'hello' to anyone. He just nodded, smiled slightly, and they moved along. With me, I don't know what happened. I thought I might be going into another episode. Everything started turning dark. It felt like there was electricity in our handshake. That's the only way I can describe it."

The Mercedes limo turned left on Avenue De Stalingrad and rolled through the night past Manneken-Pis, where the well-illuminated statue stood of the little boy known affectionately to the people of Brussels as the city's oldest citizen. Neither man acknowledged seeing the historic figure, while the black car picked up speed in its journey to the hotel which they would continue to call home for the next few days.

* * *

"Yes, Sir. We have heard those reports. The reports that there is great anger among the Iranians and Turks. Not all the murderers, it seems, are happy with the love and peace festiveness their Muslim brothers are having with Israel here in Brussels."

Yitssak spoke on the phone to someone in Tel Aviv. Tyce watched him pace in the evening's semi-darkness while the Israeli talked, his own curiosity rising.

"We must not forget our present-day prophet's words about the threat that will come from the north," the Israeli said. "Yes. He forewarned that Ezekiel's prophecy is in the making."

Steyn hesitated, listening to the caller.

"Yes. It is true. He said all the forces that do so will be destroyed, but not by our military."

Tyce sat more stiffly upright, coming to a more alert position in the back seat of the limo.

Yitssak Steyn continued to pace immediately outside the open window.

"Apparently, Ezekiel...and Tyce Greyson...believe it will be done by Israel' God, not by the IDF. At any rate, our people have just negotiated away our defense force. They trust, completely, this young...*miracle worker...*"

Again, Steyn listened to the other end of the call, before speaking.

"Yes, Sir. I will let you know if there are further...visions."

The Israeli, when he had ended the call he had received from Tel Aviv, leaned to speak to Tyce through the window.

"Bibi says the reports are true. Our intelligence tells us that there is turmoil among the Muslim crazies. They want nothing to do with the negotiations here."

"Shouldn't that make your people, the Israel contingent that is engaged in these talks, see the light?"

"In normal times, when thinking is reasonable, I would say yes. But, these aren't normal times. and the thinking of our so-called leadership, is anything but reasonable," Steyn said, opening the limo door for Yehuda Levitt.

YITSSAK HAD PROVIDED him with details of intelligence reports from Israel's north. Any attack from the Muslim horde, Bibi had told Yitssak, would be met with nuclear response. The new government would have no choice.

Within the question of how serious Israeli leadership was—absent now, the former prime minister lay the true worry. Israel's new government, if it truly was to agree to giving the nuclear stockpile to Europan and the western alliance, would have no deterrence. No defense if the many millions swarmed at them from the north.

The European had given his word among his many, great, swelling promises, that any assault against Israel would be considered a direct attack upon the western alliance. It would be met with instantaneous and total nuclear retaliation. Israel could rely on Europan, on the young European for its peace, its safety.

Yet, the prophecy had been given. Given to Ezekiel the prophet. Given through, who? Through Tyce Greyson...through *Tycus Levi?*

He again had reached the end of his day, the words beginning to blur while he worked on the manuscript.

He wished he and Yitssak could have had more time together before coming into the hotel suite, where electronic surveillance surely covered their every uttered word. ...More time to discuss more in-depth matters involving the prophecy...the foretelling of the attack on Israel that would surely come if Israeli leadership gave up its defenses...despite what the European continued to promise.

It began the moment he closed his eyes. He began falling into a bottomless, totally dark chasm, unable to straighten from the slow tumble. He sensed no fear of falling, just an ever descending slow, turning of his body while he watched the light of the upper world diminish.

The light became a pinpoint, and the pinpoint of light flashed and began burning the black veil. At the same time his body ceased to tumble, his feet settling easily on the soft surface, his body straightening, finally, to a standing posture.

He stood before the raging sea, its gargantuan waves rising and plummeting with crashing violence. Lightning electrified the boiling sky, thunder crescendo painfully within his transfixed brain.

He expected it. The monstrous beast. The Leviathan with its shimmering, scaly body rising amidst the tumult.

His vision-oriented thinking was mistaken. The sea's raged subsided to a near calm. the clouds above dissipated, the thunder and lightning no longer threatening.

Something arose from the calming waters before him while he stood gawking from the shore.

A human figure stood, walked toward him and, finally, stood in front of him, glaring at him.

He was dumbstruck, unable to move any part of his body. He could but return the unbreakable gaze coming from the eyes of Rabbi Elias Coahn.

* * *

"Yitssak, I don't know what it was all about. I've never had such a... an episode. I just remember staring at him and him staring back. I don't remember what happened next."

Steyn studied Tyce's bearded face. "That was all there was to the dream?"

"It was no dream. It was an episode...a vision."

"There's nothing else to it that you remember?"

"There was much more. But, I don't know what it entailed. It's like I have a block of some sort. But, I know there is more...Much, much more."

The Israeli let his eyes wander, taking in the distant Brussels' inner-city sites while they sat eating lunch. He looked again at Tyce. The American leaned forward on the wrought-iron table to hear him better among the sounds of the city streets and people gathered at the Al-Fresco cafe.

"If it is truly a vision, it is given by the same higher power as always," Steyn said. "You will know the full meaning at some future time."

Tyce smiled behind the beard. "Always the optimist," he said with a subdued laugh.

"Just a realist. You have been sent to us...Chosen, as Rabbi Coahn put it... As Eli and Moshi put it. You will know what is involved in due course."

It was true. He knew it in his core being. The things of the *dark Rabbi* would be revealed when, as Eli and Moshi had said...When the time was right.

Both men came to alert posture when a commotion broke out in the crowd of pedestrians near their table.

People began running, scattering in all directions.

They watched, then stood, as a man approached at a trot. He looked at Tyce, his eyes wide, a snarl upon his lips.

They saw then the weapons He held a semi-automatic pistol in one hand and a machete-like blade in the other.

The disheveled man, who stopped 10 feet from them, shouted something in Dutch, concluding his shout with a growling grunt while starting to lunge at Greyson.

An orb of tremendous brightness suddenly engulfed the attacker. The light disappeared as quickly as it had appeared. The attacker lay on the cement walkway, obviously dead.

* * *

EVEN UNDER THE pressing matter of dealing with the assault and the way the attacker was stopped, the vision-image of Elias Coahn couldn't be shaken from his thoughts. What were the deep things the Rabbi said to him in the dream-vision of the early morning hours? The things he couldn't remember...

It was as if miniscule drops of the revelations the Rabbi divulged were leading a drip at a time into his conscious moments. But the drips failed to produce a pool of thought that formed even one complete recollection. Not a single, remembered, explanation of the Rabbi's words to him.

Yet, he knew things had been told to him during the dream-vision. Things of profound, even eternal, import. But, they would not come. the thoughts would not come...

"The officer said it wasn't related to ISIS or any terrorist group. The man was mentally deranged," Yitssak said after walking through the door to the City-Ixelle office.

Tyce stood from the chair in the police waiting room to meet Steyn.

"They don't have any more than that on him?"

"They are still checking background. But, it looks like he was one of a growing number of people who have just gone insane. The psychologists attribute it to all that has happened since the disappearances."

"You saw it in his eyes. He chose me to attack, out of all the people there," Tyce said.

"They think he just saw your religious dress, and that's why he chose you. That is what set him off"

"What about the light...did they say...?"

"When I asked about the light and the man's means of death, the captain said they were now seeing it happen not only at crime scenes in Brussels, but there are reports from around city police forces all over Europe. When there are attacks like this, the light orbs encapsulate the perpetrators and they die. He wouldn't say how they die...what kills them."

"The European said that they were here to offer peace or else. I guess this was a case of *or else*," Tyce said while they walked to the awaiting limousine.

* * *

Yitssak called to him in Hebrew when Tyce started toward a door in the basement parking garage.

"What?" He turned to face the approaching Steyn, who continued to explain in Hebrew.

"I haven't a clue of what you're saying," Greyson said.

"I said that you are headed in the wrong direction. We must enter in those doors," the Israeli said in English, pointing to the doors against wall 20 feet to the left of the doors Tyce was about to enter.

"I couldn't understand a word of what you said," Tyce repeated, thinking on what it meant.

Before, he understood and spoke Hebrew fluently. Now, he was clueless as to what Yitssak had spoken.

The Israeli, too, took a few seconds to reflect, finally asking, "Have you been able to understand me to this point, whenever we are together?"

"Come to think of it, we never speak to each other in Hebrew, other than when we are in the presence of others speaking Hebrew."

"You are right. This is a puzzlement," Yitssak said, accompanying Tyce to the doors.

"Do you *think* in Hebrew? I mean when reading, or when by yourself?"

"No. I can't say that I do."

"Whatever the problem, the source that gave you the ability must have reasons," the Israeli said, holding the door open for Tyce to enter the building's bottom floor.

Tyce wondered inwardly at his companion's unwavering confidence. Yitssak Steyn had faith. He claimed to not necessarily believe in Israel's traditional God....in *Yahweh,* but his faith was strong that the *higher power* or *greater power,* as he put it, was somehow directing his, Yehuda Levitt's—Tyce Greyson's—way, controlling circumstances while he sought to fulfill the mission. Whatever that mission might be in the final analysis.

They began walking up steps to the elevator they would catch on the first floor. Yitssak turned to speak to Tyce while they ascended.

"I have a theory about the language matter."

The Israeli watched as Tyce stopped, then crumpled to the steps. The Israeli threw down the brief bags he carried, quickly reaching to keep the American's robed body from tumbling down the steps.

Tyce's body was tumbling, none-the-less. A familiar, inner-being, slowly turning motion through blackness that ended with a soft touch-down on sand he recognized as seashore.

He looked through expectant senses at the vast seascape in front of him. A calm, not turbulent sea as in other times.

The wind blew in his face, but a gentle, not violent wind, while he scanned the waters' horizon.

The sea-beast. It would appear at any moment. The leviathan, its ten horns, and seven heads, with fangs gnashing.

*"Tycus Levi."*

The voice abruptly snapped his attention back to the shore where he stood. A familiar voice.

*"You shall encounter a multitudinous meeting of Israel's House, overshadowed by a strange being, Tycus Levi."*

His eyes met those of Eli, then those of Moshi. He was strangely comforted by the recognition, despite his astonishment.

He started to speak, but Eli's words preempted. He is met again, through a vision, with the two anciently-robed Jewish figures. They tell him that the God of Israel is with him as he goes through the things he must experience. He is on a mission to accomplish a specific Divine Purpose.

*"Do not think to be other than Yehuda Levitt when facing the one who is pre-destined to fulfill the purposes for which you are chosen."*

The two men stepped forward, as if gliding on a cushion of air, he thought, his senses of alertness heightened when contact with their fingertips was felt upon his arms.

*"You shall follow the directive, Tycus Levi. You shall be led into the pathway lighted by Divine Directive."*

\* \* \*

YITSSAK HAD TO FIGHT IMPATIENCE. He looked into Tyce's eyes, seeing the pupils shrink to normal size. He helped Greyson to the sink of the men's room.

He had questions, many questions. But, first he must help Tyce to fully regain sensibility.

"This should help," he said, applying a cold, wet, paper towel to Tyce's forehead.

"Yes. That helps," Greyson said, taking over the holding of the makeshift compress to his forehead.

"Eli and Moshi," he said weakly. "It was Eli and Moshi...another vision. This time I remember what was said."

"Tell me," the Israeli said, having reached the limits of patience.

"They said I will have an encounter, a meeting with someone. That I should not think to be other than Yehuda Levitt at that time."

He took a moment to clear his thinking, and after running the compress of wet, paper towels over his face, said, "They said my pathway would be lighted through the *Divine Directive*"

Both men considered the possible meaning of the vision. Finally, Yitssak spoke.

"Let us see, then, what this...*Divine Directive*... holds in store for Israel."

COMPLETELY RECOVERED, Tyce felt bolstered by the stair-well episode, by the words given him by Eli and Moshi. Yitssak Steyn's obvious confidence that Tyce's pathway would indeed be lightened as he moved forward, too, emboldened *Yehuda Levitt* while he and his assistant carrying the brief cases walked into the meeting.

The thought had not struck until this moment. What of the loss of ability to speak Hebrew? What did this mean in the accomplishment of his mission on behalf of the *Divine Directive?*

The thought wasn't daunting to him. Maybe Yitssak's faith was infectious...

"My brother," the smiling man said, reaching to take Tyce's right hand. " This is a day for which we can all be thankful. We begin the healing process together!"

Krashna Hari briefly embraced him and led him by the elbow toward a group of ecumenically-attired men and women. The Hindu cleric introduced him to each one individually.

There were no fellow Jewish clergy among the group. Hebrew would, therefore, not be necessary, he thought, thinking how whomever or whatever the source of the Divine Directive, the way seemed clear; he would not need to know Hebrew.

At that moment Krashna Hari looked past him.

"Ah! Your fellow Rabbis..."

Tyce turned to see the three men, dressed much like himself, approaching, their eyes affixed on his own.

He didn't have time to think of what his next move should be. He had forgotten his once-memorized response about the nausea as an escape alternative. He no longer had the piece of paper that had the excuse written in phonetic Hebrew...

"Shalom," he said as the men approached. He instantly realized that the Hebrew was back.

Yehuda Levitt sat with his fellow Rabbis. Their conversation had been pleasant, not probing or prying as to who he was or what his role in the forum. All were jubilant, but the three Rabbis a little less so than most of the religionists present. Several thousand years of anti-Jewish anger and treachery would take something more than promises to overcome. They were here to try to achieve overcoming those millennia of treachery if such achievement was to be had.

A conversational buzz began from one side of the large chamber. It came from near a huge, arched doorway through which several people in colorful cler-ical robes now passed.

Soon the word reached where Tyce sat. The European would attend the meeting and would speak.

When the man could be seen approaching with a delegation of Europan leaders, the crowd nearest the doors stood and began applauding. Soon, those where Tyce sat arose to their feet and joined the applause, while the group of men, led by the young European, strode to the podium 20 feet to the left of Tyce and those around him.

The young man came to the lectern while the other Europan leaders stood in near proximity behind him.

When all were again seated, the European looked the room of religionists over and took several seconds to make sure all were settled.

He began in English only slightly tinged by a European accent Tyce could never quite identify.

"Our coming together today is perhaps for the most important purpose ever intended in the history of man. Upon how you in this assembly react to and conform with that intended purpose depends on the fate of, the destiny of mankind."

The European paused, looking over the gathered ecclesiastical leadership of the world's religions, before continuing.

"The *Dimension of Light* awaits your decision. Their question: *Will the many faiths, under your leadership, work together to bring peace and security to this otherwise doomed planet?"*

The chamber erupted, the hundreds of religious leaders jumping to their feet in thunderous applause.

When the congregants finally settled, he spoke again.

"Throughout history, the Jewish race has been accused of being the hold-up against peace. They have been seen as interlopers, as oppressors to the peoples indigenous to the areas in and surrounding the holy land. The people of the house of Israel have been hunted and hated and the victims of genocide and of holo-caust..." His audience sat in utter silence. Tyce looked around to see reaction to the European's words by the many Islamists in the room. Their faces reflected only stoic expressions as they awaited the man's next words.

"I tell you here, today, that the Jew, that Israel, has not only the right, but the commission from the brothers of light to live in peace and safety."

Still there was no visible or audible reaction from the Islamists.

"The Jew is, by my direction this day, given the right by Europan Commission authority to construct their building of worship on Mount Moriah. This will be a symbol of the coming together of mankind. the brothers of light thereby have validation that the new order of peace and security that is to soothe the distresses of Planet Earth will be pursued."

Still, he saw no change of expression on the faces of the Muslims throughout the chamber. It was if they were paralyzed in their stoicism—their stony countenances frozen in place.

"The Palestinians hereby are granted their long-sought nation-state. Jerusalem is their Capital. The city is divided, with permitted interaction between all the sections. There will be no partitions or walls."

The religionists again came to their feet in a crescendo of approval.

The room settled again and the young European spoke.

"Israel, for her part in making peace and safety for all of mankind a reality, has the honor of one of her own being made head of the world-wide worship system. He will head *Gospel of Dimension,* the global worship system."

More applause erupted and the European held up both hands, palms-out to silence the ecstatic audience.

"And now I present this man of G...O...D..." He said each letter, bringing appreciative laughter for its tone of mocking cleverness. "I give you Rabbi Elias Coahn!"

The small Rabbi shuffled to the lectern from some-where within the crowd of European leaders gathered behind the man who introduced him. He smiled at the young European, who shook his hand and, with a returned smile, gestured for him to proceed to the microphones.

\* \* \*

RABBI COAHN HAD SPENT much of his time reassuring the Jews that he had their back...That the European consor-tium—*Europan*—had the best interest of everyone on the planet on their hearts and minds. It was going to be, he assured, Heaven on Earth.

*Gospel of Dimension* would be the all-in-all for all of mankind.

Tyce reflected on the man's words. The man who had ignited his own fascination with prophecy…with Bible prophecy…with the Rabbi telling at the Wailing Wall that Israel as the sign of the end.

"What is this meeting's purpose?"

Yitssak Steyn's question pulled him from his intro-spection. He was thinking about finding his way to his interest in prophecy—about Israel's part in all of it.

"I was told it is to be part of some sort of panel before a global audience. The members of *Gospel of Dimension*—ten of us, will discuss the new faith, the new, global reli-gion, in a panel forum."

"Who asked you to be a part of it?"

There was concern in the Israeli's tone.

"A guy who said he was an emissary from Rabbi Coahn," Tyce said.

Yitssak appeared in deep thought.

"Why the concerned expression? You have something I should know?"

"No… No," the Israeli said, shaking his head nega-tively. "I'm just trying to figure why you would be invited out of the thousands of attendees."

"Have faith, Yitssak. That's what you always imply I should do in these things," Tyce said lightly.

"Yes. We must trust whoever…whatever is directing all of this. You are there for some purpose determined by that greater power, be it Yahweh…or whoever or whatever."

\* \* \*

It was a truly stunning set. Tyce looked over the large studio. It was designed for *Europan's* future broadcasts. For its world-wide audience.

It glittered with gold paint, with purple highlights throughout its motif. Shimmering jewels, diamonds, emeralds, and rubies, set encrusted within the walls at various places.

Large, luxuriant, high back, swivel chairs covered in deep purple velvet material were arranged in a circle atop a 12 inch-high, rounded, elegantly-carpeted platform.

Television cameras of the latest technology were suspended above the chairs by long, metallic arms that allowed the technicians and operators to take shots from every conceivable angle.

He had spoken to no one except the emissary who said he was sent by Rabbi Coahn to invite him, Rabbi Yehuda Levitt, to be a part of the 10-person panel.

The question that at first had bothered him, had bothered Yitssak Steyn as well, was: Why did the Rabbi...Rabbi Elias Coahn, seemed to have not recognized Yehuda Levitt?

Other questions fired within his synapses now. Why did Coahn not recognize him? What would be the result if he *did* recognize the American journalist, Tyce Greyson?

*Faith...* Faith, he thought to himself. The...*source*...that had him now put in this strange position would have to see him through whatsoever came his way.

The thought soothed his nerves, while he was ushered, along with the other nine, religiously-garbed men, into the center of the studio and up onto the platform.

He and the others seated themselves in the plush,

velour-covered chairs. Tyce watched the TV cameras above the ten men while they whirred and turned, being positioned by the program's director for the opening shots of the first presentation from this *Europan* broadcast facility.

New technologies, he had learned, would allow *Europan* to broadcast in every language of the people around the world able to receive the program. He was told to speak in Hebrew. They wanted the Jewish people of the world to know he was representing them in this spectacular show of unity of all religious leaders.

Rabbi Elias Coahn would be host. He would call upon each panelist, individually. Next, each man would be allowed to engage in the overall questions posed by the host.

Each in their turn answered questions put by Rabbi Coahn. All questions and answers involved the need for uniting all under the brotherhood of man. Thus, to produce peace and security for people everywhere. Peace and safety under the religious auspices each of the robed religionists represented.

It was as if Yehuda Levitt was deliberately saved for last to be questioned. Tyce knew, in the deepest of his being, that this was the moment for which he had been called by...by the *source that was the higher power.*

Rabbi Elias Coahn's image was on all the monitors around the walls within the huge studio. He smiled ever so faintly while making his thoughts and question, spoken in Hebrew, heard to the Jewish Rabbi and the audiences of Planet Earth.

"Israel is at the center of all controversy. This new start, instituted by *Dimension of Light,* and by *Europan,* offers our people...yours and mine...an opportunity to prove the Jew is a truly caring, loving citizen of the world, and of the cosmos. What do you have to say in that regard on behalf of all Jews, everywhere? What is your message as Rabbi, responsible for bringing all of Judaism to within Gospel *of Dimension?*"

Tyce felt it coming on. He knew, was calmly resolved, through supernaturally-given assurance. This was the moment for which he had been born. The shining purpose for which he was *chosen*.

The glittering brightness of the studio began to turn dark, the brilliantly shining spotlights above dimming to blackness. When the ebony veil had reached its deepest hue, the familiar spark, the pinpoint of light ignited at its center.

Before him was revealed behind the burning veil a scene that staggered his inner-cerebral senses.

Thousands upon thousands of young men knelt before his astonished gaze into their midst. Above the throng was a creature of immense light. A figure with a massive wingspan that spread across their entire gathering. The face of the creature was that of a magnificently beautiful being. A human, yet beyond human, face.

The creature grew in effulgence until its radiance outshone the sun, causing the mass of kneeling young men to become part of the radiance created.

He knew he was speaking to the young men that knelt within the now blinding radiance...That they were there specifically to hear his message.

* * *

WHEN TYCE CAME out of the trance the voices of the people in the studio were fading into the background.

He was being hustled away from the group who

shouted angrily. A woman's voice said, "Quickly! This way..."

Yitssak Sterne urged him to move more swiftly, partly holding him upright by the elbow while they moved, the shouts fading as they moved.

"What happened?" Tyce's weakly given question met with no reply.

"Let's just keep going. We must get away from here.

"In here," the woman's voice said. Tyce saw her, then, his senses having cleared enough to finally see his surroundings. He blinked and shook his head to assure himself he wasn't hallucinating. He didn't say the name. He wanted to say the name, but something, internally, prevented him from doing so. The name he was none-the-less saying silently within his quickly recovering senses...

*Marial?*

# CHAPTER 20

"We are safe for now," Yitssak said, working to help Tyce recover. He mopped the journalist's brow with a wet towel.

"Where is she?"

His question was week, distressed, having passed in and out of consciousness for the past several minutes.

"The woman left after she assured me that this was a safe place."

"It's...Marial," Tyce said, his eyes wide, trying to focus on his surroundings, looking for the woman.

"Tyce, you were hallucinating. Who did you think you saw?"

"Marial. She's the..."

"She's the one you've been talking about? Marial Gunn?"

Tyce nodded, trying to come fully to consciousness, struggling to catch his breath.

"Yes...It was Marial...I've got to find her."

"She has helped us. She is trying to keep us from being located by those back there," the Israeli said.

"Why are they looking for us?"

"What you said when you entered the...trance. The things you said set them in a rage."

Tyce tried to think through his confused state, sitting up on the side of the small sofa.

"What did I say?"

"You said that the things that the people of Europan were being told, that things proclaimed by the European...By Elias Coahn, are all lies. You told a world-wide audience...before they could stop the broad-cast...that this was a deadly peace arrangement meant to destroy Israel...to destroy the world."

Tyce looked at Steyn, a dumfounded expression emanating from his eyes. He spoke after several seconds of trying to understand.

"I saw a massive number of young men...thousands of them... all kneeling and looking skyward," he said, with a look that questioned whether Yitssak had an explanation.

"There was this enormous creature of light...with wings that spanned the entire width of the thousands of young men on their knees."

The telling of the vision seemed to spark a remem-brance with Steyn.

"That must be the reason you began to say the things you proclaimed."

"What did I say?"

"You said...'*you must go into all the world with the Gospel of the Kingdom.*'"

He thought further on Tyce's words during the trans-state, then said, "You said '*Preach the Gospel unto the Jew and to the Gentile.*'"

\* \* \*

MARIAL CAME into the room and Tyce's heart leaped in his chest. It was Marial!

"You need to come with me right away," she said, motioning for them to follow her.

Tyce began to feel weak, his knees almost buckling. She didn't recognize him. The emotional wrenching that followed made him feel as if he would fall, having lost much of the sensation in his legs.

"Where are we going?" Yitssak asked while following her through a door other than the one through which they had entered the room 20 minutes earlier.

"There's no time to talk now," Marial said, hurrying along a long hallway.

Tyce kept his eyes on her as she led the way. He wanted to embrace her, kiss her, to love her...

But he heard inner voices... Those of Eli and Moshi.

*"You must not stop being Yehuda Levitt."*

Why did she not recognize him? When would they be allowed by...by whomever, by whatever, to be together?...

Momentarily the three of them were descending a stairwell that opened at its bottom into the parking garage somewhere beneath the European Union Head-quarters Building.

"It's over here."

Marial led the way to one corner of the private underground parking section.

She said nothing further, opening the door to the back seat of the small, European sedan.

"I've been assured we won't be followed," she said, glancing in the rearview mirror while driving quickly through the parking garage and emerging into the Brus-sels night.

"How can you be certain," the Israeli said.

"A couple of men I trust. Men who said to tell you their names," she said.

"Who," Steyn said.

"Eli and Moshi," Marial said, picking up speed beneath the night sky filled with the pulsing, moving orbs of light.

* * *

SHE LOOKED at him with those green eyes that couldn't see him. Couldn't see Tyce Greyson. Rather saw only Rabbi Yehuda Levitt.

He knew it wasn't the beard, the Kipah, the priestly get-up. She couldn't see Tyce Greyson because the *source* of all that happened to him...had happened to *them,* had decreed that it be so.

He knew, viscerally, that it must be this way for now, even though his overwhelming desire was to rip the beard from his face...to throw aside the Kipah, and to open his arms to the one being on the plant he loved more than life itself.

Yitssak, too, knew there were elements beyond the normal at play. He would not give away who his Rabbi friend really was to this girl that had rescued them. Rescued them from the grasp of Europan forces now in a rage to find them, to keep them from doing further damage to their plans for Israel...To their plans for the world.

"How did you meet Eli and Moshi," Sterne asked, wanting to know more about the intrigues of all the strange things happening at such a rapid pace.

"You will have trouble believing it. I still can't believe it," Marial said, looking in several directions to negotiate turns upon Brussels city streets.

"They first came to me...in a dream. Crazy, huh?"

Neither man said anything, each of them intensely tuned to what came next.

"They just appeared in my sleep and said to me that I would know it wasn't a dream but a vision. I would know, they said, because I would soon meet them personally. I would be given instructions on what to do once I met them during waking hours."

"And you did meet them." Tyce said, emphatically, not in questioning tone.

""To say I met them is an understatement of all understatements," she said. "I was walking toward a building in London after parking. It was almost dark. I decided to take a short cut through an alley to go into the side door. Two men grabbed me out of the shadows and pulled me into a building next to the building where I was going. They began ripping at my clothing..."

She hesitated, the reliving the experience of terror.

"Suddenly, a light grew in this dark room where they were attacking me. It grew...became a large ball of light. Eli and Moshi stepped out of the light.

She paused to remember, before telling what happened in an incredulous tone.

"The attackers became paralyzed. They couldn't move."

She then said, as if she still couldn't believe what happened, "Eli and Moshi spoke to me. They said that I am chosen by...by...God...to accomplish His Will."

When she didn't speak for several seconds, Tyce said, "And, what happened next?"

"I was both dumbfounded and thankful to be rescued. When I next looked around me, I was inside the building I was going into before those men grabbed me. And...

My clothing was just as it was before the attack. Nothing at all torn. It was as if the attack had never happened."

"How did you know about helping us?"

The Israeli's tone was almost clinical, unemotional.

"Eli and Moshi appeared in another dream. They told me that I was to perform a mission for the Almighty...as they termed it... I would know when and where."

She started sobbing quietly, her eyes filling with tears while she drove.

"I... I betrayed someone I love...Who meant everything to me. I did it because they said if I didn't help them locate him...locate those around him, they would kill him when they found him. They wanted him for their own purposes and would keep him alive for that purpose. But, not if I didn't help. They would find him and kill him on the spot. I helped them. I betrayed him."

She wiped the tears away while she drove, unable to say more for the moment."

Tyce felt his own tears welling. He fought them back, asking through a throat constricting with emotion, "And, when did you know that it was our rescue that was your...mission?"

"Not until several minutes before it happened. They appeared to me. Eli and Moshi appeared in the hallway while I was walking toward the studio. They just stepped from that ball of bright light to right in front of me. Eli said that I was to take a Jewish Rabbi and the man with him into a certain room. I was then to drive them to a place that would be designated. That I would know where. They said to just trust and drive."

"And you said that they...Eli and Moshi...said that you are to tell us that they are directing all this," Yitssak said.

"Yes. They said I must tell you that Eli and Moshi were near at all time and to trust in the God of Israel..."

"And, they said you...we...would know where we are to be taken?" The Israeli said.

"Yes. Eli said there would be no mistaking the Lord's direction for our travel. I was just to get you in the car and start driving."

"Then, it will be done. His will accomplished," Tyce said, knowing at once that whatever happened, all would eventuate as it should.

* * *

THEY DROVE at a high rate of speed once outside of the city. Tyce watched out of the window seeing orbs of light suddenly appear in the night sky. The orbs seemed to be moving at the speed of the car.

"The things are tracking us," he said, looking behind and again out the window to his left.

"They are everywhere," Marial said in a panicked tone from behind the wheel.

"They can't let us go uncaptured," Steyn said, looking out the window to his right. "We shall see if ...Israel's God...is still at work like in the Red Sea incident."

His words were lightly put, but their meaning was grasped, while the discs of light appeared in greater numbers while the car raced along the broad highway.

Marial saw it first, and gave a startled, but stifled scream.

A huge light orb sat on the highway ahead, seeming to breathe in and out brightly—awaiting their movement into its pulsing sphere.

Behind them, Tyce saw an orb pursuing and getting larger by the second.

"What should I do?" Marial said in a panic.

"Just drive ahead," Tyce said. "You were told by Eli to drive."

She did as instructed, pushing the accelerator further toward the floorboard. The light was blinding as they pierced into its outer effulgence.

* * *

FOR WHAT WERE to them mere seconds, the light grew even brighter, it's radiance warming them. But it was a calming, comforting warmth that penetrated to their inner-most sense of being.

Their ability to see returned while the light dimmed until they stood together within its misty glow.

The car was gone. They stood on soft clay-like surface, staring into the halo of light.

Two figures walked from the mist to stand facing them.

"Eli?"

Tyce looked into the intensive, piercing eyes of the older man.

"Tycus Levi," Eli said, his voice echoing within the strange, radiant, ambience. "You have delivered the message faithfully. The one hundred forty-four thousand witnesses of Israel's House have been set upon their mission of the salvation offered by the Eternal Kingdom. Michael is with them. Well done, good, faithful servant."

"But, I did nothing. I just followed..."

"That is key to serving," the old man interrupted. "What is needed is followers who will go when sent."

"Earth-dwellers now follow the beasts," Moshi said. "The choice is theirs. The Elect follow the Spirit of Light. This is the message you have initiated with your service to the King."

"Who is the King?" Yitssak said, looking into the eyes of the two men standing before them.

"Jesus," Marial said, before the men could respond.

"Indeed, Daughter. You have spoken truly," Eli said, a brief smile crossing his lips.

"The king? Of what kingdom?"

The Israeli's question reflected genuine confusion.

"Of the world," Tyce said. "of the Jews...Of Israel."

"Jesus of Nazareth...the messiah?"

Yitssak Steyn's question, offered in a soft, emotional voice, started tears trickling from his eyes.

"This is the message for the Jew...For the world of those who will repent and accept the Great king, the lord Jesus Christ," Moshi said.

"'You have all been instrumental on heaven's behalf," Eli said. "Daughter, behold who stands at your side."

Marial looked into the Rabbi's eyes. The Rabbi who no longer stood at her side, rather Tyce Greyson.

"Marial," Tyce said, seeing the beautiful, green eyes fill with tears of joy.

# EPILOGUE I

"**T**here you are," the doctor said, a brief smile passing her lips while she spoke in an uplifted tone.

"Don't try to talk for now," she said. "let's just let things come back slowly."

He looked at her face, seeing genuine appreciation in the doctor's smile. She was pleased her patient had finally recovered consciousness.

"Where are they?"

His words brought a look of not understanding.

"Who?"

"Marial...Yitssak...Eli and Moshi..."

"You've been in coma for almost two weeks, Mr. Greyson," she said. "You are in Boston General Hospital. You were brought here for the accident you suffered in Greece."

"Accident?"

"You were bitten by a snake. A very rare species," the doctor said.

"What about Marial...the others?"

"I'm sorry, but I don't know anything about anyone by those names. You've been in my care for almost two weeks. You were quite critical when you came to us."

Tyce lay his head back on the pillow and stared into nothingness toward the hospital room ceiling.

"Two weeks," he said in a whisper, to himself.

"They brought you here after two days in an Athens hospital," she said. "We have the facilities to deal with the type of thing that happened to you. We almost lost you on several occasions," she said. "But, Thank God, it looks like you will be just fine."

Tyce looked at her, his mind racing back to ...to what? To two weeks of hallucinating?...

"Yes," he said quietly. "Thank God..."

# EPILOGUE II

My phone rang while I was sitting at my desk thinking on some writing as a deadline drew near. I placed the ever-present mug of coffee on the little hot-plate coffee warmer, then picked up the phone receiver.

"I'm Tyce Greyson," the voice said after Tyce greeted me by name. "Do you remember me, I'm the reporter who interviewed you some weeks ago. I was with Channel eleven."

"Sure, I remember you," I said. "You were headed for Patmos to pursue your fascination with Bible prophecy."

"Yes, Sir. And, that's what I'm calling about. I was wondering if we could meet at your office at some point soon. There things I want to tell you, to go over...Well," he interrupted himself. "I'll just save it for when we can get together, if that's possible."

The remembered meeting with him and our hand-shake when he left my study that day made me know that the meeting was not only okay. It was necessary.

"Sure. Whenever you can come by."

"How about tomorrow morning?"

"That's good for me. How about around nine?"

"Yes, Sir. Nine will be great."

Next morning when we met, I could tell he wanted to quickly get through the formalities of greeting. He was, it seemed to me, bursting at the seams to get something off his mind and into mine.

"I'm sorry, sir, but this whole thing is some-thing...Something beyond anything I can fully...can tell in a minute or two. It is too...fantastic to grasp in a single meeting...in a single setting."

I could tell by his tone that he was distressed, perhaps over taking up too much of my time. He knew it would take longer than I, likely, would be able or willing to spend in listening to him.

He paced back and forth. I could tell that he was searching for words to get started.

"Just sit down and take it easy, Tyce, I said, gesturing toward a chair across from the one in which I had just seated myself. "I have plenty of time. I'm quite interested to find out what you've got for me."

He sat, but I could tell, even not being able to see him, that he was leaning forward, not sitting back in a posture of relaxation.

"I went to Patmos after leaving here," he began. "I hope you will believe ...will take all I'm about to say as truth..."

"I believe you, Tyce," I said, trying to reassure. "Just tell me."

"I went to a cave on Patmos, taken there by a native of the Island. He took me to what he called the *real* cave of the Apocalypse. I decided to go there and take in the traditional cave—the one for tourists later."

He paused to gather his thoughts for several seconds, then got to his feet and began pacing again.

"While in the cave... And it *was* the real cave used by the prophet John as he wrote things of the Apocalypse. I have no doubt."

"Oh? And, how do you know with such certainty?"

My question opened the floodgate that was holding back his need to release everything he had been through. It all came gushing at me in a torrent of emotion-filled revelations.

"That's what this...this story...is all about. It started, while I was in that cave looking around...It began with a bite by a snake..." He told me everything. How he saw the tremendous storm, the beast from the sea. How he awoke in the hospital in Boston. How he had visions during the broadcast. How he predicted things that came true in every case.

He told the whole story, barely pausing to catch a breath. The betrayal by the girl he loved, the move to Israel, the meeting of the two, strange, Jewish men. The threats to Israel, to himself.

He told of warning Israel of the young European leader and his promises of peace. How he had visions that clued him to what the *false* peace was going to do to the Jews, to Israel.

He told me that the whole time he was apparently in a coma was more real than while talking to me now, while he paced my study carpet.

He told of the visions from which he broadcast or foretold things to come with one-hundred percent accuracy. How those vision were even more real to him than even the entire story while in the coma and now while speaking to me.

He told of the orbs of lights, of the strange things

promised by the young European and his partner in bringing Israel to accept the deadly peace...the Rabbi that first bent his ear while he visited the Wailing Wall in Jerusalem.

How the Dimension *of Light* was the source of the orbs. The orbs that threatened mankind, like Klaatu and Gort in the film *The Day the Earth Stood Still.*

He told of the girl he loved, who he thought had betrayed him, helping them escape, not recognizing him because of his supernatural disguise as a Jewish Rabbi. How the orbs pursued them while escaping following the vision-induced broadcast in which he forewarned Israel...Forewarned the world and told the thousands of Jewish young men about their mission... The mission that would be empowered with the assistance of a magnificent creature of light named Michael.

How they had entered the enormous ball of light on the highway leading from Brussels. The time when he was apparently in coma ending with the face to face meeting with the two Jewish men, Eli and Moshi.

Finally, he sat down across from me and was silent. I spoke first following the silence.

"You say they called you...gave as your real name, *Tycus Levi?*"

"Yes. I was told that my mother and father were killed in a plane accident. That I am a Jew by birth."

"And, you've checked this out?"

"I was raised from birth in a family through adoption," he said. "I've never checked on my biological roots."

"I suggest you do so, Tyce. This is all so relevant to these times," I said with purposeful gravity in my tone.

"Relevant, how?"

"These are the end of days," I said. "If your heritage is

indeed Jewish...Then the scripture might apply that fore-tells that Israel's young men shall have visions."

"I know the scripture. It came to me a number of times while in the coma..."

"I've always thought of that scripture as being for the Tribulation era, but that is open to interpretation. This prophecy about young men seeing visions and old men having dreams might be for the time we are in now. The time before the Rapture."

"Rapture!" The word sparked a further revelation.

"I forgot to say that one of my prophecies when broadcasting through the visions was that millions of people would disappear across the world."

"And, did it happen?"

"Yes. It is what triggered all of the light orbs, and the story by the young European involving why they were there...to govern mankind and to help people of earth live in peace and security."

My mind was reeling by this time, his story so profound that I knew it had to be told. No matter it's believability to most who would hear or read about it. It had to be told.

"What do you think should be done with your story?" I asked.

"I was hoping you could help me know what to do with it, Sir," he said. "I'm a journalist, not a story-teller, if you know what I mean."

"You think this could...should be told in the form of fiction, in the form of a novel," I asked.

"That's why I wanted you to hear it. Bible prophecy is your area of expertise. You write in every form. I've read your stuff...your work."

I said nothing, waiting for him to say more. "My friends won't read anything to do with religious nonfiction. This is something I believe is meant to be shared."

"Yes," I agreed. "We are at the end of days."

He said, "They will read novels...will read fiction. Maybe we could present it in fictional form."

"Like the *Left Behind* series of novels?"

"Yes. They got out an important message, didn't they?"

"Assuredly," I agreed.

We wrapped up our early morning meeting. It was after noon when he said he had to catch a plane to New York by 3 o'clock.

"I want you to meet someone before you go, Tyce," I said, holding him by the arm and leading him back toward my desk.

I pushed the intercom button on the desk.

"I want you to meet my beautiful niece. She helps her old uncle in the writing business."

I pressed the button again.

"Yes?" Her voice sounded in reply on the intercom speaker.

"Marial, I want you to meet someone."

## A LOOK AT: THE RAPTURE DIALOGUES: DARK DIMENSION

### BY TERRY JAMES

Set in the era from the 1947 Roswell UFO incident, to the terror attacks of 9/11, "The Rapture Dialogues" sets the stage for biblically prophesied events.

USAF Fighter pilot James Morgan finds himself in supernatural conflict that suctions his wife, Laura and daughter, Lori, into clandestine governmental intrigues of terrifying dimension.

Mark Lancing, a young Marine fighter pilot, finds his life intertwined with the plight of the Morgans, through a growing love for Lori, night-marish intrusion by hellish creatures and explosive involvement with Israel's spiritual and physical wars for survival.

***COMING SOON***

# ABOUT TERRY JAMES

**Terry James** is author, general editor, and co-author of numerous books on Bible prophecy, hundreds of thousands of which have been sold worldwide. James is a frequent lecturer on the study of end time phenomena, and interviews often with national and international media on topics involving world issues and events as they might relate to Bible prophecy.

He has appeared in major documentaries and media forums, in all media formats, in America, Europe, and Asia.

He appeared in the History Channel series, The Nostradamus Effect.

He is an active member of the PreTrib Research Center Study Group, a prophecy research think-tank founded by Dr. Tim LaHaye, the co-author of the multi-million selling "Left Behind" series of novels. He is a regular participant in the annual Tulsa mid-America prophecy conference, where he speaks, and holds a Question and Answer series of sessions on current world events as they might relate to Bible prophecy.

Terry James has been blind since 1993 due to a degenerative retinal disease (retinitis pigmentosa). He uses the Jobs Accessible Word System (JAWS) –which is voice synthesis—to write and conduct business over the Internet.

His former profession was in public relations, advertising, marketing, and publicity and promotion.

He received his education from Arkansas Polytechnic Institute, Memphis Academy of Arts, and University of Arkansas at Little Rock.

He served in both corporate and government positions for 25 years, before becoming a full-time writer.

James also served in the United States Air Force from October 1966 through October 1970.) He served at Randolph AFB, Texas, in the T-38 section, a mission dedicated to training pilots in high-performance jet fighter-trainers.

Terry James and his wife, Margaret, live near Little Rock, Arkansas.

Made in the USA
Las Vegas, NV
12 December 2023

82611770R00194